A Season for Strength

A Season for Strength

Laurel Mouritsen

Covenant Communications, Inc.

Covenant

Library of Congress Catalog Number: 91–072632
A Season for Strength
Covenant Communications, Inc.
Printed August 1991
ISBN 55503–361–X

But ye are a chosen generation, a royal priesthood, an holy nation, a peculiar people; that ye should shew forth the praises of him who hath called you out of darkness into his marvellous light

1 Peter 2:9

CHAPTER ONE

A fierce January wind tore at the cabin. Lydia opened the shutter on a window-sized hole hewn out of the rough logs and peered outside with an anxious frown. Fanned by the gusting winds, the snow swirled about the farmyard like a flock of frightened sparrows. The barn, located not more than a few yards from the house, was swallowed up in the storm, and the garden and fields beyond had long since vanished from sight.

Shivering, Lydia drew her shawl closer around her shoulders. The familiar knot in the pit of her stomach tightened. She tried to relax, but the worry bottled up inside her made it impossible. A savage blast of wind drove a sheet of snow through the open window; in the rush of cold air, a candle's flame flickered. Lydia quickly closed and latched the shutter.

Cupping her hand around its feeble light, Lydia carried the candle to the far end of the room where a tattered blanket hung from two hooks driven into the ceiling, serving as a divider between the cabin's living and sleeping quarters. Lydia pushed the blanket aside and slipped through. In the dim light the few objects which all but filled the tiny enclosure took on ghostly dimensions. She tiptoed to the trundle bed and bent to tuck the quilts around her two still children.

"Night, Mama," came a child's voice.

"Aren't you asleep yet, 'Lizabeth?" asked Lydia quietly.

"Almost. James has been keepin' me awake with his tossin' and turnin'," the girl complained.

Lydia felt the forehead of the little boy lying next to his sister. It was warm to her touch—too warm. "I hope he's not comin' down with somethin'. Now you hush and go to sleep."

"Mama?"

"What?"

"The wind's real wild tonight, isn't it? It scares me when it whines."

Lydia sat down on the bed and took her daughter's hand. The warm, trusting fingers of the child helped to quiet her own concerns. "There's not a thing to be frightened of, 'Lizabeth. It's just old Father Wind doin' his best to scatter the snow so as to make it easier for the spring to come in."

"But why does Father Wind make such an awful noise, like wolves howlin' at our door?"

Lydia smiled at her precocious five-year-old. "It's the sound the wind makes when it's workin' hard. Here now, let me cover you up tight so the wind won't shoosh under the blankets and tickle your toes."

Elizabeth giggled and lay still while her mother tucked the covers snugly around her.

"Night, angel. You sleep now. Let's not wake your brother."

Lydia left the children and returned to the outer room. The cabin was growing colder. She went to the hearth, intending to feed more wood to the fire, but only three short pieces remained in the woodbox. She felt a quick surge of annoyance. Abraham had neglected to bring wood in from the shed before he left.

She tossed two of the pieces onto the fire. If Abraham didn't return soon, she would have to go outside to the woodshed herself. She did not relish that thought. The wind hammered against the door and whistled through the chinks and cracks between the logs where pieces of wattle had loosened and washed away during the fall rains. Abraham had not yet repaired the gaps nor plastered the interior walls as he'd promised.

Lydia dropped wearily into a chair beside the table and let her fingers play at the pages of a book she had been reading earlier and set aside. Glancing down, she pulled the bulky leather-bound Bible closer and began to read, her lips moving silently with the rhythm of the words:

Who can find a virtuous woman? for her price is far above rubies.

The heart of her husband doth safely trust in her, so that he shall have no need of spoil.

She will do him good and not evil all the days of her life.

She seeketh wool, and flax, and worketh willingly with her hands.

She is like the merchants' ships; she bringeth her food from afar.

She riseth also while it is yet night, and giveth meat to her household, and a portion to her maidens.

She considereth a field, and buyeth it: with the fruit of her hands she planteth a vineyard.

Lydia's mind wandered from the page in spite of the fact that this was one of her favorite passages.

She considereth a field, and buyeth it: with the fruit of her hands she planteth a vineyard. . . .

Six years ago she and Abraham, newly married, had purchased their fifteen acres in Green County, Illinois, built the small cabin, and planted ten acres of wheat and five of corn. She smiled as she recalled the happiness of those early days. Abraham had been affectionate and attentive, and she had been content working alongside him in the fields.

She couldn't remember when she'd first met Abraham Dawson; she simply had always known him. Her family and his had resided in Green County for generations. The first time she became aware of him, however, was the night he asked her to dance at the harvest social. That was in 1825. She remembered the year because it was the summer of her fifteenth birthday.

She married Abraham two years later in the old stone Baptist church in the middle of the town square. Abraham's father was a logger, as were Abraham and his three brothers. Abraham was the oldest of the boys and the most headstrong. A few months after they wed, Abraham quit his work as a log cutter after a bitter argument with his father, took Lydia, who was two months pregnant, and moved to the fringes of the county. He cleared the land, planted it, and built the cabin himself. Lydia bore their two children, Elizabeth Ann and James, in the drafty, one-room shelter.

She sighed softly. What had gone wrong since then she couldn't quite frame into words. Abraham had grown distant and surly, and she sensed that his ardor for her had cooled. His whiskey and card playing seemed to isolate her further. The preceding spring he had been forced to take out a mortgage on the farm in order to pay his gaming debts, and almost the entire summer's crop had been forfeited as a result of "a run of bad luck," as Abraham termed it. Lydia feared they would be turned out of their home before the winter was over. The knot in her stomach clenched into an iron fist.

A ferocious gust of wind shook the wooden shutters, interrupting Lydia's dark thoughts. Feeling utterly discouraged, she threw the remaining log onto the dying fire.

Slumped in her chair, Lydia felt a jarring hand on her shoulder. She awoke to find Abraham standing over her, his dark brows knit together in displeasure.

"The fire's out. It's cold as a tomb in here, Lydia."

She motioned to the firewood box. His eyes followed unsteadily; Lydia noticed they were puffy and shot with red.

"Somethin' wrong with your legs? Why didn't you fetch some?"

"I asked you to bring more wood in 'fore you left this evenin'," Lydia replied.

Abraham's scowl deepened but he said nothing further. He pulled off his snow-covered coat and beaver hat and hung them on a peg beside the door. Lydia watched the melting snow from his clothing trickle onto the dirt floor.

Abraham blew on his cold hands, then briskly rubbed them together. They were big hands, strong hands. He was powerfully built, blocky and broad-shouldered. Abraham's black hair curled at the nape of his neck, and his short, curly beard hid the proud set of his jaw. His complexion was swarthy, his mouth full, and his eyes were like two glittering black stones.

Cold and tired, Lydia went into the makeshift bedroom to

change into warm nightclothes. She heard Abraham in the other room, grunting as he fumbled with his trousers and coarse woolen shirt. In a moment he appeared, clad in his long johns.

"I'll git wood in the mornin'," Abraham told her curtly. As he prepared to climb into bed, he struck his shin on the corner of the bunk.

"Damnation!" he bellowed.

"Hush, or you'll wake the young'uns. I'm afraid James is comin' down with somethin'. He's feverish."

Abraham muttered some reply.

Lydia hurriedly climbed into bed and lay on her back, staring into the darkness. She could hear Abraham mumbling and punching his pillow into a more comfortable position. She lay still, listening to the wind. It seemed to be increasing in its frenzy.

"I been worried about you. Where you been so late—at Ira's place?" she asked, turning onto her side to face him.

"Don't start on me tonight, Lydia."

"I was only askin'."

"Well, don't. Saturday's my night out same as always. Ain't no concern of yours how I choose to spend it. You got Sunday to use as you see fit, though it's a waste of time in my opinion to spend it goin' to meetins'," he added sourly.

"Maybe if you went with me once in awhile you might see it differently."

Abraham snorted and flopped over onto his stomach.

"Abraham?"

"What?"

"If James is sick tomorrow, you'll watch him close while I'm at meetin'?"

"Stop yappin', woman. Can't you see I'm all wore out?"

His curt reply stung Lydia. She wiggled as far away from him as she could manage in the narrow bed. Before long, she heard his nasal snore. Lydia turned over and gazed at her husband. In the pale moonlight she could just make out the rugged line of his profile. She closed her eyes tightly, wishing there were some way to rekindle the fire they'd once felt.

CHAPTER TWO

At breakfast, Elizabeth kept up a stream of chatter. Lydia listened to her with one ear as she cradled three-year-old James in her lap. She was concerned about the boy. He was still unusually warm and his slender face was flushed. Lydia brushed his black wavy hair out of his eyes and kissed him on the forehead.

As she rocked James, her gaze fell on the hearth, where a fire burned brightly. The woodbox, too, was filled. She glanced at Abraham, who was engrossed in his flapjacks. After he had come home late the night before in a questionable state of sobriety, she was surprised that he'd risen before sunup to attend to his chores.

"Mama, look at all the snow!" exclaimed Elizabeth. "Can I go outside? Please!"

"Not yet. Later, maybe. Pass me the flapjacks, will you?"

Elizabeth handed her mother the platter of round pan-fried cakes and a small crock of molasses. Lydia offered a bite to James, but he refused to take it.

"James is fretful, Mama, and won't eat his cakes," Elizabeth told her matter-of-factly.

"I know. He hasn't swallowed a mouthful all morning." James sat passively in Lydia's lap, sucking his fingers and staring out of listless brown eyes.

When she'd finished her breakfast, Lydia set James on a chair and prepared to clear the dishes from the table.

"I'll do that," Abraham said. "You best git ready for meetin'."

Lydia's eyebrows hooked up in surprise. "You sure?"

He nodded and took her empty plate to a bucket filled with soapy water.

"All right."

Lydia removed her Bible from its place on the cupboard shelf and went into the adjoining room to dress. She slipped on the same plain homespun she wore every Sunday. The coarse cloth scratched her cheeks as Lydia pulled the dress over her head. She smoothed the wrinkles out of the skirt with the palm of her hand, then deftly began coiling her long copper hair into a knot at the nape of her neck. In went the metal hair pins to hold it in place—three, four, five of them in rapid succession. She fingered the finished product, and then paused to study her reflection in the chipped and rippling old mirror fastened on top of her maple chest of drawers.

Her wide blue eyes went over every detail of her appearance, from her petite nose to the tip of her high-buttoned shoes. She noted with some satisfaction that she was still slender-waisted and pale of complexion. She was glad she'd always been careful to keep her bonnet on in the sun. She wished Elizabeth would be as conscientious. It was almost impossible to keep Elizabeth's golden curls confined beneath a bonnet, for she tossed it aside the moment she was out of Lydia's sight. The child's ruddy and freckled cheeks testified to that.

Lydia's eyes left the mirror and lingered on the handsome chest of drawers. She ran her hand over its smooth grain, savoring the silky feel of the wood underneath her fingers. The chest of drawers was a wedding gift from Abraham's parents. Everything else in the cabin Abraham had made himself: the cupboard where she stored her kitchenware, a chest for linens, the rude table and chairs, and her favorite slat-backed rocker.

"Mama, the Johanssens are here," Elizabeth sang from the next room.

"I'll be right there."

The Johanssens, Lydia and Abraham's nearest neighbors, took Lydia with them each Sunday to the renovated barn which served as a meetinghouse for all denominations in the backwoods area. Niels and Gerta Johanssen and their five children practiced the Universalist religion, but the gospel preached in the old converted barn was general enough to please nearly everyone.

Lydia believed strongly in God and strived to obey his word as she understood it. Ever since she was a young girl, she had studied and pondered the Bible. From her searching, she had developed her own ideas as to certain points of doctrine. Lydia's parents were staunch Baptists, and although in her judgment the Baptist religion did not answer all of her questions, she preferred it to other sects with which she was acquainted.

On occasion she'd attended camp meetings, or revivals, where traveling ministers preached the gospel with great emotional fervor. She was not convinced, however, that the outcries, jerkings, and contortions of the congregation which occurred at such gatherings were evidence of God's spirit. For Lydia, spiritual comfort and insight came from reading the scriptures and committing select passages to memory, such as the one in the thirty-first chapter of Proverbs.

Lydia wrapped a warm shawl around her shoulders, and grasping her Bible firmly in hand, started for the door.

"Behave while I'm gone," she instructed the children.

As she turned to leave, Abraham took hold of her arm and said quietly, "I'll be wantin' to talk to you when you git back."

"About what?"

"It'll keep," he replied.

Niels Johanssen was tramping a path through the deep snow from the house to the waiting sled to make the way easier for Lydia. The two chestnut horses hitched to the sleigh snorted and tossed their heads in the crystalline air. As she picked her way to the sleigh, Lydia wondered what Abraham wanted to discuss with her. It would likely be something she'd disapprove of—that explained his cooperative behavior this morning.

"Careful, Mrs. Dawson. Itsa deep," Niels Johanssen said in his lilting Scandinavian accent. When he extended a hand, she grasped it and climbed into the sled alongside Niel's plump, blue-eyed wife.

"Liddy, you have never seen such snow, huh!" Gerta Johanssen exclaimed. "Niels could scarce get ta sleigh out of ta barn this morning it vas piled up so high. And the vind, roaring through as it did!" Mrs. Johanssen rolled her eyes.

Lydia nodded in agreement. "I was worried about Abraham gettin' home in the storm."

Mrs. Johanssen cast Lydia a sympathetic look. "This snow vill slow us and I wanted to get to meeting early to meet ta preacher ta Reverend invited to—stop that, Inge!" Mrs. Johanssen gave her youngest daughter's hand a stinging slap while it was still in contact with her sister's long yellow braid.

All five of the Johanssen children were blue-eyed and tow-headed, miniature replicas of their mother. The three daughters sat in a row in the rear seat of the sled, clothed in matching green woolen dresses which came below their ankles, their yellow-white hair parted in the center of their heads and divided into two shoulder-length braids tied with green ribbons. The oldest girl, Johanna, held a hefty, round-faced baby on her lap, who was sucking happily on his thumb. The girls' older brother, thirteen-year-old Jens, sat between his parents, a frown on his pugnacious face.

"What preacher is that, Gerta?" asked Lydia.

"Haven't you heard, child? Some preacher from Ohio, making quite a stir with his new gospel. Says God has sent the people a prophet and a new Bible."

"A new Bible?"

"Yah. Their prophet dug it out of the ground, if you can imagine that."

Lydia couldn't and so she remained silent, content to wait and hear what the preacher had to say about it all.

The sled slipped easily over the sparkling, unmarked snow. Whitefrocked trees—beech, maple and hemlock—slid past, showing off their snowy gowns. In the distance, a rail fence snaked to the south, enclosing a large area of cleared ground—-Ira Slater's homestead. Lydia frowned as she thought of the weasel-eyed farmer. She couldn't imagine why Abraham enjoyed his company. She found Slater to be crude and unprincipled.

Within an hour they arrived at the meetinghouse. Niels

Johanssen brought the horses to a halt, jumped from the sled, and tied the reins securely to the hitching post. Then he helped the ladies and children inside where they found seats near the rear of the crowded room.

The Reverend John Russell had already begun the service and was in the midst of introducing his guest preacher. Lydia removed her shawl and listened closely.

"—he hailed previously from Kirtland, Ohio," the preacher was saying, "but has since removed to the area of Colesville, on the western boundary of Missouri. Mr. Pratt and his companion, Mr. McLellin, have been preaching in our neighborhood for several weeks. Many of our friends and neighbors have listened with interest to their message. Brother Calvin, whom you all know and respect, has become a hearer of the word and welcomed these gentlemen into his home. With great pleasure, may I introduce Mr. Parley P. Pratt."

With a flourish of his hands, the Reverend Russell indicated a well built, tall young man with dark, wavy hair and dark, somber eyes. There was a look of determination about his jaw and in the set of his wide mouth. Mr. Pratt rose to his feet and began in a loud voice:

"Thank you, Brother Russell. I am here to relate to you and your friends the particulars of my message and the nature of my commission. A young man in the state of New York, whose name is Joseph Smith, was visited by an angel of God, and, after several visions and much instruction, was enabled to obtain an ancient record, written by men of old on the American continent, and containing the history, prophecies and gospel in plainness, as revealed to them by Jesus and his messengers. This same Joseph Smith and others were also commissioned by the angels and ordained to the apostleship, with authority to organize the Church of Jesus Christ, to administer the ordinances, and to ordain others, and thus cause the full, plain gospel in its purity to be preached in all the world.

"By these Apostles thus commissioned, I have been sent forth to minister in the name of Jesus Christ the baptism of repentance for remission of sins; and to administer the gift of the Holy Ghost, to heal the sick, to comfort the mourner, bind up the broken in heart, and proclaim the gospel in its fullness."

Lydia's jaw dropped in astonishment. She'd never heard such a sermon as this, nor one preached with as much conviction. The preacher's voice was mellow and rhythmic, and he spoke with assurance. He appeared to be about twenty-five or twenty-six, yet his bearing and manner were characteristic of a more mature man. Lydia sensed an authority, almost a power about him, and it awed her. She leaned forward, concentrating on his words.

"We read in the New Testament that certain definite principles existed, which constituted the Christian Church; namely, an inspired priesthood authorized to administer salvation in the name of Jesus, faith on the part of those who received their words, reformation of life, baptism by immersion for the remission of sin, and the laying on of hands to receive the gift of the Holy Ghost."

Pratt stood with his feet planted firmly apart, his broad hands gesturing as he spoke. "It may be presumed that every portion of the professed Christian Church will readily agree that the five principles just named did exist and did constitute the Christian Church. Either these same principles would be required to constitute the Church in all succeeding ages, or else the New Testament must cease to be a standard. If the ancient model or pattern is the standard, then the entire world is unchristianized, for we nowhere find such a pattern in the world today."

Lydia frowned as she considered Pratt's supposition. What was he getting at? His words stirred up questions and anxieties that she thought she had put to rest. She clenched her hands into a tight ball in her lap.

"But suppose, upon opening our eyes, we search and find a great and glorious discovery? Suppose Jesus Christ and his apostles and prophets have unveiled the truth, the pattern as it were, once again to man? Suppose Christ's church has again been restored with every principle and ordinance as it was in days of the ancient prophets?"

The preacher's eyes glowed as if lighted by some hidden fire, and his voice thundered in Lydia's ears. "I testify to you, my brothers and sisters who dwell in a state of darkness and despair, I testify to you in the name of Jesus Christ that a new dispensation has been revealed from heaven, by the ministration of angels and the power and gifts of God, which will result in the overthrow of all mystery, darkness, ignorance and corruption, and the ushering in of the universal reign of peace and truth. I solemnly bear witness that the truth has been restored to the earth again in all its fullness, beauty, majesty and purity."

Lydia's skin prickled as Pratt's testimony burned into her heart. Was it possible that this new religion was literally Christ's church, restored again? If that were true, what a marvelous blessing it would be for mankind, for her personally —for Abraham. Her spirit soared as she contemplated the glorious possibilities of such a gospel. Perhaps this was the key to draw Abraham close to her again.

She felt Gerta's hand on her arm and turned to find the older woman's eyes bulging and her mouth agape. Wrapped in her own thoughts, Lydia hadn't noticed the congregation responding. Questions began to pelt the preacher from all quarters of the room.

"Do you mean to tell us angels revealed this new gospel?" asked one man incredulously.

"And showed themselves to a mortal man?" another cried.

"Seems unlikely," a woman sitting near Lydia muttered.

Lydia listened to the comments around her. She wanted to believe the preacher, but it was all so incredible. Had the man, Joseph Smith, truly seen an angel? And if so, why had God chosen *him* to receive such a miracle? Of the reality of angels, Lydia had no doubt—Jacob of old had wrestled with one. But she was skeptical of an ancient record containing the Lord's gospel. Was that record the new Bible Gerta had mentioned, she wondered. She didn't believe in any sort of new Bible; everything the Lord intended to reveal to his people, he had already revealed in the Old and New Testaments. She had been taught that since childhood. Mr. Pratt spoke for some time and Lydia was captivated, her attention totally focused on him.

All too soon he concluded, "My friends, I have long detained you. I have much to impart to you concerning the details of the commencement of this restoration revealed from the heavens and of the subsequent organization and movements of the Church of the Saints. If you desire, we will hold another meeting tomorrow evening."

Cries of "Aye, aye!" and "We'll listen to you, preacher," echoed around the room.

"My home's open for meetin', Brother Pratt," shouted Mr. Calvin, jumping to his feet.

"Very well," said Pratt, holding up his hands in a gesture of silence. "Tomorrow evening at seven o'clock at the home of Brother Calvin. May the spirit of the Lord Jesus Christ rest upon you, my brothers and sisters, that you may receive and know the truth. Amen."

As Mr. Pratt concluded, his companion Mr. McLellin stood and came to his side. Together they started toward the rear of the meetinghouse, escorted by the Reverend Russell, shaking hands as they progressed down the aisle. As they approached the last row of pews where Lydia sat, Pratt's glance fell upon her. He paused and regarded her with a solemn expression. She had the strange sensation that his clear, dark eyes gazed into her very soul. Her heart quickened, and in that instant she resolved to attend his meeting on the morrow.

"Abraham? Abraham, where are you?" Lydia called as she shut the door of the log house behind her.

"Here," he answered, stepping from behind the divider.

Lydia hastily removed her shawl and bonnet and tossed them over a chair. "Abraham, you can't imagine the things I've heard today. The Reverend invited a guest preacher to speak, and he talked about angels revealin' the gospel just as it was in Christ's time, and about a book a Mr. Smith has that tells—"

"Slow down, Lydia. I don't know what you're talkin' about. A book, you say?"

"Yes. A book that tells about the people who used to live here before the white men came." Lydia's words tumbled over one another in her eagerness to share them with Abraham.

"Ain't nobody lived here 'fore that but the redskins," Abraham remarked, seating himself on a chair next to the table.

Lydia took the chair across from him. "I know it sounds

peculiar, but if you'd heard this preacher . . . Abraham, he wasn't like any I've ever listened to before."

"Did you say his name was Smith? Wasn't Joe Smith, was it?" Abraham asked suspiciously.

"No, Joseph Smith is the man who found the book. The preacher's name is Pratt." Some of her enthusiasm faded under Abraham's stern stare. "You've heard of Joseph Smith?"

"Mormons! You been listenin' to the d—n Mormons, Lydia."

"The who?"

"Mormons. Been spreadin' their lies all up and down the country. I heard about 'em."

"When?"

"There's talk in town. Heard more of it last night, in fact. They're a passel of liars and thieves led by Joe Smith. Tellin' folks about some gold book Smith says he dug up. Did your preacher mention that?"

"He didn't say anything about gold," she answered, trying to ignore the sarcasm in her husband's voice.

"Well, I'm tellin' you Smith is a fraud and a treasure hunter. Probably crazy, too. Claims to have visions and dreams, and says he's conversed with God himself." Abraham raked his fingers through his jet black hair. "You stay away from 'em, Lydia. You don't want nothin' to do with them Mormons."

"But Mr. Pratt is holdin' another meetin' tomorrow evenin' and—"

"You ain't goin'."

"Maybe it's true what you say about the Mormons, but I'd like to hear about it for myself."

"You ain't goin', Lydia. That's the end of it."

Abraham stood up and thrust his hands in his pockets. Lydia looked up at him, exasperated by his refusal to discuss the matter any further. Surely he was wrong about Joseph Smith and the Mormons. If only he'd been there to hear the Mormon preacher speak. She and Gerta had talked of nothing else throughout the cold ride home. And Niels, who did not take easily to new ideas, was keenly interested. Gerta would be disappointed she was not going with her to the meeting.

"Lydia?"

She looked up. Abraham was watching her closely. "Are you so stirred up over that meetin' that you got no thought for your young?"

Startled by his words, Lydia glanced quickly about the room. "Where is 'Lizabeth?"

"'Lizabeth is outside playin'. It's James that needs tendin' to."

"James? Is he worse?" Alarmed, she sprang up and started for the other room.

"I been in there for a better part of an hour spongin' him," Abraham called after her as she disappeared behind the ragged blanket hanging from the ceiling.

James lay on his small bed, a damp rag across his forehead. Lydia knelt beside him and took his hand. "James, honey, how you feelin'?"

"Hurts," he answered, pointing to his head.

She removed the cloth and brushed the damp hair from off his brow. "Should Mama get you a cool drink of water?"

James shook his dark curls. "No, Mama."

"Does your stomach hurt too?"

He didn't answer, only looked at her out of eyes underscored with dark circles.

She rinsed the cloth in a bucket of cool water Abraham had placed beside the bed and wiped the child's face and arms with it. He was burning with fever. She talked soothingly as she sponged him, hiding the fear rearing up inside her. When she'd finished, she fluffed his pillow and did what she could to make him comfortable.

"How's that?" she smiled.

"James hurts," he repeated.

"I know, angel, but I'm sure you'll feel better tomorrow. You must try to sleep now. Shall I sing you a lullaby?"

He nodded and as he did so the wet cloth slipped down over one big brown eye. Lydia adjusted it as she began singing a favorite old Irish tune. She was only halfway through the second verse when his eyelids began to droop. She kissed him and quietly went out. Abraham was seated at the table, waiting for her.

"I'm worried about him, Abraham. He's hot as coals."

"Been that way all mornin'," Abraham replied. "Sit down

here, Liddy. I been waitin' to talk to you." He took her hand and pulled her into the chair next to him.

"What is it?"

He took a deep breath. "Liddy, you know the fix we're in what with the bank holdin' our mortgage and all. I figure I can make one, maybe two more payments, but that's it. There's no more cash. Either we got to sell this place or I got to come up with some extra money."

All the fear and worry Lydia had been harboring flooded to the surface. She felt her eyes sting with tears. She turned away, her mouth set in a rigid line.

"Last night Ira was tellin' me about some minin' goin' on in the upper part of the state. They're pullin' enough lead out of the mines around Galena to pay for our farm a hundred times over. Ira and me figure we could make upwards of three hundred dollars apiece in three or four months' time. That would give us enough money to pay off the mortgage and buy seed for fall plantin'."

"Galena? That's over two hundred miles away! You want to leave us here while you run off prospectin' for four months?"

"Might not be that long. Just long enough to git ourselves out of debt. I don't like being beholden' to anyone, includin' the bank, and I know you ain't gonna want to give up the farm. So where's the harm? It's a good idea to my way of thinkin'."

"What do you know about lead minin'?"

"Not much, but Ira used to do some minin' years ago. He says it ain't such a bad life and I'd take to it fast."

"I don't like it," Lydia said.

"Well, then, you figure out somethin'," Abraham replied.

She frowned, trying desperately to think of another solution, one that wouldn't take Abraham miles away from her. She hated the idea of being left alone with sole responsibility for the farm and the children. It frightened her.

"How soon 'til you'd be wantin' to leave?" she asked.

"Soon as the snows melt—a month, maybe six weeks." He scratched his shaggy beard. "Ira's seein' to the supplies."

Ira Slater owned seventy acres of good ground a few miles

south of their own homestead and was farming it success-fully. Lydia wondered why he would want to leave it to work in the mines.

"I know what you're thinkin', Liddy. There'll be no one here to look after you."

"Or the children," she snapped.

"I'll ask Niels to keep an eye on the place and see to it that you got everythin' you need."

Lydia's mouth turned down at the corners.

"Come on, Liddy. You'll be fine. You can take care of the farm for a few weeks without me. You got 'Lizabeth to help you."

"She's just a child."

"But she's strong, like you." Abraham stood up, hooked his thumbs in the pockets of his trousers, and glanced out the cabin window. "I guess that's all that needs sayin' for now. I'll be out back doin' chores."

She watched him as he strode toward the door. The Mormon meeting scheduled for the following evening was now no longer important. With James sick and Abraham planning to leave, she had enough to contend with.

"Abraham?" He paused, his hand on the latch. "We need you here. I hope you'll change your mind about goin'."

"I'll send 'Lizabeth in to help you with supper." He lifted the latch and walked out.

CHAPTER THREE

A light snow fell throughout the day and dense gray clouds blotted out the sun. The writhing smoke from the cabin's chimney climbed into the dark sky and disappeared beyond the fringe of heavy forest. Lydia had passed the morning by washing her family's laundry and hanging it to dry on a line of rope stretched in front of the fireplace. The fire in the hearth sizzled and cracked, and the room was muggy from the damp clothing.

Elizabeth sat near the hearth, hunched over her slate. Carefully she formed the letters of the alphabet with her stump of chalk, printing each one over and over across the slate. Lydia glanced at her as she set a large black kettle over the fire to heat.

"How you doin', 'Lizabeth?"

"Fine," Elizabeth mumbled.

"Let me see. Oops, your K is facin' wrongside. Looks like he's walkin' backwards? Turn him around, darlin'."

Elizabeth scrubbed the misshapen letter off the board and started it again. Lydia watched her a moment longer. Satisfied, she went to the cupboard where she removed a box containing tallow, wicks, and beeswax and placed it on the table beside several heavy candle molds. Then she put a quantity of wax and tallow inside the hot kettle. Lydia performed the tasks mechanically, her mind dwelling on James, not on the work before her. Despite her nursing, James continued to suffer with fever and chills. Her gaze returned to the corner where the child lay sleeping fitfully.

The bubbling mixture inside the kettle forced Lydia's attention back to the chore at hand. She readied the molds and began to pour steaming liquid into them. She'd just finished the first one when the sound of an approaching sled drew her eyes to the window. Elizabeth set her slate aside and looked up expectantly. The Johanssens' sleigh, pulled by their two big chestnut mares, slid to a stop at Lydia's door. Lydia put the kettle down and stepped out onto the porch.

"Morning, Liddy," Gerta Johanssen's husky voice rang out. She climbed down from the sleigh, carrying eighteen-month-old Lars in the crook of one arm. "Come along, Inge," she said impatiently, handing her daughter out.

Inge shyly hung her head while her mother situated the baby onto her hip, grabbed her hand and started through the snow.

Elizabeth ran to the door. "Inge!" she shouted delightedly.

The other girl's face broke into a smile. She jerked her hand from her mother's grasp and dashed ahead, nearly slipping on the snow, which was packed and frozen at the doorstep. Elizabeth hugged her, took her by the hand, and led her to a spot near the fire.

"Careful, Gerta, it's icy," Lydia cautioned the older woman. She grasped Gerta's arm and helped her inside.

"Do you think it will ever stop snowing?" Gerta shook the snowflakes off her winter shawl and handed the baby to Lydia.

"Not for a few weeks, anyway," Lydia answered, smiling. Lydia removed the baby's coat and cap, planted a kiss on his fat, rosy cheek, and set him on the floor to play. "I'm glad you've come in spite of it. 'Lizabeth and I can use some company. Abraham's been gone since early this mornin' checkin' his traps. I don't suppose he'll be back 'fore dark."

Gerta nodded her head, "Yah, vinter can get to be a mite long in these voods. Most days ta only visiting I do is vith some bushy-tailed squirrel." Gerta spoke the words brusquely. Though short and stout, she was a vigorous woman for her years. She always wore her long yellow hair in a single braid, wound around her head.

"Vasn't yust for the company I came, however. I brought you some tonic for Yames." She reached into her skirt and took out a small bottle filled with gritty brown liquid. She pulled out the cork stopper and sniffed the contents. Wrinkling her nose, she continued, "Smells like vet chickens, but this remedy vill cure most anything. Made it up myself out of powdered bark, herbs, and molasses syrup. It should do Yames good."

She replaced the stopper and thrust the bottle into Lydia's hands. Lydia eyed it hopefully. "Thank you. Nothin' I been doin' seems to help."

"Is he any better today?"

Lydia shook her head.

"Vell, you give the boy a spoonful of that tonic night and morning," Gerta instructed.

Lydia took the tonic and a spoon and went to James' bedside with it. James had awakened at the sound of the Johanssens' arrival and was lying passively on his bed. Lydia seated him on her lap. She poured a spoonful of the medicine and gave it to the child to drink. He took the bitter liquid willingly, but made a sour face as it slithered down his throat.

"This will make you well, angel," she said, smiling and smoothing his hair away from his fevered brow.

James didn't protest or whimper when she tucked him back into bed. She kissed his cheek, then returned to the outer room, where Gerta waited.

Lydia took up her work at the table again. Gerta, keeping one eye on baby Lars, held the forms while Lydia poured in the hot wax.

"Did my candlemaking a vhile back," Gerta said conversationally. "Been vaiting on Niels to get me some calico yardage so I can make up a new smock for Yohanna. That girl is growing more than I can keep up vith."

"She's near eleven, isn't she?"

"Vill be in the spring. She has a fine hand. It von't be long until she makes all her own clothes."

Lydia smiled and continued pouring the candle mixture into the molds.

"Yohanna pulls her load, but getting Kirstine to do chores is like getting a mule to dance ta Irish yig. It takes her three days to get done vhat ta rest of us can do in an afternoon. I've a mind to take a strap to that child."

"Kirstine just moves at a slower pace, that's all."

"Huh!" Gerta snorted. "She'd dawdle if the house vas afire."

The two girls sitting near the hearth burst into a peal of laughter, evidently over something Elizabeth had drawn on her slate.

Gerta glanced over at them. "Your Elizabeth is goot for Inge. Nobody can draw Inge out of that shell of hers like Elizabeth can."

"There's not much that stops 'Lizabeth from doin' or sayin' what she's got a mind to," Lydia agreed. "She's like her father in that respect." Lydia's brow furrowed slightly as she thought about Abraham. Although nothing more had been said about his plan to work the lead mines, she knew his mind was set and he was going forward with the preparations. She wanted to discuss her feelings about it with Gerta. Lydia had scarcely completed the thought when Gerta abruptly set aside the molds.

"Child, I vas hoping Abraham vould be avay so ve'd have a chance to talk. I've been aching to tell you about ta meeting at Mr. Calvin's." Gerta spoke in a hushed tone and her clear blue eyes shone.

The Mormon meeting, of course. Lydia had completely forgotten about it. Gerta and Niels had stopped for her the evening before and Abraham had curtly told them she wasn't going before they'd even exchanged a word of greeting. She'd explained that James was sick and she couldn't leave him, but she suspected Gerta knew the full reason why she was staying away.

"What happened, Gerta? What did Mr. Pratt say?"

Gerta pulled her chair closer to Lydia's. "Mr. McLellin first spoke about ta book. He called it ta Book of Mormon and said it vas vritten in a strange tongue on plates of gold. Mr. Smith deciphered ta tongue vith ta help of a seer-stone, and published it." Gerta went on to tell her about the contents of the book, how it described an ancient people who were at first a righteous nation, but later grew in wickedness. This book was a record of the people and their prophets and their relationship with the Lord.

Lydia sat without speaking, fascinated by Gerta's account.

"God commanded their prophet to bury ta book so ta vicked vouldn't lay hands on it and so as to preserve it. This book is ta same one Yoseph Smith dug up, right in ta spot where ta ancient prophet buried it."

Gerta's brow broke out in a thin line of perspiration and her eyes burned with an intensity Lydia had never seen in them before as she continued her narration. "After Mr. McLellin finished speaking, Mr. Pratt stood up to preach. Before he could say a vord, that Baptist preacher from Rock Spring . . . vhat's his name? Ta one who puts out ta Baptist paper?"

"You mean Reverend Peck?"

"Yah, that's him. He yumps up, all red in ta face, and starts shouting at Mr. McLellin and Mr. Pratt that their Mormon Bible is a hoax."

"What was Reverend Peck doin' there?"

"I gathered ta Reverend Mr. Dotson invited him down. Ta both of them been doing all they can to turn folks against ta Mormons. Mr. Peck starts raving about how there's nary a sign of ancient remains in America such as ta book describes; no ruined cities nor monuments of any sort to show civilized folks once lived here. He says further that ta book talks about horses, oxen and cows when everybody knows there vas none vhen ta Europeans first come. He said a lot more trying to discredit ta preachers."

"What did Mr. Pratt say in defense of the book, Gerta?"

"I'm getting to that." Gerta's attention became momentarily distracted by baby Lars, who was scooting himself along the floor. "Inge, vatch that babe. He's getting too near ta fire." Returning to her narrative, she continued, "Mr. Pratt stood up and said as calm and cool as a spring morn, 'Vhat are vild buffalo if they aren't ta descendants of cattle of ancient inhabitants?' Then he asks, 'How did horse tracks get imbedded in ta petrified rock of Kentucky vithout a horse to make them?' Vell, Mr. Peck couldn't answer either question. He yust sat back down and let Mr. Pratt finish."

Lydia's eyes widened and she smiled to herself.

"Mr. Pratt vent on to say a number of remarkable things. He told us to take hold of ta truth as he gave it, learn ta scriptures, obey ta commandments of God, and seek for ta Holy

Spirit to guide us into ta vay of truth."

"What else, Gerta?"

"Vell, he spoke some on ta second coming of Jesus and ta fulfilling of ancient prophecies."

"Oh, I wish I'd been there," Lydia said softly. "Gerta, do you believe the things he told you?"

"Liddy, I handled a copy of that book myself, and Niels read a portion of it aloud. I can't explain the feelings that come over me vhile I listened to ta words. It vas as if my heart leaped in my bosom. Niels and me been asking ourselves that same question and I've prayed over it. I'm inclined to believe ve've heard ta truth."

Lydia fell silent, pondering Gerta's words. The things she'd heard stirred up a host of emotions, all swirling inside her. She wanted, desperately, to know for herself the truth of these things.

In spite of Gerta's tonic, James continued to get worse. He progressed from fever and chills to fits of thrashing upon his bed, his little body bathed in perspiration. As the days passed, he became increasingly disoriented, with fewer lucid moments.

Lydia was out of her mind with worry. She'd been on her knees for lengthy intervals, pleading with the Lord to make James well, but the Lord seemed unwilling to answer her supplications. The day before, she'd sent Elizabeth to the settlement to stay with her parents, over her daughter's petulant protests. She was terrified Elizabeth would come down with the sickness too.

As Lydia prepared a simple meal of soup and cornbread, her thoughts lingered on James. It wasn't long, however, before Abraham's heavy step at the door put an end to her contemplation. He lunged inside, slamming the door behind him. His beaver coat and cap were caked with snow, and ice clung to his beard.

"Supper ready?" he asked, shedding his coat and stamping the snow off his boots.

Lydia nodded. She dished the thin soup into bowls and set them on the table. Abraham placed his squirrel gun beside the hearth and then extended his broad hands beside the fire.

"How's the boy?" he asked, his back to her.

"No better. Worse if anythin'."

"You ain't heard from Doc Reynolds yet?" he asked as he pulled a chair up to the table.

She shrugged. "He's still on rounds somewhere in the county."

"That does us a h—l of a lot of good, don't it?" Abraham began eating his soup noisily. The melting snow in his beard glistened in the dancing light of the fire.

Lydia joined him at the table. "Did you get anythin'?"

He jerked his thumb toward the cabin door. "A rabbit. It's outside. It's the only one I seen, though. Ain't another sign of game in those woods."

"Maybe you'll find somethin' more tomorrow."

"Don't think so," Abraham mumbled, his mouth full of cornbread. She looked at him questioningly.

"I'm goin' into town tomorrow for supplies. Powder for the gun is almost gone and I'm near out of shot, too."

"We'll be needin' some salt and flour."

He nodded in acknowledgement.

"Maybe someone in town will know where Doc Reynolds is," Lydia suggested hopefully.

"I'll ask."

Lydia put her elbow on the table and rested her chin in her hand. A steaming bowl of soup sat before her, but she had no appetite for it. She eyed it glumly, her thoughts on James. She knew there was a strong possibility he might die, even if the doctor were located. Casualties along the frontier were common, particularly among children. Lydia's own mother had lost four of her seven children before they'd outgrown childhood. She shuddered at that unspeakable thought.

Abraham, finished with his meal, leaned back in his chair and wiped his mouth with his sleeve. "I'll be leavin' at first light and try to be back by nightfall." He stood and stretched, then retrieved his gun from the hearthside and began to clean the barrel with an old rag.

Lydia silently removed the dishes from the table, then poured a bowl of soup for James and carried it into the corner where he lay sleeping.

"James, honey, can you wake up for Mama and eat a little somethin'?"

The child moaned and his eyelids fluttered open. Lydia propped a pillow behind him and pulled the blankets up under his chin. "Have some of this nice soup, darlin'."

James tried, but the soup only trickled out of the corner of his mouth as fast as Lydia spooned it in.

"You got to swallow it, James. Try some more now." Lydia held another spoonful to his lips, but the boy turned his head away and no amount of coaxing could get him to open his mouth or unclench his teeth. Lydia finally set the bowl aside. She sponged him with cool water from a bucket and brushed through his curly, dark hair. As Abraham toiled over his gun in the next room, Lydia cradled her son and fervently uttered another silent prayer.

Abraham left the following morning before Lydia awoke. She spent the morning doing light chores and encouraging James to eat. By early afternoon she was exhausted. She dropped into the slat-backed rocker, closed her eyes and wept. She must have dozed after that, for a sudden rap at the door jerked her to her feet. Thinking it was Abraham home early from his trip to town, she swung the door open wide. Instead, she was startled to find Gerta Johanssen on her doorstep accompanied by a tall man. Both were bundled up to their noses and covered with snow.

"Liddy, Abraham stopped by our place this morning on his vay into town and told Niels that your boy was doing poorly. I took ta liberty of inviting Mr. Pratt over to see Yames. He might be able to help, child."

Lydia stared at the young man on her porch. All she could see of him was his dark, strong eyes. The rest of his face was hidden beneath a woolen muffler and low-fitting hat. "Come in," she said hesitantly.

Lydia closed the door against the swirling snow, briefly wondering if Abraham were warm and safely indoors. She motioned the pair to be seated. "How can you help, Mr. Pratt?" she asked in a defensive tone of voice. "Are you a doctor as well as a preacher?"

"No, I'm not, Mrs. Dawson, but I may be able to render some assistance nonetheless."

Lydia's look clearly conveyed her doubt. "I don't need preachin' right now, Mr. Pratt," she answered after a long pause.

"He's not come to preach, Liddy. He's come to heal Yames. I believe he can, child. Give him a chance —"

"Heal James!" Lydia cried. "Ain't nobody goin' to heal that child but the Lord himself. He's dyin', Gerta!" Overcome with emotion, she buried her face in her hands and sobbed.

The sober young man stepped to Lydia's side and put a hand on her heaving shoulder. "Mrs. Dawson, do you recall Sunday last when you attended meeting?" he asked.

Lydia nodded, her face still hidden in her hands.

"I noticed you as that meeting adjourned. You struck me as a woman of singular courage and faith. Mrs. Johanssen tells me you're affiliated with the Baptists. Is that correct?"

She nodded again.

"I, too, professed to be a Baptist at one point. I had a very great desire to be saved from my sins. I believed in Jesus Christ and wanted to serve him and keep his commandments. It seemed to me at the time that the Baptist religion followed more closely the teachings of the Bible than any other sect I was acquainted with. But still it occurred to me that there was one great key lacking, and that was the authority to minister in holy ordinances."

Lydia raised her head and looked up at the tall, dark man at her shoulder. He stood regarding her with that same intensity of expression she had noted at the conclusion of the Sunday meeting. She trembled slightly under that powerful gaze. His words stirred something in her heart, but she failed to understand what relevance they carried for herself or for James. What difference did authority make to a child who was near death?

"I do not lay claim to medical training, Mrs. Dawson," Pratt continued in a quiet, assured voice, "but I do possess something far more valuable. I speak of the Holy Priesthood of God—the power and authority which God bestows upon men to act in his name—conferred upon me by one having

the authority to do so, in an unbroken chain from the Lord himself. By and through that priesthood given to benefit mankind, the blind see, the lame walk, the sick are healed."

"Are you sayin' you can heal my boy, Mr. Pratt?"

"As you said earlier, Mrs. Dawson, only the Lord can heal your son."

Lydia's heart raced as she comprehended his meaning. She searched his face in an effort to determine if he spoke the truth. Could he be a messenger from the Lord in answer to her prayers?

"Do you have faith enough to believe your son can be made well, Mrs. Dawson?"

She wavered, wanting desperately to believe, hoping, yet not daring to hope. She darted a glance at Gerta. The older woman's eyes were moist and she was silently nodding her head. Lydia shut her eyes and said in a whisper, "The Lord God healed the leper and raised the dead. I place my faith and trust in him." She opened her eyes and said with confidence, "Ask God to heal my son, Mr. Pratt."

Parley Pratt helped Lydia to her feet and gave her shoulder an encouraging squeeze. She led him to the bed where James lay. The child's cheeks were flaming and perspiration ran in rivulets down his brow, pasting his dark curls to his face. He moaned and tossed upon the bed.

Pratt gazed at him for several moments before saying or doing anything. Then he placed the palms of his hands upon the boy's head, and in the name of Jesus Christ prayed, "James Dawson, I bless you that your body will be made well and whole from this hour forth, to be no longer afflicted with disease, but to be restored to its natural and normal state of health, that you might be a blessing and a light to your parents, Amen."

Lydia could barely see through the tears that blurred her eyes. She picked up James and held him tightly against her. His feverish, tense body relaxed in her embrace. Her eyes lifted to Pratt's face. A peace and assurance seemed to flow from him—a warmth and spiritual strength Lydia could *feel.*

"Thank you," Lydia whispered. "Thank you."

Wherefore, this is the land of Promise, and the place for the city of Zion

D & C 57:2

CHAPTER FOUR

Christian Kent folded his arms and leaned back against a barrel full of dried beans as he listened intently to the conversation going on in the mercantile.

"I'm telling you, Sidney, if South Carolina doesn't rescind the ordinance, Jackson will not hesitate to send troops in and end the crisis by force."

"I don't believe the President will do that," Sidney Gilbert answered. The short, spare proprietor of the store took a swipe across his forehead and frowned slightly. "Old Hickory doesn't want to start a civil war and that's what he'd be doing if he tries sending troops into Charleston. Jackson wants to maintain peace and keep the Union intact. I believe he'll go to any peaceable lengths to do so."

The other man, older and stouter, with balding pate and gray eyes, rapped his fist on the counter. "Why in tarnation, then, has he readied two hundred thousand men just waiting for his signal?"

"Hold on now, John. The President claims he can raise that number of men. He hasn't actually done it." Gilbert stood behind the counter, with a flour sack tied around his waist for an apron. Behind him were rows of shelves stacked with goods.

John Corrill shook his head and muttered under his breath. "You're burying your head in the sand, Sidney, if you think Jackson won't act."

Christian silently contemplated both sides of the argument. His face bore a slight frown, which emphasized the notch in his chin. Christian was well aware of the controversy swirling around South Carolina's "Ordinance of Nullification," an action which had grown out of the fiery debate over states' rights.

"The whole issue," Sidney Gilbert was saying, "revolves around the question, Does a state have the right to resist federal authority?"

"No!" Corrill thundered. "Nullification can only lead to disunion and chaos. In my book that's treason. Those southern states' righters are treading on dangerous ground. Mark my words, nothing will come of this whole mess but more trouble." He shook his head sourly.

"You haven't said anything, Christian. What's your opinion?"

Christian considered Gilbert's question carefully before answering. He spoke slowly, choosing his words. "It's true the President has said that disunion constitutes treason and that the people of Carolina are in violation of the Constitution. Personally, I agree with that. I think you can depend on Jackson doing everything in his power to prevent South Carolina from seceding."

"Including ordering troops in," Corrill nodded with a look of satisfaction.

"Jackson is determined to enforce the law," Christian Kent said, eyeing the two men calmly. "If that means resorting to armed force, I don't think he'll hesitate. He didn't gain the moniker 'Hero of New Orleans' by issuing empty threats."

"And that's the root of his problem, Christian," Sidney Gilbert said. "He's never forgotten how to behave like a soldier."

Christian laughed and straightened to his full height. He was a head taller than either of the other two men. "You may be right."

"Of course I'm right. Admit it, Christian. That old soldier was never cut out to be president."

"You won't get him to admit to that," Corrill said. "I've never heard Christian criticize a single action the President's taken. Old Hickory's his hero—next to Brother Joseph."

"I do admire Jackson because he's concerned about people, not politics. He's as anxious for the welfare of the common man as he is for the wealthy and influential," Christian said with conviction.

"And Christian can quote doctrine to substantiate it,"

laughed the lean proprietor of the store.

"It's all those newspapers Christian peruses," Corrill said with a twinkle springing to his eye. "He scrutinizes every scrap of paper that comes into the printing office."

Christian smiled and slapped his friend on the back. "And if I don't get back to the office, William is going to ask for my resignation."

"William would never let you go without the Prophet's say-so." Sidney Gilbert spoke the sentence lightly, but there was an edge to his voice.

"I'd rather not give him the excuse, if you don't mind," Christian returned with a grin. "I believe you wanted to see that upcoming issue of the *Star*, Brother Corrill, or do you intend to stay here and argue politics with Sidney?"

Christian and John Corrill crossed the rutted and muddy street and made their way down the block. Christian slowed his stride to match the older man's. At twenty-four, he was more than a dozen years Corrill's junior. His long legs easily covered the distance to the printing house. They climbed the outside stairs of the brick building and let themselves into the office. William Phelps glanced up from his desk as they entered.

"I ran into Brother Corrill at Gilbert & Whitney's Mercantile. He was on his way here to look at the galleys for the January issue of the *Star*."

Phelps stood up and shook hands with the portly fellow at Christian's side. "I'm glad you've come, Brother Corrill. We're ready to go to press. Oliver's in the back now setting the type. Come and I'll show you."

The three of them started to the rear of the house where the Church's printing press was situated. A thin, tall man of about Christian's age was bent over the press, arranging type in the pan.

"Afternoon, Brother Cowdery," John Corrill said, putting a hand on the man's shoulder. Oliver Cowdery looked up from his work. His was a pale, solemn face, topped by a shock of black hair combed back to reveal a high forehead. His eyes were dark, his nose sharp, and his lips thin and narrow.

"Hello, John," Cowdery replied. A smile flickered across

his mouth and disappeared. He straightened and wiped his ink-stained fingers on the front of his printer's apron. The two men shook hands and exchanged a moment of pleasantries.

"William tells me you're ready to begin printing."

"That's correct." Oliver reached to a nearby table where a manuscript copy of the *Evening and the Morning Star* lay, dated January 1833. He handed the paper to Corrill.

"Ummm," Corrill murmured as he scanned the manuscript. "Continue to stress that the gathering be accomplished in an orderly manner as you've done here, Oliver," he suggested, tapping the page which carried the caption "Let Every Man Learn His Duty." "The Saints need to be reminded that the gathering to Zion is not to be made in haste nor without proper preparation."

"Many Saints arrive with only the barest of necessities," Oliver replied. "They suppose their needs will be provided once they reach Missouri."

"Continue to educate them. That's one of the purposes of the *Star.*"

Cowdery nodded in agreement.

Corrill leafed through the next few pages of paper, his lips moving silently as he read. "You've included the testimony of the witnesses. Good."

Christian reflected on the testimonies to which he referred, testimonies borne by Oliver Cowdery and others of the truthfulness and divinity of the Book of Mormon. These men had seen and handled the golden plates from which Joseph Smith translated.

Christian's breath quickened even now as he recalled receiving his own copy of the book. He'd been working in Ohio, writing for a small newspaper, the *Ohio Sentinel.* From the moment his newspaper filed an account about Joseph Smith and his fabulous book of golden plates, Christian had been fascinated. He'd decided to learn more about the story for himself. He'd ridden to the Johnson home in Hiram, where Joseph and his family were staying, and conducted an interview with the Prophet. He'd liked Joseph Smith immediately and the two had talked until late into the evening.

It was then that Joseph told him of seeing the Father and

the Son in a glorious vision, of the angel Moroni's visit to him, and of later securing the book of ancient scripture under Moroni's direction. He spoke of the persecutions he had suffered since that time, the trials involved in translating the plates, and the subsequent establishment of Christ's church, together with the restoration of the keys of the holy priesthood. He bore solemn testimony to the divinity of the work and presented Christian with a copy of the Book of Mormon. Christian returned home the next morning with a changed heart.

Corrill glanced over the remaining pages of the newspaper. "I see your handiwork here, Christian. 'Rebellion in South Carolina.'" Corrill chuckled.

"William requested that I delete the better part of the article I had prepared on that topic," Christian answered with a grin.

"Good for him," Corrill said.

Corrill handed the paper back to Cowdery. "It looks fine, William. I'll inform Bishop Partridge."

William Phelps nodded vigorously. "I'll be bringing the tithes to the Lord's storehouse in a day or two. You can mention that to Bishop Partridge."

"I know the Bishop is pleased with the way you've handled your stewardship, Brother Phelps. He remarked to Brother Morley and me the other day that the printing establishment was bringing in a good surplus and he commended you for your faithfulness."

Phelps' chest swelled with pride at the compliment. "The Lord has seen fit to bless us abundantly, Brother Corrill."

"Good." Corrill smiled briefly and then turned to Christian, who was standing at his elbow. "Has any further progress been made with regard to the Book of Commandments?"

Christian hesitated. "Publication of the book is still pending, John."

"What problems are you encountering? You've received all the revelations and commandments from Brother Joseph?"

Christian looked at his employer uncomfortably.

"We've received them, Brother Corrill, but we haven't had as yet an opportunity to print all of them," Phelps answered quickly. "The project has taken longer than anticipated."

Corrill said nothing for several seconds. Christian kept his eyes downcast, pretending to study a scrap of paper near his toe.

"Well, then, brethren, I'll be looking forward to receiving a copy of the *Star*. Goodbye, Oliver." Corrill extended his hand to the reedy young man.

William Phelps walked with him to the front part of the house. They paused as they reached the stairs and Corrill put his hand on Phelps' shoulder and spoke to him in a quiet voice.

Christian watched their exchange with growing uneasiness. He went to his desk and began going through papers he had been working on earlier. He tried to keep his mind on his work. But an unsettling feeling nagged at him, a feeling he found impossible to shrug off.

By five o'clock that afternoon, Christian had scrubbed the ink from his hands, changed into a shirt of the same rich shade of chestnut brown as his eyes and hair, and was well on his way to the town of Liberty, Clay County, Missouri. He was looking forward to his evening there and would have been entertaining only the most pleasant thoughts had it not been for John Corrill's visit to the printing house.

Corrill stopped at the publishing office frequently, for it was part of his assignment to keep abreast of the printing done for the Church and report its progress to Bishop Edward Partridge, the presiding Church authority in Independence. Corrill, along with another man by the name of Isaac Morley, were Bishop Partridge's counselors in the center stake of Zion. As such, they held responsibility for the physical and material welfare of the Saints, as well as their spiritual needs.

Corrill's questions concerning the publication of the Book of Commandments triggered disturbing thoughts that Christian had tried for some time to ignore. More than eight months ago, the Prophet Joseph Smith had given Phelps and Cowdery stewardship over a collection of sacred revelations to be published at the printing firm in Independence. Phelps was editor and publisher, and the establishment was housed in the upper story of his brick home. What Phelps had said was true—he had not had sufficient time to finish the printing of all the revelations. However, Christian surmised that other matters had, of late, occupied his attention.

Christian ran a restless hand through his longish brown hair. He knew that Phelps, along with many of the Saints at Independence, had fallen prey to feelings of jealousy and rivalry directed at the members headquartered in Kirtland, Ohio. It was there that Brother Joseph resided, not at Independence. Several of the brethren in Independence felt that the Prophet should be in their midst and strongly expressed that opinion. Phelps himself had recently written Joseph a letter, urging him to come to Missouri. It had been rumored among the Missouri Saints that Joseph considered them spiritually lacking in comparison with the members in Ohio. This, along with other misunderstandings, had spawned discontent and suspicions. Christian was not completely purged of these feelings himself, but he suspected that the brethren were carrying their suppositions and jealousies to an extreme. For his own part, he was determined not to speak against the Prophet.

For Joseph Smith was, in truth, God's prophet. Christian knew that as surely as he knew the sun rose and set. The Spirit had borne him that witness more than a year ago when he joined the Church of Christ. The Church had its roots in New York State, but Joseph received a revelation designating Independence, Jackson County, Missouri, as the gathering place and the center stake of the Church for the Lord's Saints. This was Zion, the land of promise. Joseph accordingly called seven high priests from Kirtland to settle in Jackson County and build up Zion. Other members of the Church joined them as quickly as they could dispose of their property and migrate to Jackson County. Christian, recently converted and baptized in Ohio, was among them.

As Christian approached the town of Liberty, his tensions eased. He stopped in front of an imposing two-story brick home, tethered his horse, and bounded the three steps to the porch. When he rapped with the heavy brass knocker, a big-faced negress swung open the door.

Christian spoke first. "Hello, Matty! How are you?"

"I's tolerable well, Mis't Kent," the plump woman beamed.

The negress wore a plain dark smock and white apron, with a turban wound around her head. In her arms she carried a huge bundle of laundry. "Come in heah, Mis't Kent, Miss Mary Ann's awaitin' fo' you."

She ushered Christian inside and directed him to a chair in the parlor. Christian removed his hat and coat and handed them to the woman. "When are you going to sit still long enough for me to make that sketch of you, Matty?"

"I knows you joshin' me, Mis't Kent. You don't want no picture of this heah darkie."

"I certainly do. You have extraordinary eyes. I want to capture them in charcoal."

The black woman waved his answer aside with a sweep of her big hand.

"You gwine on now, Mis't Kent."

Christian chuckled and took a seat on a rose-colored velvet chair. "I don't give up easily, Matty. Next time I come I'll bring my drawing paper."

Matty shook her turbaned head and turned to leave, but not before Christian caught sight of her beaming smile.

The room where Christian waited was large and richly furnished. The trappings of wealth added to his pleasure when he visited Mary Ann. Christian had been seeing Mary Ann Stewart for several months and had become a frequent dinner guest in her father's home. Her father, Josiah Stewart, was a wealthy Eastern banker who had come west to open a state bank. Mary Ann was his youngest and prettiest daughter. She had eyes the color of Missouri grass and hair as yellow as honey.

As Christian's eye traced the contours of a fine old English clock resting atop the mantlepiece, there came a rustling of skirts at the parlor door. Christian jumped to his feet as Mary Ann swept into the room.

"Christian, you naughty boy. I thought you'd never get here!" Mary Ann glided to his side and slipped her small hand into the crook of Christian's arm. Her tawny hair brushed his cheek. The smell of it was sweet and fresh. She smiled up at him with teasing eyes. "I hope you haven't been waiting here long all by yourself."

"No, as a matter of fact I've been engrossed in conversation with Matty," he said with a grin.

"Oh, Christian, I hope you didn't bring up the subject of drawing her likeness again. You shouldn't encourage her. She's much too uppity as it is."

"I'm serious. I really would like to do a drawing of her."

"Oh, pooh."

Christian laughed. "That's what I like about you—ever charitable to those less fortunate than yourself."

"Don't be silly. Matty's just a darkie. Come along now. Papa's in the dining room and growing more cranky by the moment."

"Oh no," groaned Christian. "I don't have much success with your father when he's in the best of humor."

Mary Ann patted his hand. "Just try not to irritate him."

"An impossibility."

"Come along," Mary Ann laughed, guiding him out of the parlor. She prattled happily as they walked arm in arm down the wide hallway toward the dining room. The pressure of her arm against his brought a spot of color to his cheek and he thought her the most beautiful and exciting girl he'd ever met.

"Are you planning to ask me to the concert in Independence?" Mary Ann asked, her voice smooth as corn silk.

Christian stopped short. "Now, how did you hear about that?"

"A girl reads the newspapers, silly. Even if it's not the *Star*."

Christian chuckled. "Yes, I'm planning to ask you. I just thought the asking was going to be *my* idea."

"I know how much you dislike sitting through a classical performance. I didn't want you to forget it was coming, that's all," she added, peeping up at him under long lashes.

"I hadn't forgotten, and neither have I forgotten how much you enjoy that infernal operatic racket."

Mary Ann giggled and hugged Christian's arm. "I thought you'd have developed more of a taste for the arts, growing up in Philadelphia," she teased him.

"I'm afraid I didn't absorb many of the city's values. My mother despairs to this day over my lack of cultural appreciation."

"Well, I shan't stop trying to instill it into you."

As they reached the entrance of the dining room, Christian paused to allow Mary Ann to enter ahead of him. She reached for his hand and playfully pulled him inside. His eager smile faded when he caught sight of Josiah Stewart standing at the head of the room, a frown on his florid face and his arms folded resolutely over his chest.

"Good evening, Sir."

"Kent." The word was more of an acknowledgement than a greeting.

"Papa, Christian's just arrived and we're famished. When will Mother be down?"

"Momentarily," Stewart answered. He gave Christian a look of distaste. His gray eyes were all but hidden by bushy red brows, and his hair was reddish gray as well. He had on a striped silk waistcoat, flawlessly cut trousers, and boots of polished leather. His impeccable appearance attested to the success he enjoyed in the business community. Stewart managed the newly formed Bank of Missouri and took an active role in the political affairs of Clay County. He eyed Christian testily as Christian held the chair for Mary Ann to be seated.

"Thank you," Mary Ann murmured as she slipped into her seat. Christian stood stiffly at her side, trying to think of an appropriate remark to make to Mr. Stewart.

Reaching into a vest pocket, Stewart withdrew a shiny gold-plated cigar case. "Cigar, Kent?"

"Thank you." Christian hastily chose a cigar and put it to his lips. Stewart selected one for himself, struck a match and lit both cigars. They were an expensive brand and strong of flavor. Stewart took several deep draughts before exhaling the smoke. The two smoked in silence for some moments. Stewart had moved to the head of the table and made himself comfortable in a chair. Christian hesitated to sit without being invited. He remained standing at Mary Ann's side, feeling ill at ease.

Stewart evidently enjoyed his discomfiture. The slightest trace of a smirk appeared on his face. "Tell me, Kent. How is the newspaper business?"

"It's going well, Sir. We're busy and continue to attract a few new subscribers each month."

"Gentile subscribers, do you mean?"

Christian knew the remark was meant to goad him. "Some of them."

Stewart's smirk deepened.

"An issue of the *Washington Globe* came into our office the other day," Christian said in an attempt to divert the conversation into another path. "It had quite a piece about the banking establishment."

Stewart's eyebrows shot up in interest.

"It seems Mr. Biddle is still intent on pursuing his course with regard to the state banks."

Stewart's fist slammed the table in a fit of fury. "That devil is determined to ruin us all. If his policies continue, soon there won't be a bank left in the country able to make a loan."

"Most bankers would probably agree with you. Biddle has boasted he can destroy nearly any bank in the United States."

"Let the scoundrel boast all he likes. Jackson will put an end to him and his blasted regulations." Stewart chewed furiously on the end of his cigar.

"Josiah?"

Both men started at the sound of Mrs. Stewart's voice. She stood in the doorway of the dining room, her mouth poised in a practiced smile.

"Josiah, I hope you haven't been unpleasant company." She spoke the sentence lightly, but her tone was unmistakably condescending.

Stewart put out his cigar and stood up. Mrs. Stewart entered the dining room and glided past him to her seat at the table. She was tall and willow thin, and carried herself in a stately manner.

"How are you this evening, Mr. Kent?" she asked as she removed her linen napkin and folded it across her lap.

"Very well, Mrs. Stewart. Thank you."

She nodded slightly. "Please be seated, gentlemen."

Christian doused his cigar and sat down at the place Mrs. Stewart indicated for him. Mary Ann smiled brightly from across the table.

Immediately a slim young black woman appeared, carrying a silver tray with a large tureen of soup resting upon it. The serving girl set the bowl in front of her mistress and disappeared back into the kitchen.

Mrs. Stewart spooned soup into delicate china bowls and handed them around the table. Mary Ann chattered freely as they ate. Her talk relieved Christian's uneasiness and he settled back more comfortably into his chair.

"Mother, Christian's invited me to Mrs. Ludendorff's concert in Independence. May I go?" Mary Ann asked.

"Foreigners," Josiah Stewart mumbled under his breath. "Taking over the whole d—n country."

Christian couldn't help stifling a smile. He knew Stewart's comment stemmed from the fact that several foreigners held stock in the National Bank. Stewart was apparently still fuming over the topic of their earlier conversation. He was emphatically against the idea of a national bank.

Christian reviewed in his mind the facts he knew about the situation: In 1823 Nicholas Biddle had become president of the National Bank. Biddle realized he could regulate the availability of credit all over the nation by controlling the lending policies of state banks. Eventually, much of the paper money of the local banks came across the counter of the National Bank. In collecting these notes and presenting them for conversion into specie, Biddle could compel the local banks to maintain adequate reserves of gold and silver. By doing so, Biddle was prohibiting the smaller banks from lending freely, thus limiting their profits. Stewart's bank was among those smarting under Biddle's policies.

"Oh, Papa," Mary Ann was saying, "Mrs. Ludendorff is a famous vocalist."

"Fattening herself at the expense of American pocketbooks," Stewart snapped.

"Papa, that's unreasonable."

"Unreasonable?" Stewart shouted. "You consider it reasonable for foreigners to be involved in American finance?"

"I wasn't aware that we were discussing politics," Mary Ann said, her tone icy.

"That's exactly what we are discussing here," her father returned. "Politics and money—the twin pillars of American business. Politics and money—that's what determines success or failure. Take the National Bank for example—"

"Oh, for heaven's sake," Mrs. Stewart exclaimed.

"Take the Bank, for example," he continued, glaring his wife into silence. "It's become a purely political issue. Congress passed a bill for recharter of the Bank, and Jackson vetoed it out of hand. And for good reason. Jackson knows the danger of supporting a private monopoly that allows a few plutocrats to accumulate millions of dollars."

Stewart looked fiercely around the table, ready to pounce on anyone foolish enough to disagree with him. No one did.

"You're a good Jacksonian, Kent. What I've said is true, isn't it?"

Christian hesitated. He didn't wish to be drawn into the fire. He cleared his throat.

"Well, Kent?"

"Basically, I agree with you, Sir. I think Jackson was right in vetoing the bill as it stood."

"As it stood? What do you mean by that?"

"Only that the President might consider reforming the Bank instead of destroying it entirely. Perhaps take it out of private hands."

"Then you support the idea of a central bank!" Stewart exploded.

"No, Sir. I didn't say that. I only suggested there might be another solution."

"Don't be ridiculous, Kent. There's only one solution and Jackson stated it succinctly. 'We must strangle this hydra of corruption.'"

Christian said nothing more, hoping Stewart would let the matter drop. But the elder man persisted.

"I might have expected a comment like that from you, Kent."

Christian looked up from his plate, surprised by the personal attack.

"Those religious tenets you adhere to seem to have warped your thinking."

Christian felt his face redden. "I don't believe my religious views have anything to do with banking, Mr. Stewart."

"I think they do. With all of your people swarming into the area, you might take it into your heads to change the whole political complexion of this county."

"We're not interested in changing anyone's political views nor trampling anyone's freedom of political expression."

"Come on, boy. You people are notorious for trying to impose your views on others!"

"You're wrong about that, Sir. We're only interested in sharing what we believe to be true and allowing others to make up their own minds."

"Don't spout that rubbish to me, Kent. Everyone knows you Mormonites have little tolerance for those who won't accept your beliefs. Your own newspaper preaches damnation to those who don't submit to baptism at your hands." Stewart was openly hostile.

"There's not another people on earth who respect religious freedom more than we do, Mr. Stewart. It's our people who are being ridiculed and persecuted for what they believe in," replied Christian with feeling.

"You bring it on yourselves! With your self-righteous attitude and your blasphemous doctrines, what sort of treatment do you expect to receive?"

"We expect to be permitted to worship as we see fit. Our forefathers fled to this continent to avoid religious persecution. They believed men should be allowed to worship when and how they choose. We expect that same God-given right."

"And you deem it your right to take possession of the entire county of Jackson." Stewart's voice was sour with sarcasm.

"We believe the Lord has given us this place for an eventual inheritance. But we don't plan on taking anything, not without fair payment."

"What makes you think the settlers are willing to sell? Or do you plan to convert us all first?"

Mary Ann was squirming in her chair, trying to get Christian's attention. When she'd caught his eye, she frowned and shook her head in warning to let the matter drop. He glanced from Mary Ann to her mother. Mrs. Stewart had a curious expression on her face, as if she would enjoy hearing his answer.

Christian swallowed and ran a hand across his forehead. "I apologize, Sir. I didn't mean to be disagreeable."

Mrs. Stewart looked disappointed. "Why don't we all finish our supper," she said primly.

Mary Ann was silent for the remainder of the meal. Christian knew she was angry with him, yet he felt offended by her anger. He had said what he had to. It would have been unconscionable to let Stewart attack him in that manner and not defend what he knew to be right. In spite of that, a feeling of gloom settled over him. He tried to recall exactly when the conversation had veered out of control. He should have been on his guard to avoid it. What little remaining conversation took place at the table was strained, and Christian longed for the meal's conclusion.

At last Mr. and Mrs. Stewart put aside their dinner napkins and left the dining room, leaving Christian and Mary Ann to themselves. As soon as they were out of earshot, Mary Ann hissed, "Christian, why do you argue with Papa? You know it makes him angry with you."

"He was angry with me before I even arrived."

"You only succeed in annoying him further by bringing up the subject of your religion." Mary Ann's cheeks were growing pink.

"I didn't bring the subject up. Your father did," Christian protested.

"Oh Christian, surely you don't believe all those ridiculous notions your church professes."

He stared at her for several seconds. "I don't consider them to be ridiculous," he answered quietly. "And yes, I believe everything the Church teaches. I hoped that you would eventually come to accept the gospel too."

The look of scorn on Mary Ann's face caused Christian to drop his gaze. Suddenly he felt foolish for expressing his feelings. Instead of the pleasant visit he'd anticipated, the whole evening with the Stewarts had gone awry.

CHAPTER FIVE

The frontier town of Independence sat on the broad and fertile prairie of western Missouri, bounded by the Big Blue River on the west and the Little Blue on the east. Independence was the last outpost for traders and travelers embarking for the west along the Santa Fe trail. It was a busy, growing town, boasting a courthouse, a saw mill, a blacksmith shop, the Gilbert and Whitney store, and the *Star* printing office. A few homes were built of brick, but most were rough dwellings hewn from logs.

Christian picked his way through the mud and muck which was Main Street, his thoughts on an article he was contemplating for the next edition of the *Star*. He wanted to discuss his ideas with a friend who worked at the mill. It was noon and the sun was struggling to shine through the gray clouds concealing the bleak January sky. He'd ridden home from Mary Ann's the evening before in a torrent of rain, and now the roads were nearly impassable.

Despite the soggy weather, the town was buzzing with its usual activity. All around him were the sights and sounds of building. The ring of hammers and the twang of saws formed a melody against which all the other noises of the street played their accompaniment—the rustle of ladies' long skirts, children's giddy shouts, the rumble of heavy wagons careening through the muddy roads, the snap of reins across a horse's rump, raucous laughter from a saloon across the way. Christian breathed it all in, savoring the strength and vitality of the burgeoning town.

As Christian approached the mill, he scanned the faces of the half-dozen men working out in the yard. Most were in their shirt sleeves, despite the cold weather. A couple of the men were hauling logs with a rope and pulley; two others cut at a length of oak with a double-handled saw. Christian greeted several of them as he walked through the yard and into the shed-like building. It took a moment for his eyes to adjust to the dim interior. The pleasant odor of newly cut lumber hung in the air.

A big, burly man with an ax slung over his shoulder passed Christian on his way out of the building.

"Is Seth around?" he asked the big man.

The man jerked his thumb over his shoulder. "Back there."

"Thanks."

Christian strode to the far end of the building and found his friend bent over a rough piece of furniture, working the wood with an awl.

"Don't you ever take a break?"

"Christian! How are you?" Seth Whitfield replied in a pleased tone, clapping his friend on the back.

"Not bad. It looks like they're keeping you busy."

"Yes. Walters received four new orders this week." Seth put down his tool and wiped a sleeve across his forehead. He was a handsome man of twenty-three, several inches shorter than Christian and of slighter build. His hair was brown and worn long to his collar. Curly side whiskers reached almost to his chin. He had chocolate brown eyes, an aquiline nose, and a full mouth. "Pull up a chair," Seth offered.

Christian sat down on a stump of wood, stirring up a miniature swirl of sawdust with his boots.

"What brings you down here?" Seth asked. "You looking for advice on how to handle that gal of yours?"

Christian laughed. "Not from you. Things are bad enough as it is."

"What happened now?"

"I had dinner with Mary Ann and her parents last night. I'm afraid I spoiled her father's evening."

"Don't tell me you got into another disagreement with him?" Seth shook his head in a bemused way. "You've got to learn to get along with the old gentlemen if you want to get along with his daughter."

"You're a fine one to talk. Didn't I hear something about Carrie's father once running you off his place at the end of a pitchfork?"

"That was before he came to realize what an exceptional fellow I am." Both of them chuckled, then Seth continued in a more serious tone. "I believe I have them both convinced, however. Looks like there's going to be a wedding this spring."

"Good for you! Congratulations, Seth."

"Thanks. I know you didn't come here to discuss my plans. What's on your mind, Christian?"

"I wanted to show you something," Christian answered, taking a folded piece of newsprint from his vest pocket. He unfolded the paper, smoothed it out and handed it to Seth.

"What's this?"

"It's a piece from the *London Gazette* written by a Colonel Galindo from Central America. Read it and tell me what you think."

Seth slowly read aloud:

> The neighboring country for many leagues distant, contains remains of the ancient labors of its people, bridges, reservoirs, monumental inscriptions, subterranean edifices, etc. Everything bears testimony that these surprising people were not physically dissimilar from the present Indians; but their civilization far surpassed that of the Mexicans and Peruvians; they must have existed long prior to the fourteenth century.

Seth issued a long, low whistle. "Well, what do you know."

"This is the first substantial piece of evidence I've seen for the existence of Book of Mormon people. Do you know what that means, Seth? Those skeptics who claim that a high level of civilization never existed in America will have to choke on their words. This is going to change a lot of people's minds concerning the authenticity of the Book of Mormon." Christian chuckled delightedly.

Seth quickly scanned the remainder of the article. "It's a good case for us."

"You bet it is and it's just the beginning. There'll be more people like this Colonel Galindo turning up with evidence to verify the account in the Book of Mormon. You can be assured of that."

"One more testimony to the truthfulness of the work. It's great stuff, Christian. Are you going to print it in the *Star?*"

"I thought I'd run it along with a few verses out of Helaman describing the cities and dwellings of the Nephites. What do you think?"

"I think it's a fine idea, but it's not my opinion that matters. What does William say about it?"

"He likes it. It's just a question of having enough space. He had something else in mind for the February issue."

"Well, talk him into it. I think the Gentiles would find it enlightening." Seth handed the sheet back to Christian.

Christian refolded it and slipped it back into his pocket. "Why don't you stop by the printing office when you're through and we'll go get some supper?"

"Can't. Carrie and I are invited to the Whitmers for supper tonight. If you'd get yourself a girl of the right religion you'd probably receive more social invitations," Seth said in jest.

"And I suppose you'd be the proper one to pick her out for me?"

"I've got good taste in that area. No doubt about it. Just look at Carrie."

Christian indulged in the banter with a smile, but inwardly he was troubled. The evening spent with Mary Ann had gone badly and he was frustrated with their relationship. He realized the chances were slim that Mary Ann would ever embrace the gospel. She was far too proud and she had her heart set on the things of the world. The problem was that he was smitten with her. Whenever he was in the company of another girl, he found himself comparing her to Mary Ann. And inevitably the other girl came out wanting.

"We won't be long at the Whitmers. Drop by my place later in the evening," Seth suggested. "We'll play a few hands of cards."

"I don't think so, Seth. Thanks anyway."

"All right." Seth picked up the awl and returned to his

work. "You should print that article. Tell it straight out, Cicero," he said in parting.

Christian left the sawmill feeling discontented. He walked the several blocks back to the printing house, thinking about his conversation with Seth. His excitement over the article in the *Gazette* was beginning to ebb, and he felt oddly alone even though the streets were filled with people. He plodded on toward the office but halted when he heard his name called. He looked around to find Sidney Gilbert signaling him from the porch steps of his store.

"Hello, Sidney."

"You look a little down in the mouth. Come here. I've something to fix that."

Christian crossed the street, his boots making sucking noises in the sticky mud with each step. Sidney ducked inside his store and reappeared a moment later with something round and red. "Here," he said, thrusting it into Christian's hand.

"Where did you get apples this time of the year?"

"I have a few saved for a rainy day," Sidney replied.

Christian shined the apple on his coat sleeve and then bit into it. It was crisp and juicy. He smiled appreciatively.

"A good one, is it?"

"Umm," Christian replied, his mouth full of the fruit.

"Are you out on a news-gathering detail?" Sidney asked him in a conversational tone.

"Sort of. I've been at the mill talking with Seth."

"How is Brother Whitfield?"

"Fine," Christian mumbled, taking another bite of the apple.

"Have you seen John today?" The question was phrased innocently enough, but Christian detected a note of tension behind it.

"John Corrill? No, I haven't. Why?"

"I was just wondering if he'd said anything more to you— about our discussion yesterday, I mean."

"Only that he was sorry he lost his temper."

"I'd call it more than merely losing his temper."

Christian was becoming annoyed at Sidney's hooded implications "What are you getting at, Sidney?"

"You heard how he spoke to me, Christian. He acted as if I wasn't entitled to an opinion of my own about this whole affair with Jackson and states' rights. He sounded as if he'd received a revelation from God on the subject." Sidney's face darkened and he lowered his voice. "I don't think Brother Corrill is quite as humble as he'd have us believe."

"I don't agree. I think John says what's in his heart."

"That's a perfect example of it right there!" Sidney cried. "He's even got you bamboozled into thinking whatever he utters is gospel. If the Prophet were here, he'd set John in his place."

"Brother Joseph has set John in his place, and that place is as high priest and counselor over the Church in Zion. I don't believe John aspires to anything more."

"Only more authority and more influence. The whole lot of them are getting too smug for their own good," Sidney breathed.

Christian was shocked by his friend's accusations. "What lot are you referring to?" he asked, taking a menacing step forward.

"I've never been one to speak out against the Prophet. I've supported his decisions from the moment I joined the Church. But frankly, Christian, I'm beginning to wonder about Joseph's motives. He's surrounded himself with those new converts from Kirtland—that Kimball fellow and the Young brothers, Joseph and Brigham. With his new friends backing him, Joseph seems bent on accumulating more power and prestige."

"I'd hardly call Joseph's position prestigious—that is unless you consider being imprisoned, tarred and feathered, and having your name slandered as indications of public esteem," Christian answered coldly.

"He's attempting to rewrite the whole canon of scripture! What would you call that?"

"I'd call it a marvelous blessing for mankind. He's correcting passages of the Bible which have caused men to stumble and lose their way for hundreds of years. He's restoring plain and precious truths that have been corrupted by scribes who did not possess the God-given power to translate!" Christian was trembling with emotion. He'd heard several of the brethren in Independence make the same sort of insinuations, but none as blatant as Sidney's.

Christian threw his partially eaten apple with a vengeance into a barrel standing on the porch. "Thanks for the apple, Sidney." He jammed his hands into his pockets and stalked off down the street. He was still fuming when he stepped inside the printing house. He yanked off his overcoat and hat, flung off some mud clinging to his boot, and slammed down into a chair. William Phelps looked up from his desk.

"Something the matter?"

"You're darn right there is. It's this atmosphere of suspicion and apostasy that's affecting the brethren. Their disloyalty is appalling. I'm telling you, William, it's poisoning the Saints."

The week passed with its normal share of difficulties in publishing and distributing the *Evening and the Morning Star*. Christian and the others working at the printing house spent long hours refining the manuscript and preparing the type for printing. Then came the process of screwing the clamp tightly down on the newsprint to make a copy. The hand-operated press made a single copy at a time, a laborious process, but one in which the men found satisfaction. The Church-owned press published the only newspaper in Jackson County and the first religious sheet to gain wide circulation.

The *Star* was devoted to gospel themes for the purpose of instructing the Saints and spreading the gospel of Christ throughout the world. Since its inception in June of 1832, the *Star* had met with criticism by many outside the Church. They labeled the Church and its doctrines, as expressed through the newspaper, blasphemous. Joseph Smith's printed revelations were received with scorn and ridicule. In addition, the paper's repeated call for the Saints to come to Zion and take up their inheritance antagonized the original settlers who owned property in Jackson County. The settlers feared for their economic and political influence as Saints continued to flood the state.

Bad feelings between the Saints and their neighbors seemed to be escalating, as Christian was acutely aware through his association with the Stewarts. Many of the townspeople were openly hostile, including members of the clergy, who were especially vocal in their attacks.

Joseph advised the brethren in Zion to suffer patiently under this yoke of persecution. Christian would have enjoyed giving vent to his indignation through the medium of the *Star*. Instead, he put his efforts into preparing fresh material for the paper. He had in mind an explanation of the quickest route to Zion for Saints coming from the East, and he planned to print a portion of the article written by Colonel Galindo.

Friday afternoon Christian left the printing house earlier than usual and trudged through the street to his cabin. He lived in the same log structure he'd built upon his arrival in Jackson County over a year ago. The cabin was small and crude, but it served his needs. It housed a fireplace and cupboard, a bed, an old chest of drawers, and a bookshelf overflowing with books and newspapers. In a corner lay his drawing materials. Christian spent little time there, only enough to eat and sleep. Most of his reading, writing and studying were done before and after hours at the printing house.

He put on his white high-collared shirt and black coat, combed his hair, which fell well over the edge of his collar, and then left the cabin. Two hours later he and Mary Ann were seated at Mrs. Ludendorff 's concert in the courthouse at Independence. Seth and his fiancee, Carrie Harris, sat beside them. Carrie was a pale, thin wisp of a girl with light-colored hair and large blue eyes. She and Seth snuggled close together, more interested in one another than in the celebrated vocalist.

The selection Eva Ludendorff was in the midst of rendering went on and on. The incessant rise and fall of the plump woman's voice began to wear on Christian's nerves. Finding it impossible to keep his attention fixed on the musical dynamics, he fished into his breast pocket and withdrew a small sketching pad and pencil. Balancing the pad on his knee, he quickly sketched a likeness of the German soprano. He flipped the sheet over and started a second drawing, this one a caricature of the first. Mrs. Ludendorff's nose took on enormous proportions and her frizzled hair shot out in every direction. Mary Ann glanced at the drawing and winced. Christian put his signature to the paper, quietly tore off the sheet, folded it, and presented it to Mary Ann.

"Thanks," Mary Ann mouthed ruefully.

"My pleasure," Christian whispered. He took her hand and settled deeper into his chair.

The rows of benches lining the courthouse were filled to capacity. Independence seldom experienced the honor of hosting an artist the caliber of Eva Ludendorff. All the important families of the town were in attendance, dressed in their finery. Most of the gentlemen wore black trousers, coat, and top hat. The ladies were dressed in full skirts, with colorful bonnets and fringed shawls draped around their shoulders. A fire burning in the pot-bellied coal stove sizzled and snapped, adding more heat to the already close room.

Christian loosened his cravat with the tip of his finger and wiped a bead of perspiration from his brow. The heat and the frustratingly endless run of notes made him edgy. He longed to be outside in the open air.

Apparently Seth was feeling the same, for at that moment he tapped Christian's shoulder and motioned toward the door. Christian nodded.

"I'm going to step outside for a breath of air," he whispered in Mary Ann's ear.

"Now? Christian, don't. You'll disturb everyone," she answered in hushed tones.

"It's either now or I'll have to be carried out at the conclusion. Don't worry, I'll be discreet." He grinned and patted her hand.

"Don't be long," she said petulantly.

Christian excused himself as he made his way along the row with Seth at his heels. The two tiptoed toward the door and slipped outside.

The air was cool and fresh, and a stiff breeze blew from the direction of the river. Christian drew a deep breath and let it out slowly.

"Five more minutes in there and I would have been ready to leap out of my skin," exclaimed Seth.

"I know exactly what you mean."

Seth clasped his hands together in an attitude of mock earnestness and his face took on a prissy look. "La, la, la, la, la," he sang in a falsetto.

Christian laughed and jabbed his friend in the ribs. "Be quiet. They'll hear you."

"And we paid to listen to that!"

"What a man won't do to get on the good side of a woman," Christian lamented.

Seth withdrew a small tin of tobacco from his pocket, opened it, and placed a wad inside his cheek. "Well, I suppose we should be grateful that Mrs. Ludendorff is the worst of our troubles."

Christian looked at his friend questioningly.

"I don't know about you, but I've been feeling a bit jumpy over this states' rights mess," Seth said.

Christian nodded. "It appears President Jackson's hard-line attitude has paid off. None of the other southern states has supported South Carolina in her bid for nullification. I'm glad to see Carolina back off. I hope it ends there." The crisp air penetrated Christian's thin frock coat. He shivered and shoved his hands into his pockets.

Inside the building, the audience suddenly burst into applause. The two men glanced through the window nearest them. People began leaving their seats and moving toward a small table where refreshments were being served.

"Let's go get some punch for the ladies," Christian suggested. Seth spit a jet of tobacco juice from his mouth and started with Christian toward the door. As they approached it, a group of three men came out. The man in the lead, a big burly fellow, looked surprised to see Christian and Seth on the porch.

"Well, lookee who's here, boys," he said to his companions. "If it ain't Kent and Whitfield."

"Hello, Barnes," Christian returned coldly. He attempted to pass by the men who were standing in the doorway, but one of them barred his way.

"Hold on, now. What's your hurry?" the man asked Christian.

"Let me by, Chiles."

"What are you boys doing out here? You been up to some sort of mischief?" The man put a rough hand on Christian's shoulder. Henry Chiles was a prominent attorney in town and one of the Saints' bitterest opponents. He was relentless in pursuing litigation against Church members involved in civil disputes.

"Get out of the way, Chiles," Seth said coldly.

Chiles' black brows came together and his eyes narrowed into slits. "You ask nice and polite-like, Whitfield, and I'll be happy to step aside."

From the periphery of his vision, Christian saw the other two men stealthily move into a position which put Seth and himself in the center of all three of them.

"If you want trouble, I'll be happy to oblige you," Seth threatened.

"Who says we want any trouble?" the big, lumbering man named Barnes asked. "We're just wonderin' what's goin' on here."

"I think these fellas have been out here conversin' with angels and don't want us to know about it," the third man jeered. Christian didn't recognize the man, but he immediately disliked him.

"That'd be jist like 'em now, wouldn't it? Conversin' with angels and not invitin' us Gentiles to join in," Barnes said with a shake of his shaggy head. "What a selfish lot."

Seth took a menacing step forward.

"Or maybe they've been digging up gold plates," said Chiles, his voice thick with sarcasm.

"I'll bet that's it," the unfamiliar man said, snapping his fingers. "Didn't I just read in your newspaper about those fellows who swore they saw them golden plates with their own eyes? Wasn't one of them fellows you, Kent?"

Christian's expression hardened and his hands clenched into tight fists. "I'd be careful about what I said if I were you."

"Why is that? You ain't plannin' to call down hell fire on us, are you?" The other two men guffawed at their companion's remark.

Chiles moved away from the door and took a step nearer Christian. Christian could smell the odor of whiskey on his breath. "I'd suggest you boys be more prudent about what you print in that paper of yours," Chiles said with deliberate slowness. "You might offend some folks. It would be a pity to wake up some morning and find your printing house in ashes."

Chiles' menacing words sent a chill down Christian's spine.

"Is that some kind of threat?" Seth breathed.

"That's what it is, boy. I can't paint the picture any clearer.

We don't want you Mormons around here." Chiles glared at the two of them and then roughly pushed Seth out of his way.

Like lightning, Seth's right fist shot out and made solid contact with Chiles' jaw. The man staggered backward and fell sprawling onto the porch steps.

Before Christian saw the blow coming, Barnes punched him hard in the stomach. He doubled over, the wind knocked out of him. Seeing his friend's dilemma, Seth hammered the back of Barnes' neck and the burly man dropped to his knees. But then the third man, spewing profanity, grabbed Seth's arms and pinned them behind him. By this time, Chiles had recovered his senses. He rose to his feet and rammed a fist into Seth's unprotected belly. Seth cried out in pain.

Struggling to regain his breath, Christian drew back his fist and aimed a blow to Barnes' head, but it glanced off his temple. Barnes whirled around and followed through with a sharp uppercut to Christian's jaw. Christian felt his teeth rip into his upper lip.

Seth was sustaining punch after punch as Chiles' companion continued to hold him fast. Christian struggled with Barnes, dodging and ducking his blows.

The commotion outside the courthouse attracted the attention of several men lounging beside the punch bowl. A knot of them threw open the door, startled to see the five men scuffling on the porch steps. One of the men, John Whitmer, rushed forward to put a stop to the fighting.

"What the devil's going on here?" he cried as he pried loose the man's hold on Seth. Once released, Seth sank to the ground.

Several others hurried forward, two grabbing hold of Christian, and the others grappling with Chiles.

"Stop it," Whitmer commanded. "What's the matter with you men?"

With an oath, Christian shook off the men holding him and hurried to Seth's side. Seth's eyes were closed and he was moaning softly.

"How badly is he hurt?" John Whitmer asked, bending over Christian's shoulder.

"I don't know. Have these men move back, will you?"

"All right. Let's clear out. Go back inside." Whitmer ushered the men back into the building. The last to enter was Henry Chiles. As Christian glanced back over his shoulder, he saw the hatred glimmering in Chiles' eyes.

Seth was beginning to come around. He murmured something incoherent and struggled to sit upright. John and Christian assisted him and in a few moments he was able to speak.

"How do you feel?" Christian asked anxiously.

"I wouldn't care to run any foot races, if that's what you mean," he answered in a groggy voice.

"Any broken bones?" Whitmer asked.

Seth gingerly moved his arms and legs. "I don't think so." He looked closely at Christian. "I hope I don't look as bad as you do."

For the first time since the altercation, Christian became aware of his own injuries. His head suddenly began to throb and his stomach ached. He recognized the taste of dried blood on his swollen lips. His right brow, too, was cut and bleeding.

"I'm all right. It's you I'm worried about. You took quite a beating."

"Yeah." Seth rose shakily to his feet, leaning on Whitmer for support.

John Whitmer took off his frock coat and put it around Seth's shoulders. "What on earth possessed the two of you to tangle with Chiles and his cronies?"

"Don't ask," Seth groaned.

Christian drew his handkerchief from his pocket and wiped the blood from his mouth with it. "John, do us a favor, will you? Go inside and ask Carrie and Mary Ann to meet us out by the carriage."

"Are you sure you're not hurt?" Whitmer asked.

Both men nodded. Whitmer disappeared inside the building and the two men limped over to where their carriage and horse was tied.

"I'm sorry I got you into this, Christian. I shouldn't have let Chiles get to me like he did."

"Don't apologize. If you hadn't thrown the first punch, I would have."

"How are we going to explain this to the ladies?"

Christian smiled wryly. The movement stung his lip. "Ouch," he grimaced. He pressed the handkerchief to his swollen mouth.

A moment later Mary Ann and Carrie came hurrying out of the courthouse, carrying the men's topcoats in their arms. When they saw them standing next to the carriage, the girls broke into a run.

"Seth!" Carrie cried.

"I'm fine, fine," he answered hastily, taking her into his arms. Her eyes filled with tears as she scanned his bruised face. Seth kissed her and held her tight.

"Christian? What happened? Your friend said there'd been a—oh, you look awful!" Mary Ann blurted out.

Christian tried to draw Mary Ann to him, but she resisted. "Everything's fine. It was just a misunderstanding, that's all."

"A misunderstanding? About what?"

Carrie looked expectantly from Seth to Christian. Intuitively, she grasped what had occurred. "I don't think we need to hear the reasons right now. Let's go home," she said.

"Wait a minute. I think we have a right to know what happened." There was impatience and a hint of arrogance in Mary Ann's voice.

"We'll talk about it later." Christian took Mary Ann firmly by the arm and helped her into the carriage. He climbed in next to her while Seth and Carrie took their places in the front. Mary Ann sat stiffly beside him, her green eyes flashing in the glow of the burning street lamps.

Seth snapped the reins and the carriage lurched forward.

"I'm sorry we had to leave the performance early. I know how much you were looking forward to this evening. I apologize for spoiling it," Christian said simply.

"I don't believe you're sorry at all," Mary Ann snapped.

Christian was taken aback by her remark. "What do you mean by that?"

"I thought you intended to step outside for a breath of air. Instead I find you've been street brawling like some common—" She stopped, leaving the sentence hanging.

"Go ahead, finish what you were about to say. Some common what?" Christian challenged her. He was sore and upset, and vexed with Mary Ann for not being sympathetic.

She pursed her lips together in silence.

"Why don't you admit the real reason why you're angry? My behavior embarrassed you, didn't it?"

"I thought leaving during the performance was in bad taste."

"Appearances—that's what's really important to you," Christian said with disgust.

Carrie listened with consternation to their exchange. Finally, she squeezed Seth's arm meaningfully.

"Hold on, you two," Seth cut in. "I don't think we're accomplishing anything here. In the first place, Mary Ann, we weren't brawling. We were provoked by that scoundrel Chiles. We had no choice but to defend ourselves."

"Why would a respectable attorney like Mr. Chiles want to fight with you?" she retorted.

"Don't bother to answer that, Seth. She wouldn't understand anyway."

Mary Ann shot Christian a withering look. "I suspect you're going to tell me it had something to do with your religious views. I should think you'd value your life more than your religion."

"Our religion *is* our life, Mary Ann. That's what you don't seem to understand," Carrie said quietly. "Christian and Seth did what they had to do."

There was no more discussion of the matter during the long ride home. When Christian walked Mary Ann to her doorstep, she tartly told him goodnight and slammed the door.

The next morning Christian awakened with his head pounding. He groaned and rolled onto his side. The cut above his right brow hurt fiercely. He sat up on the edge of the bed, his throbbing head in his hands. The cabin floor was freezing. Bleary-eyed, he pulled on his socks and boots, and fumbled with the buttons on his shirt. When he'd completed dressing, he stoked up the fire in the hearth and warmed himself beside it. He felt miserable. Not only did his body ache, but his emotions were battered as well. He regretted his quarrel with Mary Ann the evening before and was disappointed that they hadn't been able to settle their differences before he left her.

Ignoring the gnaw in his belly, Christian threw on his over-coat, put out the fire, and left the cabin.

The day was bleak and cold. Gray clouds hid the sky and a chilling wind buffeted him as he walked the few blocks to the printing house. He'd slept late and could look forward to Phelps' reprimand. When he entered the office, he found the outer room empty and no one seemed to be about. Christian removed his coat and hung it on the back of a chair. The door to Phelps' personal office was closed, but as Christian drew near it, he heard men talking in low voices.

He tapped on the door. "William?"

There was a sound of shuffling feet and a moment later Oliver opened the door for him. Christian expected him to comment on the appearance of his swollen face, but Oliver merely nodded for him to come inside. William was sitting at his desk, his expression sober. Oliver sat down across from him and pulled up a chair for Christian.

"Sit down, Christian," said Phelps in a tired voice.

Christian's body tensed. "What's happened?"

Phelps picked up a letter that had been lying on his desk. It consisted of several pages of closely spaced handwriting. "This arrived late yesterday afternoon. It's from Joseph and the brethren in Kirtland." He handed the pages of correspondence to Christian.

Christian glanced at Oliver for a clue to the letter's contents. Oliver's thin face was more ashen than usual. Christian quickly read the opening paragraphs.

Brother William W. Phelps:

I send you the "olive leaf" which we have plucked from the Tree of Paradise, the Lord's message of peace to us; for though our brethren in Zion indulge in feelings toward us, which are not according to the requirements of the new covenant, yet, we have the satisfaction of knowing that the Lord approves of us, and has accepted us, and established His name in Kirtland for the salvation of the nations; for the Lord will have a place whence His word will go forth, in these last days, in purity; for if Zion will not purify herself, so as to be approved of in all things, in His sight, He will seek another people. . . .

Christian gripped the paper tighter and read on,

> Our hearts are greatly grieved at the spirit which is breathed both in your letter and that of Brother Gilbert's, the very spirit which is wasting the strength of Zion like a pestilence; and if it is not detected and driven from you, it will ripen Zion for the threatened judgments of God.

Christian laid aside the first page of the letter and shook his head. "I was afraid of this very thing," he said slowly. Phelps looked at him with an air of resignation. Christian handed the pages back to him. "I don't need to read any further. I can deduce the rest."

"There's another letter in the same vein addressed to Bishop Partridge," Oliver told him.

Phelps bowed his head and tented his fingers. "I'm primarily to blame for this, brethren. It was I who urged Joseph to come to Independence. It was my letter which has brought this rebuke upon us."

"Don't blame yourself, William. I'm afraid none of us are without fault," said Oliver, placing a hand on the older man's shoulder.

"Joseph is not coming to Independence, then?" Christian's inquiry was more of a statement than a question.

"No." Phelps shuffled through the pages of the letter until he located the paragraph he was searching for. He pointed to the words on the paper. "Not until Zion repents and abides by the commandments."

Christian contemplated this last bit of news.

"I'll have to take these letters to Bishop Partridge. He'll undoubtedly call a council to discuss the matter," Phelps said without lifting his eyes from the page.

"Perhaps worst of all, for us in particular, is the fact that Joseph is not pleased with our handling of the *Star*," stated Oliver.

"The *Star*?" Christian repeated, jolted. "Why not?"

"He feels our enterprise may be on the brink of failure." Oliver's shoulders sagged.

"Let me read to you exactly what he wrote," Phelps turned to the last page of the Prophet's letter. "It's here, in the postscript."

We wish you to render the *Star* as interesting as possible by setting forth the rise, progress, and faith of the Church, as well as the doctrine; for if you do not render it more interesting than at present, it will fall, and the Church suffer a great loss thereby.

Cowdery was slumped in his chair. "Have you any ideas what we might do to improve the paper?" he asked Phelps.

Phelps shook his head. "We'll have to consider it."

Christian fell silent, weighed down with the burden of his thoughts. He was pained by the fact that the Prophet, and more importantly, the Lord, were displeased with the Saints in Independence. In spite of all the revelations given with respect to Zion and her responsibilities to God and to the world, the Saints had failed. He had failed. He had not been obedient or faithful enough, not earnestly engaged enough in the work. He trembled for the judgments which God would surely pour out on his rebellious Saints in Missouri.

And in the back of his mind, to add to his despair, was the knowledge that he had also failed Mary Ann. She wasn't speaking to him—might in fact never consent to see him again. Christian felt as though his whole world were crumbling down around his head.

Trust in the Lord with all thine heart; and lean not unto thine own understanding. In all thy ways acknowledge him, and he shall direct thy paths.

Proverbs 3:5,6

CHAPTER SIX

J ames' health began to improve immediately. A few hours after Gerta and Parley Pratt left the Dawson's cabin, James felt well enough to sip a few spoonfuls of soup. By evening, he was sitting up in bed, asking for his favorite toy, a small horse Abraham had carved for him out of wood.

Lydia marveled at his recovery and the power of the Lord Pratt seemed to have at his command. He had spoken to her of the priesthood and its divine restoration, along with other keys and powers revealed from heaven. Before leaving the cabin, Pratt had given her a small book. He'd pressed it into her hand, urging her to read it and to pray as to its truthfulness. Lydia had set the book on the cupboard shelf, beside her bible.

As soon as James was tucked in bed for the night, Lydia reached for the book Pratt had left her. She studied its title by the light of the fire—the Book of Mormon. Pondering all she had heard and seen of this new religion called Mormonism, Lydia settled into a chair with the book in her hand. She pulled a candle close by. With some trepidation she turned to the first page and read:

> I, Nephi, having been born of goodly parents, therefore I was taught somewhat in all the learning of my father; and having seen many afflictions in the course of my days, nevertheless, having been highly favored of the Lord in all my days; yea, having had a great knowledge of the goodness and the mysteries of God, therefore I make a record of my proceedings in my days.

She read on, her interest pricked, and then on and on. Before she realized it, the candle burning at her side had shrunk to a stub. She set the book down and went to the cupboard for a second candle. She lit it from the dying flame of the first, then settled back in her chair. For a moment her thoughts turned to Abraham. She hoped to have a few hours yet before he returned. She picked up the book and continued to read.

Abraham did not return from town that evening as he had promised, nor the next. It wasn't until well into the afternoon of the third day that he arrived, cold, hungry, and in bad humor. Lydia helped him off with his coat and warmed him some supper.

"So the boy's well," he commented in answer to Lydia's excited explanation of their son's condition.

"Yes, he's almost his old self. I can hardly believe it."

Abraham raised his brows. "Seems sudden. You try some new tonic or somethin'?"

Lydia hesitated before answering. She knew Abraham's anger would be kindled if she told him about Pratt ministering to their son, but she also knew without a doubt that it was the reason why James was no longer ill.

"Well?" Abraham asked impatiently.

She drew a deep breath. "Gerta brought Mr. Pratt by while you were away. You remember me tellin' you about Mr. Pratt."

Abraham's eyes narrowed and his mouth took on an ugly twist.

Lydia hurried on. "Mr. Pratt said he might be able to help James. I told him to try if he thought he could do any good. I was desperate, Abraham. If there was anythin' that could be done for the boy, I was willin' to try it. Mr. Pratt laid hands on James and prayed over him and James started improvin' right after that."

"You let some Mormon devil lay ahold of my son!" Abraham exploded. "Have you lost your senses, woman?"

"Your son is well!"

"You bet he is. And it ain't got a d—n thing to do with Mormons!" Abraham bolted from his chair and glared at his wife. He was so wroth that Lydia feared he would strike her. She shielded her face with her arms.

"Don't you never let them Mormons in my house agin, do you understand me? Not ever!" He glowered at her a moment longer and then stalked off toward the fireplace.

She sat rigid in her chair, smarting under his anger. She heard him cursing as he viciously stoked the fire with the poker. Giving the poker a last ferocious thrust, Abraham hurled it to the floor. It clattered on the hearth stones and rolled over to the foot of the cupboard. He bent to retrieve it, and upon rising, spied Lydia's Book of Mormon resting on the cupboard shelf. Grabbing the book he inspected its cover, then rifled through the pages. He snarled something uncomprehendable and then threw the book into the flames leaping up in the hearth.

"No! Wait!" Lydia cried. She rushed to the hearth. Abraham seized her arm and jerked her roughly away from the orange tongues of fire licking at the pages.

The next morning Abraham left for the settlement to get Elizabeth. Lydia wanted to accompany him so she could see her parents, but Abraham refused to take her. While he was gone, she bathed James and attended to her chores.

As she worked, scenes from the book Pratt had given her ran through her mind. She had read nearly all of it while Abraham was away, and its words had sunk deep into her heart. She'd been moved by the account of the righteous Nephites and their brethren, the rebellious Lamanites. Her soul delighted in the story of Alma and the miraculous conversion of his son, and the tremendous success the four sons of King Mosiah experienced among the Lamanites. The gospel proclaimed by the prophets in the Book of Mormon was quite unlike anything Lydia had known, but it made perfect sense. She yearned to know more about this new church with its unusual doctrines, but she knew Abraham would go out of his way to prevent her from having any further contact with the Mormons.

It was nearly evening when Abraham and Elizabeth returned. The little girl raced into the cabin and threw herself into Lydia's arms.

"Oh, Mama, I've missed you so! I'm glad James is well. I don't like stayin' with Grandma."

"I missed you, too," Lydia laughed. She hugged her and kissed the top of Elizabeth's curly blonde head.

Abraham came in after stabling the horse and put Elizabeth's traveling bag on her bed. He brushed past Lydia without a word, pulled up a chair in front of the fire, and slumped into it.

"Mama, guess what Grandpa made for me?" Elizabeth continued excitedly. "A dolly with real hair!"

"Real hair? Where did Grandpa get real hair for your doll?"

"Well, not real people hair. He pulled out a bunch of strands from Old Mac's tail. Old Mac didn't like it much," Elizabeth giggled.

"I don't imagine he did." Lydia smiled as she thought of her father's feisty old mule.

"Grandma pasted them on the dolly's head with molasses and made me a yellow dress out of some scraps she had. Then Mr. Slater gave me a tiny blanket for her."

"Mr. Slater? When did you see him?" asked Lydia in surprise.

"On the way home, Papa stopped at his cabin and let me come inside too. Mr. Slater had an old shirt he was tearing up for rags. He gave me a piece for Betsy and said he'd bring me a surprise when he came by tonight. What do you think it might be?" Elizabeth asked.

Lydia was disturbed by the news of Ira Slater's impending visit. "I don't know, 'Lizabeth. You go unpack your things now. And keep still. James is sleepin'."

Elizabeth happily ran off, disappearing behind the curtain. Lydia eyed Abraham's broad back. He was hunched forward in his chair, warming himself by the fire. She walked to his side.

"Were the folks well?"

Abraham nodded.

"'Lizabeth tells me Ira's comin' by this evenin'."

"That's right."

"Shall I set an extra plate for supper?"

"Suppose so."

Knowing that was all the information she was going to get from him, Lydia began preparations for the evening meal. As she readied a portion of their meager store of potatoes and carrots, she thought about Ira Slater. She knew the reason for his visit—he and Abraham would be planning their trip up to Galena. Now that James was well and spring was coming on, Abraham would be anxious to leave. She didn't know how she could manage without him.

It wasn't an hour before Slater's knock sounded at the cabin door. Abraham answered it.

"You bring the maps?" he asked in lieu of greeting.

"Right here," Slater answered, patting a leather pouch slung over his shoulder.

Abraham stepped away from the door and Ira Slater shuffled inside.

"Evenin'," Lydia said in as friendly a tone as she could muster.

Slater swept off his beaver hat and bowed ceremoniously with it across his chest. "Right nice to see you again, Missus Dawson." He smiled broadly, revealing a black gap where two upper front teeth were missing.

"You hungry?" Abraham asked.

"If it ain't too much trouble."

"Ain't none."

Lydia spooned stew from the black kettle hanging over the fire while Abraham called the children to supper. Elizabeth came running to the table with a sleepy James in tow.

"Hello, Mr. Slater," she said excitedly. Slater extended a stubby, dirty hand and patted her head.

"I brung you somethin' like I promised." He opened his pouch, reached inside, and brought out what appeared to be some sort of amulet or charm. It consisted of a hunk of black hair attached to a round piece of worked leather. Yellow and turquoise beads formed a geometric design around the edges.

"I got this off a real Indian chieftain—traded it for a bit o' firewater." Slater grinned, obviously proud of the bargain he'd struck. Lydia suspected the Indian had gotten the poorer end of the exchange. He handed the trinket to Elizabeth.

"Golly!" Elizabeth exclaimed. She took the amulet and examined it eagerly. "Golly, thanks, Mr. Slater!" She thrust her arms around Slater's waist and gave him a squeeze. Lydia winced. The man's clothes were filthy and he reeked of sweat and grime. Slater had a wizened face, beady eyes, and stringy black hair which fell below his ears. Several days' growth of black stubble covered his chin.

Elizabeth closed her hand over her treasure.

"Let me see," James said, peering over her shoulder on tiptoe.

Elizabeth bent down and opened her fist a crack. "There, see. It belonged to an old Indian. Now it's mine."

"Can I hold it?"

"No." Elizabeth shouldered him out of the way and walked over to the table.

When they all were seated, Lydia passed around the bowls of stew. Abraham and Slater fell to discussing their mining enterprise. Lydia kept one ear cocked on the conversation while she cut James' vegetables into small pieces and saw to it that Elizabeth ate more than just the bits of meat in her bowl.

"How long you reckon it'll take us to get to Galena?" Abraham asked.

"A couple of days, I suppose. Depends on the rains. Muddy roads will slow us down some. You still got the list we made out?"

"Right here." Abraham pulled a crumpled sheet of paper out of his trouser pocket. He unfolded it and set it on the table between them.

Ira scanned the list of scribbled items. "Better pick up another lantern."

Abraham penciled it in.

"Looks fine. We should be all set," Ira commented.

Abraham nodded and shoveled a spoonful of stew into his mouth.

"What does the missus think about our business venture?" Slater asked, his beady eyes flicking toward Lydia.

Abraham glanced up at her and shrugged. "She don't have much to say one way or t'other."

Lydia bit her tongue to keep from making a tart reply.

"That's good. A smart woman leaves such matters to men-folk."

Lydia flashed Slater a contemptuous look. His remark brought to mind an image of Slater's wife. Lydia had seen her

only once. She was a thin, haggard-looking woman with lus-
terless eyes.

Slater removed a couple of maps from his pouch and spread
them on the table. Pointing to a speck on one of them he said,
"This here's where we can replenish our supplies if need be."

Abraham bent over the spot Slater indicated.

"I ain't been up north for some time, but as I recall there's a
spring that runs along here." Slater traced a line eastward on
the map with a stubby finger, and the two men continued to
pore over the maps as they discussed their plans.

Lydia began clearing the dishes from the table. "You finished?" she asked Slater, her hand on the bowl in front of him.

"Yes, Ma'am. And thank ye. It was a mighty fine meal." He
put a clammy hand over hers. "Your missus is a fine cook,
Abraham. Purty, too. It must be nice havin' a woman like yours
to warm your bed at night." His hand moved slowly up her arm.

Abraham looked up briefly from the maps, his expression
indifferent.

Slater's touch made Lydia's skin crawl. She shook free of his
hold, then took his bowl and put it with the other supper
dishes. After she'd finished cleaning up, she helped the children prepare for bed. When she returned to the outer room, the
men were still hunched over their maps. A bottle of whiskey
and two cups rested on the table between them.

As Lydia sat by the fire with her mending, she listened in
silence to their plans. She tried not to let her distress show,
keeping a stoic countenance against the hard knot wrenching
her stomach.

The following weeks brought clear skies and warmer tem-
peratures. Lydia couldn't wait to get outside in the sunshine.
She'd asked Abraham several times to take her and the children for an outing in the sleigh, but he always refused,
claiming to be too busy with chores. Finally, she decided to
drive the sleigh herself. She bundled up the children, hitched
the big farm horse to the sled, and set out across the snowy
fields.

The snow spread around her, clean and unspoiled as far as
Lydia could see, and the sky was a brilliant shade of blue.

Lydia breathed in the beauty and freshness. The sight of a chipmunk scampering up a nearby tree brought squeals of delight from the children. Lydia watched a bluejay wheel and sail in the air above her head.

Before long they neared the Johanssen's cabin. Lydia hadn't intended to stop, but it seemed a good time to pay a long overdue visit to her friend. She pulled up in front of the snug house, helped James and Elizabeth out of the sleigh, and rapped on the door.

Ten-year-old Johanna swung it open wide. Of all Gerta's children, Johanna resembled her mother the most. She had the same round, ruddy face and no-nonsense manner.

"Why, hello, Mrs. Dawson. Come in. Mama's just puttin' the babe down for a nap."

"She can take her time, Johanna. We're in no hurry."

Lydia removed James' coat and cap while Elizabeth sped off to find Inge.

"He's growin' like a rabbit," Johanna remarked as she eyed James affectionately.

"That he is."

Johanna held out her arms and James scurried over to her. She picked him up and balanced him on her hip. Kirstine, who'd been curled up in a chair with a book, came over and planted a kiss on his chubby cheek.

Though Lydia was fond of all of Gerta's daughters, she had a special spot in her heart for gentle, eight-year-old Kirstine. The girl was prettier than either of her sisters, and there was a sweetness and sensitivity about her. Kirstine's slim figure, soft flaxen hair, and pale eyes promised the blooming of a lovely young woman.

"Kirstine, you look real nice in that dress. Did your Ma make it for you out of her new cloth?" Lydia asked with a smile.

"Yes, Ma'am, she did. Thank you." Kirstine curtsied and smiled shyly.

"Liddy! I vas afraid ve vould not see you again soon," Gerta cried as she swept briskly into the room.

Lydia laughed and answered, "You can't get rid of me, Gerta."

"Nor vould I vant to, child." Gerta hugged her, then she patted her friend on the back. "You vant some sveetcake now, huh!"

"That sounds delicious. I'd love some."

Gerta led her to a huge hickory table in the center of the room. The Johanssen's cabin was much larger than Lydia's own, with plastered and whitewashed walls and a wooden floor. Yellow curtains hung at the windows and a yellow and white checkered cloth covered the table. Several pieces of fine needlework, crafted in the Scandinavian tradition, hung in frames on the walls.

"Glad I am to see Yames with roses in his cheeks again," Gerta said, her braided head bobbing up and down.

Lydia put a hand on the older woman's arm, "I haven't thanked you properly for all you did for us, Gerta. If you hadn't brought Mr. Pratt by that afternoon . . . well, I don't know what would have happened to James." Lydia's eyes filled. She blinked back the tears and the lump that formed in her throat.

"I vas happy to do vhat I could, child."

Gerta sliced a big serving of cake for each of them and they sat down together at the table.

"Have you been to any more of the meetin's?" Lydia asked eagerly.

"Nearly every one, Liddy. I've been bursting to tell you ta news. Niels and I vill be baptized as soon as ta ice is broken up on ta river." Gerta's eyes shined with excitement.

Lydia sucked in her breath. "Gerta, are you sure you're doin' the right thing?"

"As sure as spring follows vinter. Ve've been brought ta truth, Lydia! Ta Lord's gospel in its plainness has been restored. His church is once again on ta earth yust as it vus in ta days of ta ancient apostles, and ta goot Lord has seen fit to send ta vorld a prophet. Vhat a glorious blessing, Liddy! How grateful I am to be privileged to hear his vord. God be praised!" Gerta clasped her hands to her bosom. "Open your heart, child. Let the Lord's spirit vhisper ta truth of these things to you."

"Oh, Gerta, if I could only be certain."

"You can! I promise you." Gerta took Lydia's hand and squeezed it tightly. "You come vith me to meeting this Sunday," she said, nodding her head vigorously.

"I can't. Abraham forbade me."

Gerta's snapping blue eyes softened. "A vay vill open up, child. Trust in ta Lord."

That was the end of their conversation, for just then Elizabeth and Inge came bounding to the table.

"Mama, can Elizabeth and I have some cake too?"

"Have you been goot girls?" Gerta asked them with feigned sternness.

"Yes, ma' am," Elizabeth promptly replied.

"Vell, then a nice big piece you can have."

"Yippee!" the girls shouted in unison.

Lydia laughed and pulled two chairs over to the table for them to sit on.

The remainder of the afternoon slipped away far too quickly to suit Lydia. She realized it was time to leave only when Niels and Jens came in from their work.

"Afternoon, Missus Dawson. Thought that vas your sled out front."

"It is and I'm afraid I've stayed entirely too long. You men will be wantin' your supper." She rose from the chair and motioned for the children to follow.

"Stay and eat vith us, Liddy."

"Thanks, Gerta, but I need to be goin'. Abraham will be wonderin' what's become of us. Jens, you've grown six inches since I saw you last," she said, putting a hand on the boy's shoulder.

He shook it off with an almost imperceptible shrug.

"Can't you answer Missus Dawson properly, boy?" Niels asked, a hardness edging his words.

"Didn't think no answer was needed," Jens muttered. Niels' brows came together in a furious scowl.

Gerta stepped to her son and grasped him roughly by the ear. "Yes, Ma'am. Thank you," he said sullenly as he pulled away from his mother.

At thirteen, Jens was a broad-shouldered, sturdy young man. His thatch of straw-colored hair sat atop a round, florid face. He had a wide mouth, broad nose, and cold blue eyes. Lydia had never found him to be very pleasant. He was curt and surly, and Lydia had often heard Gerta complain of his disobedience.

"I'll valk you out to your sled, Missus Dawson," Niels offered. He swooped James up into his arms and took Elizabeth by the hand and led them outside.

Lydia kissed Gerta's cheek in farewell. "Come by and see me soon."

"I vill, child."

Jens held the door for Lydia as she walked out, a sour expression on his face.

"Thank you, Jens."

"You're welcome, Ma'am," he answered, deliberately emphasizing each word.

Niels already had the children seated in the sleigh. He helped Lydia in beside them. "I suspect Mrs. Johanssen told you ta goot news?" he asked as he handed Lydia the reins. Lydia noted a sparkle spring into his eyes.

"You mean about joinin' with the Mormons? Yes, she told me. Congratulations, Niels."

"Excuse me, Missus Dawson, but ve'll rightly be called Saints, not Mormons."

"I'm sorry, Niels. I'll remember that. Congratulations again."

"Yah. Nice to see you."

"Good-bye, Mr. Johanssen," Elizabeth sang out as the sled moved briskly away.

Abraham left for the lead mines the first part of March. Lydia missed him more than she had expected. It was several weeks before she became accustomed to being without him. Abraham had worked hard beforehand to prepare the ground for spring planting, and he'd brought in fresh meat and stores. Niels Johanssen came regularly to check on Lydia and the children, and he promised to bring Jens with him to help her plant the fields as soon as the weather permitted. Niels, Gerta, and the three older children had been baptized into the Church of Christ just a few days before Abraham left. Abraham had called the Johanssens "deluded fools" and hadn't permitted Lydia to attend the ceremony. She was grateful, however, that he still allowed Niels to come on their place in spite of his new affiliation.

Abraham had written a cursory note shortly after he arrived in Galena, letting Lydia know he had found quarters and would be spending a few days in town purchasing the last of his supplies. Three weeks after he'd gone, Lydia's parents came for a visit. She was overjoyed to see them. Her father helped with the outside chores and made a few repairs around the farm, while her mother filled her in on all the news of the family. Lydia's two older brothers lived in Quincy, both of them struggling farmers with large families to support. Lydia's mother reported that John's wife, Katherine, was pregnant again. That would swell their family to nine. Lydia smiled ruefully as she thought of her outspoken sister-in-law. Quiet, gentle John seldom enjoyed a moment's peace.

Lydia loved John, but she enjoyed a closer relationship with Philip, the younger of the two brothers. Like herself, Philip was redheaded and blue-eyed. When they were children they'd spent all of their free hours together, roaming the fields and streams near their home or sitting crosslegged in the tall prairie grass exchanging confidences. When Philip wed, Lydia had felt as though she'd lost her best friend. His wife, Charlotte, proved to be good natured and generous, however, and she produced a child to mark each year of their marriage. Although she'd grown stouter with each pregnancy, Charlotte was still a pretty woman with chestnut colored hair and large hazel eyes. Lydia loved them both very much.

After spending a few weeks with her, Lydia's parents returned to their home. Their absence left Lydia feeling lonely and discouraged. She missed Abraham even more than before. The spring rains came almost every day, postponing the planting and limiting social exchange. Lydia spent the time indoors teaching Elizabeth her letters, reading aloud to James, and attending to the never-ending chores.

At last the weather cleared and the sun soaked up the moisture from the earth. As he'd promised, Niels appeared one early morning in April and set to work seeding the fields. Lydia labored beside Niels and Jens throughout the week. It was tiring work. Lydia's back ached from the stooping and bending. She dropped into bed each night exhausted, and arose before sunup to complete her chores before the Johanssens arrived.

On the last day of seeding, Gerta accompanied her husband to Lydia's place.

Lydia threw her arms around the older woman. "I'm so glad to see you. How are you?"

"Goot, child. And you?"

"We're gettin' along. Surely appreciate your menfolk helpin' me like they have."

"Niels says you've been getting a heap of planting done. Almost finished."

"That's right. This is the last quarter-acre." Lydia arched her tired back and squinted at the sky. There wasn't a sign of a cloud. "If the rains will cooperate now," she added hopefully.

"Yah, I expect they vill," replied Gerta.

"Come and sit with me in the shade and we'll talk," Lydia suggested, leading the way to an old branching hickory tree. The two women sat down against its gnarled trunk. Lydia idly watched Niels drop corn kernels into each round hole.

"You have heard from Abraham?" Gerta asked.

"Just once. I hope he writes again soon. The children miss him. So do I."

"How long you expect he'll be gone?"

"Don't know. 'Til he mines what he needs, I suppose."

The two women sat in silence for a time, Lydia enjoying the rest and the cool shade of the tree.

"Hope I'm not keepin' Niels from work on your place. I know you got plantin' of your own to do."

"I been vanting to speak to you about that," Gerta said in an uncharacteristically halting voice.

Lydia sat forward in surprise. "What is it?"

"I told Niels not to say anything to you until ve vas sure."

"Sure of what? What are you tryin' to tell me, Gerta?"

"Yust that Niels and I von't be doing any planting this spring, at least not on this piece of ground. "Ve've sold ta farm. Ve're moving to Independence."

"Movin'! Why? When?" Lydia cried in confusion.

"It's ta gathering place, Liddy. Independence is. Ta Lord's vanting all his Saints to gather to Zion and build up ta church there. Niels and I vant to go and be vith the Saints."

Lydia sat still as stone, stunned by Gerta's revelation.

"I hate to leave you, child, especially vith your man gone," Gerta said with feeling. "But you can understand. Ta Lord's vork is ta most important thing there is to Niels and me."

"Where is Independence? I've never heard of it," Lydia asked as she struggled to harness her emotions.

"Missouri. A little place on ta edge of ta frontier."

"Why would God want to gather his people there?"

"Because there's vhere ta land of promise is, Liddy! Zion. Ta Lord's promised it to his Saints."

"When will you leave?"

"First of next veek. I'll be missing you, child." Gerta added in a rush of feeling.

Tears sprang to Lydia's eyes as she hugged Gerta close. "I'll miss you, too. And Kirstine and Inge and the rest of the children. You've been like family to me."

Lydia's heart ached with the news. Not only would she lose Gerta's companionship, but she would also be deprived of the only contact she had with the Mormon religion. A cold emptiness settled upon her like frost on a fall evening. Lydia had never felt more forsaken in her life.

CHAPTER SEVEN

The rains failed to come after Lydia finished putting in her crops. Nor did it rain in the following weeks. Lydia walked the dry ground anxiously, keeping an eye turned to the heavens. The sky was faultlessly blue, not a cloud in sight. She bent down and scooped up a handful of dirt and let it run through her fingers. It was dust dry. There wasn't a sign of green anywhere in the field, just clods of parched, crusty earth. She could almost see her seedlings withering and dying from lack of moisture.

She wiped the remaining dirt clinging to her hand onto her apron. If Abraham were here, he'd think of some way to aid the crop. But he wasn't. No one was. No one at all was there to help her. The feeling of helplessness made her angry. She stomped out of the fields and back toward the house. Flinging open the cabin door, she nearly stumbled over James, who was playing on the floor with a top and a bit of twine. He looked up at her, his brown eyes questioning. Lydia brushed past him without a word. She cast an angry glance at the soiled dishes littering the table and marched over to the divider and flung it aside.

"'Lizabeth, I thought I told you to finish up those supper dishes."

"I forgot, Ma." Elizabeth was clad in an old hat and dress of her mother's, with a string of beads hung around her neck.

Lydia whisked the hat off her daughter's head. "I don't want you playin' in my things, you understand?"

"Yes, Mama."

Lydia glared at her as Elizabeth quickly removed the dress and beads. "Now you get started on those dishes quick-like."

Elizabeth scurried into the outer room and set to work. Lydia sank down on the bed and put her head in her hands. She immediately regretted the harsh tone she'd taken with Elizabeth. She hated losing her temper with the children. It made her feel like an ogre. She could hear Elizabeth in the other room scraping and rinsing the dishes. When James started to complain, she heard Elizabeth scold him soundly. More than ever, she wished Abraham were home to shoulder his share of the responsibilities.

She got up from the bed, pushed aside the homespun curtains from the window, and gazed out across the fields. She seldom left the farm nowadays, and saw almost no one outside her family. The Johanssens had moved west and she knew nothing about the new owners of Niels' farm, nor had she made any attempt to make their acquaintance. Without the Johanssens to drive her to meeting on Sundays, she seldom went. She was either too tired from chores or too burdened down with loneliness to go by herself. Attending to all the extra chores was almost more than she could handle. Elizabeth and James helped as much as they could, but the bulk of the work fell on her.

Lydia fretted over the crops as the days went by and still no rain fell. She took to carrying buckets of water from the creek which ran about a quarter mile past her place and dumping them into little trenches she'd painstakingly dug in the hard ground. She'd scooped out a network of tiny ditches in an effort to save the plants. The work had taken days and her body ached with the effort. Even so, she'd not been able to salvage much of the field. As she looked out over the acres of parched earth, she realized the endeavor was hopeless. She couldn't possibly water all of it. Her muscles groaned from hefting the heavy buckets of water and the palms of her hands were blistered. Each night she dropped into bed resigned to the fact that she could do nothing more to save the crops, but the next morning she was invariably back out in the fields, struggling to bring water to her thirsty seedlings.

One muggy afternoon while James napped, Lydia put aside

her worries and her chores. "Come on," she said to Elizabeth, "let's make your dolly a new dress."

"Yippee!" Elizabeth cried.

Lydia opened the chest where she stored her linens and rummaged through it for a scrap of material. "What color do you think she'd like? Here's some blue gingham. Or what about this red plaid? It's bright and cheerful."

"No, I think she'd like the blue better," answered Elizabeth with excitement.

"Blue it is, then. You smooth out the material and I'll cut the pattern."

The two worked together, Elizabeth holding the fabric in place while Lydia cut and sewed the pieces.

"This is going to be Betsy's prettiest dress. I'll have her save it just for Sundays. It'll be her Sunday best."

"She'll look lovely to go to church with you," Lydia agreed.

"Can we make a bonnet to match?"

"I think we might have enough gingham to do that."

"Now she *will* be beautiful," Elizabeth sighed happily.

As Lydia began stitching up the bonnet, there came a rap at the cabin door. "Now who would that be?"

Elizabeth shrugged her shoulders.

"Wait here. I'll answer it." Lydia cautiously opened the heavy wooden door. A man in a dark blue uniform whipped off his cap.

"Evenin', Ma'am. My name's Lieutenant Forbes."

"Yes?" Lydia opened the door a crack wider. She could see now that the man was a soldier dressed in the navy blue of the state militia. A buff colored stripe ran down the outside seam of his trousers, and on his jacket a row of gold buttons gleamed in the spring sun.

"I got separated from my outfit a few days ago, ma' am. I was wonderin' if 'n you had any vittles you could spare. I ain't had nothin' to eat since yesterday mornin'."

Lydia eyed him guardedly. It wasn't the first time soldiers had come to the door, asking for directions or a cup of cool water. Although there was nothing in particular about this soldier to cause her alarm, still she was wary.

"You wait here. I'll get you what I can spare." She shut the door.

"Who is it, Mama?" asked Elizabeth.

"A soldier. He wants somethin' to eat." She put two slices of bread and a generous piece of jerky inside a cloth and tied the corners up into a knot, then returned to the door. When she opened it, the soldier's back was to her. Lydia had the distinct impression he was looking over her farm. The thought passed through her mind that she should have mended the broken section of fence and repaired the sagging barn door. The soldier whirled around and replaced his cap on his head. Lydia handed him the knapsack.

"Many thanks, Ma'am. You supposin' I could git myself a drink from yer pump over yonder?"

Lydia nodded.

"Right fine place you got here, Ma'am," Forbes remarked as he sauntered toward the pump. "Bet it keeps you and yer man busy." He'd reached the pump by now. He stood with one hand on the pump handle, watching Lydia out of slitted eyes. His face was pockmarked and weather-beaten, and one eye was plagued with an exasperating twitch.

Lydia didn't like the way he stared at her, or his leisurely attitude. "You get your drink and be on your way," she said.

She turned to go back inside when she heard him call out to her. "Appears yer place might need some fixin' up. I could stay on a bit if'n you need help. That is, if'n yer man don't object." The last sentence was spoken with deliberate emphasis.

A shiver ran down Lydia's spine. She tried to keep her voice free from the fear that began to build inside her. "We don't need no help. You best be on your way now."

The lieutenant grinned. "You don't fool me for a minute, little lady. You ain't got a man here abouts, do you?"

Lydia froze on the doorstep. She heard Forbes' rapid steps coming toward her.

"Mama?" Elizabeth called from inside the cabin.

Panic-stricken, Lydia darted inside and grabbed Abraham's old rifle from where it rested on hooks above the door, loaded and ready to fire. She stepped to the doorway, cocked the gun, and leveled it at the approaching soldier. He stopped in midstride.

"Don't come no closer," she breathed. Her heart was pounding so loudly she could scarcely hear herself speak.

Forbes studied her for a few seconds, trying to decide if she meant to use the gun if he persisted. He took one tentative step toward her, a false smile spread across his face.

"No closer!" Lydia cried, aiming the gun at his chest.

"Hold on now, little lady. I don't want no trouble. All I need is a few dollars. Tide me over 'til I get my wages, you know. Surely you can spare a couple of dollars." The soldier's eye twitched madly.

To her alarm, Lydia felt Elizabeth suddenly tug on her skirt. "Get back inside, 'Lizabeth," Lydia hissed, glancing down at her. But Elizabeth stayed and clung tighter to her mother.

Lydia's eyes had left the soldier's face for only a split second. Now she was horrified to find he'd crept another pace closer and was within an arm's length of her. Her breath came in rapid gasps and her heart felt as if it would burst within her breast. Forbes' eyes took on a treacherous expression. Lydia felt destruction closing in. She took aim and fired.

Elizabeth screamed. The rancid smell of burned powder temporarily blurred Lydia's senses. When the smoke cleared, Lydia realized her hands were trembling. The gun was shaking like a leaf in her grip.

There wasn't a sign of the soldier. Her aim had been true. She'd fired just above his head. Astonished, Forbes had turned and had run down the rutted road, disappearing around the bend. Lydia's legs felt rooted to the spot where she stood. If it hadn't been for Elizabeth's hysterical screaming, she didn't know how long she might have stood there. Roused by the girl's cries, Lydia stooped down and hugged her. "It's all right now, 'Lizabeth. He's gone. Don't cry."

No one slept well that night. Lydia sat up in the rocking chair, the gun in her hand and her eye fixed on the door. The night passed quietly, however, and with the morning came a welcome sight. Big black thunderheads had rolled in, and by noon it was raining great heavy drops. Lydia opened the cabin door and stepped outside into the downpour. Within seconds she was drenched. She gazed up into the darkening sky, and clasping her hands together, poured out her thanks.

Just as the sun had been relentless, now the rains were so. The glutted black clouds continued to dump their load until the ground was sodden. The ditches Lydia had so painfully dug turned into churning rivulets, sweeping away tender roots and struggling green shoots in their wake. Just as one storm abated, another burst upon its heels. Lydia kept the cabin windows shuttered against the rain, but the moisture still seeped through. The dirt floor became damp and dank, and the cabin clammy. She kept the fire burning continually. Occasionally a gust of wind shot down the chimney, setting the flames dancing. It was Elizabeth's responsibility to tend the fire and stamp out any shooting sparks. Once before, a spark had leaped from the hearth and onto the rag rug, setting it afire. They'd almost lost the cabin before Abraham had put out the blaze.

On the evening of the fourth day of continuous rain, the storm was particularly fierce. Thunder cracked and lightning split the sky in two. The children were uneasy and had stayed close to Lydia throughout the day. Every time the thunder roared, James grabbed for her skirt and hid his head in its folds. It had been a long and wearing afternoon, and Lydia anticipated getting the children to bed early. As she turned down the blankets on their bed, she heard Elizabeth scream. She ran into the outer room and found Elizabeth staring in horror at the window. A strong gust of wind had evidently loosened the shutter, flinging it open. It was swinging slowly on its leather hinges.

"What is it?" cried Lydia, grabbing Elizabeth by the shoulders. Elizabeth's eyes were wide as saucers, and she trembled from head to toe.

"It's him," she cried hoarsely. "He's back. I saw his face outside the window."

Lydia's heart froze. She pushed both the children behind her and grabbed Abraham's gun. If the soldier were indeed back, this time she would not hesitate to put a bullet into his head.

A thud sounded at the cabin door. Elizabeth let out a squeal like a frightened cat. Lydia readied the gun and backed slowly away from the door, pushing the children along behind her. Then, startled, she cocked an ear, straining to hear over the howl of the wind. She thought she'd heard her name called. "Shhh," she commanded the children. "Let me listen."

There it was again. This time she distinctly heard it. "Missus Dawson! Missus Dawson!"

Lydia approached the door cautiously. She paused, turning around to glance at her children. They were huddled in the corner, their arms thrown around one another.

"Who is it?" she shouted through the closed door.

"It's me, Ira Slater."

"Mr. Slater!" Lydia hurriedly lifted the latch and threw open the door.

"Whoa! Hold on, Missus Dawson, it's just me, old Ira," exclaimed Slater, seeing the gun in Lydia's hand.

"Mr. Slater, what are you doin' here? You frightened us to death."

"I knocked, but I guess you couldn't hear me in the storm. So I banged on the shutter. Afraid I skeered your little gal."

"Come in. Dry yourself off."

Lydia fetched him a towel. The man was thoroughly drenched. His old felt hat was sodden and his coat ran water onto the floor. When he removed his hat, his stringy black hair lay pasted onto his head.

Slater stood uneasily with his hat in his hands. His usually slack expression was replaced with a look of gravity.

Lydia looked at him expectantly. "Is Abraham with you?"

"No, he ain't. I'm afraid I got bad news for you, Missus Dawson."

Lydia caught her breath. "What is it? Tell me."

Slater glanced at Lydia's children. He hesitated and cleared his throat. "Me and Abraham been workin' a couple of weeks in the mine. The ore's real plentiful, like we was told. Hard to get out, though. Real hard. Abraham, he didn't want to quit. You know how stubborn he could be. Wanted to go right on workin', move farther and farther back into the mine." Slater paused, and ran a hand across his mouth. The gap in his teeth showed clearly in a sudden flash of lightning.

"Go on!"

"There was an accident in the mine. Abraham's dead, Missus Dawson."

"No!" Lydia cried out. "Oh, no! No!" She sank down onto

her knees, unable to bear the news Slater brought her.

"I'm sorry," Slater said lamely.

Lydia drooped forward and her eyes closed. The last thing she remembered was Slater reaching out for her as she lost consciousness.

Lydia's family came to comfort her. John brought his wife and children with him, but Philip came alone and devoted himself to Lydia. Without Philip beside her, Lydia could not have withstood the funeral and the ensuing days. Philip seemed to sense what she was feeling. When she needed a shoulder to cry on, he was there. When she needed conversation, Philip provided it. When she required rest and quiet, it was Philip who shooed family and friends away so she could sleep.

After the others returned to their homes, Philip stayed on to help her deal with some hard decisions that had to be made.

"You know Charlotte and I would like nothin' better than to have you and the children come and stay with us."

"I know, Philip, and I appreciate the offer, but I can't do that. You have your own family to take care of without us hangin' on."

"That's ridiculous . . ." Philip began, his face clouding.

"Please. I want to take care of things myself. The children and I will be fine."

"How can you stay on and take care of the farm by yourself? It's not practical, Liddy."

"Well, I've been thinking about that. We've been alone for a spell now and gotten along all right." Lydia's eyes suddenly brimmed with tears. The realization that Abraham would never be coming back stung her anew.

"Liddy," Philip said gently, taking his sister's hand. "I walked the fields yesterday. There's not a blade in sight. I'm afraid the rains have ruined your plantin'. You'll have to cultivate and reseed all over again."

Lydia dashed away her tears with the back of her hand.

"Then what about harvestin' in the fall? And takin' care of the animals and repairs around the place? You can't do all that by yourself."

Lydia looked at her brother out of red-rimmed eyes. "You

think I should sell the farm."

Philip nodded. "I think it's the best thing to do. Maybe you should reconsider the offer that scoundrel made you."

"The farm's worth far more than what Ira offered to pay for it," Lydia replied hotly.

"I know that, but under the circumstances it may be the best proposal you'll get. Times are hard, Liddy, and your farm's gonna need a lot of work to make it produce."

"I can't leave my home! It's all I've got."

Philip patted her hand. "Give it some more thought and we'll talk about it again later. Come on. I'll fix you a cup of hot coffee."

After coffee, Philip busied himself by the fireside repairing a broken harness strap. Lydia wandered outside and sat on the porch of the cabin, her chin in her hand. The sun was setting to the west, and the sky was a curtain of purple and gold. She looked out at her land and thought about the years she and Abraham had worked it together. She contemplated the early years of their marriage and the bitterness the last few years had brought. Her sorrow had not lessened. Though the shock of losing him had passed, acceptance had not yet set in. She could scarcely think of anything but Abraham.

Elizabeth, too, was grief-stricken. She'd hardly spoken a word since Abraham's passing. James was too young to fully realize his loss; Lydia had tried to explain it to him, and to her surprise, the boy accepted it without question.

Lydia's eyes ran over every corner of her farm. She thought about what Philip had said. Much as she hated to admit it, she knew he was right. She couldn't farm the land by herself. But of one thing she was determined. She would not become a burden to Philip or any other member of her family. Whatever course she took from this point on—and she had no idea what that might be—she would fend for herself. What money she received from the sale of the farm would have to sustain her until she could find some kind of work. She mentally clicked off how much it would take to provide for herself and the children. She scowled as she recalled the pittance Slater had offered.

Ira Slater had come to the house two days after Abraham's funeral with an offer to purchase Lydia's farm at a fraction of its value. She'd refused him on the spot. Perhaps she wouldn't have been so hasty if she had not detected the greediness in his eyes. He was an unscrupulous man, and she thoroughly disliked him. If she must sell the farm, Slater would be the last recourse.

"Liddy?" Philip called from inside the cabin.

Lydia's head jerked up in response to his voice. "Yes?"

"It's gettin' late. Don't go and catch cold sittin' out there."

Lydia got up from the porch and walked back inside the cabin. She put a hand on her brother's shoulder and attempted a smile.

He looked up at her from his chair. "You're gonna be all right, Sis. I'll see to it."

Lydia bent down and kissed his brow.

Philip stayed through the remainder of the week until Lydia made up her mind. Then he left to see about finding a buyer for the farm. After he'd gone, Lydia tried to keep busy, but found she could do little more than sit morosely in her chair. A few days later Philip returned. His face told Lydia everything she needed to know—he had not been able to find a buyer.

"All the farmers in these parts are hurtin'. They barely got enough to make ends meet as it is. I couldn't find any one interested in buyin' more land."

"I was afraid of that," Lydia replied. "Listen to me, Philip. I want you to go home to your family. You been here long enough. They'll be needin' you. Let me have some time to mull over what's to be done."

"I'm not leavin' you here alone, Liddy."

"Even if I promise to come stay a spell at your place?"

"How soon 'til you'll come?" he asked skeptically.

"A few weeks, maybe a month. Soon as I get things settled here."

"I'll leave only if you swear you'll stay with us as you say."

Lydia laughed. "Don't you believe me?"

Philip shook his head.

"I promise I won't do anything without lettin' you know. Don't look so glum. We'll be all right."

Philip scrutinized her face. "I'll be comin' with my wagon

for you. No more than four weeks, remember."

Lydia nodded.

"You think about that offer of Slater's."

"I will."

"I'll ask around some more when I get to Quincy."

"That'll be fine."

Philip leaned over and kissed Lydia's cheek.

By noon the following day, Philip was on his way back to Quincy. He'd wanted to take James with him, but Lydia couldn't bear to let the boy go, even for a few days. Lydia accomplished the tasks that needed to be done almost automatically, her thoughts always lingering on Abraham and the enormous void he'd left in her life. As far as the farm was concerned, she vacillated from one day to the next as to what she should do. She paced the barren fields again and again. If she sold the farm, where would she go? What would she do?

Late one afternoon, weary with the weight of indecision, Lydia retreated to a far corner of the field and sat to rest under the shade of an ancient elm. Mindlessly, she traced circles in the dusty ground with her finger. Her thoughts wandered over the six seasons of planting and harvesting she and Abraham had done since they'd bought the farm. She thought particularly of this last planting. She recalled how Niels had been so kind to help her and—Niels! Why, Niels and Gerta weren't even aware of Abraham's passing. Somehow, that thought grieved her almost more than she could bear. At that moment she would have given anything to pour out her grief on Gerta's sturdy shoulders. She could almost hear Gerta say, "There now, child, don't fret. A way will open up. Trust in the Lord."

Trust in the Lord. Hadn't she done just that? And it hadn't helped her at all. Abraham was dead just the same. What good was trusting in a God who would allow her husband to die when she needed him so desperately? A pang of guilt assailed her as she considered that last unspoken thought. God had listened to her prayers; he had spared James. But maybe he had only exchanged one life for another. She put a fist to her forehead. Her head ached with the impossibility of unraveling the reasons why. It did no good to think about it. The reality was stark and simple—Abraham was gone and she must struggle on by herself. She must do whatever needed doing for herself and her children. That would be the advice Gerta would offer her. Struggle on. A way will open up. Trust in the Lord. A scripture from Proverbs stuck in her mind: "Trust in the Lord with all thine heart; and lean not unto thine own understanding. In all thy ways acknowledge him, and he shall direct thy paths." She bowed her head in silent prayer, the tears coursing down her cheeks.

As she sat there hunched over in the dirt, her shoulders heaving in grief and the intensity of her prayer, a new thought crept into her mind, imperceptibly at first, so that she hardly noticed it was there. Gradually it impressed itself upon her. She straightened, pondering the curious possibility that had presented itself. Slowly she rose to her feet, a stirring of hope fluttering through her. She stood in the ruined field, thinking, considering. Of course! It was the perfect solution. Why hadn't she thought of it before?

She shook away the dirt clinging to her skirt and resolutely strode toward the house. She swept in, breathless. Elizabeth and James looked questioningly up at her.

"Get me your belongin's, children. You can help pack them in the trunk."

The children passed a startled look between them. "Are we goin' somewhere, Mama?" Elizabeth asked.

"Yes, 'Lizabeth, we are. We're goin' to Missouri."

"On the 27th, we transacted considerable business
for the salvation of the Saints, who were settling
among a ferocious set of mobbers, like lambs
among wolves"

Joseph Smith

CHAPTER EIGHT

ishop Edward Partridge appointed a solemn assembly to be held in each of the branches of Zion after receiving Joseph's letter of rebuke. The Bishop went from branch to branch reproving the Saints and calling them to repentance. In the meeting Christian attended, Bishop Partridge's message was powerfully, yet humbly, delivered. Afterwards, confessions were heard and testimonies borne. The spirit of love and harmony among the Saints which was manifested on that occasion left a deep impression on Christian. He'd been profoundly touched by Sidney Gilbert's expressions of penitence. Sidney voiced his desire to rededicate himself to the Lord and asked forgiveness from any he may have wronged.

After the several solemn assemblies had taken place, Christian and the others at the printing house discussed changes that needed to be made in the format of the *Star*. Following Joseph's direction, they resolved to print more particulars concerning the restoration of the gospel and the growth of the Church. In addition, the *Star* would carry letters written by elders preaching the gospel abroad, so that the Saints would know of the Church's progress. Christian felt good about the changes and hoped Brother Joseph would be pleased. He worked hard on his material, rewriting and perfecting it to the best of his ability, so that it would be acceptable to the Prophet and to the Lord.

Christian was immersed in his work at the publishing house, and the weeks passed quickly for him. He had taken the day off, however, in the latter part of March to attend Seth's and Carrie's wedding. He hadn't seen much of Seth since that day. The couple spent every free moment together and Christian disliked intruding. A week or two before, though, Seth had stopped at Christian's place on his way home. They'd visited briefly, exchanging a few bits of personal news, and Seth told him about a new assignment he and Carrie had received from Bishop Partridge. The two of them were working with the new Saints coming into the county. Seth related how they went to the ferry landing each week to welcome the incoming Saints and assist them in finding quarters until they were able to make more permanent arrangements. Christian had chuckled as Seth told him about inviting a family of nine to stay with him and Carrie in their tiny cabin.

Besides his occasional visits with Seth and Carrie, Christian did not often go out socially. It had been some time since he'd been to see Mary Ann Stewart, and now as he rode over the rutted roads in a buggy he'd borrowed from Seth, he had misgivings about the afternoon that lay ahead of him. He'd invited Mary Ann out for a buggy ride and picnic. He hoped they could spend the day together without disagreement. Although he'd made amends with Mary Ann after their argument on the night of the performance in Independence, their relationship had not assumed its old familiarity. Mary Ann was distant with him and more easily annoyed. Christian had to weigh every word he spoke to her.

He pulled up in front of the Stewart's imposing home and gave the reins to a groom who instantly appeared. Christian climbed the few steps to the porch and waited longer than usual before the door opened to his knock. Instead of Matty's friendly face, Josiah Stewart stood in the doorway.

"Good evening, Sir," Christian stuttered.

"Come in, Kent."

Christian stepped inside. Stewart eyed him for some seconds, and then with a nod of his head indicated for Christian to follow him.

The two of them walked a short distance down the hallway, and then Stewart opened a door on his left which led into a semi-darkened room. He strode inside and flung open the heavy draperies covering the windows. In the flood of sunlight, Christian saw that the room served as a library. The walls were lined with shelves filled with bulky leather-bound books. In the center of the room sat a massive mahogany desk.

"Sit down," Stewart commanded.

Stewart took his own seat behind the desk. He sat down heavily and began fishing in one of the desk drawers for his cigars. He drew out two of them.

"Cigar, Kent?"

"No, thank you, Sir."

"Why not?"

"I wouldn't care for one, Sir."

"You always have before. Why not now?" Stewart demanded.

Christian wriggled in his chair, but before he could articulate a satisfactory answer, Stewart exclaimed, "I hope this doesn't have to do with another of your blamed religious tenets!"

Christian felt himself redden. It was true he was refusing the tobacco on religious grounds. Two months before, the Prophet had received a revelation from the Lord, advising the Saints against substances that are not good for the body. Tobacco was one of those substances expressly mentioned. When he learned of the revelation, Christian had decided to abstain from cigars.

Stewart snatched back the proffered cigar and jammed both of them back into the drawer, slamming it shut. "Never mind, Kent. I don't want to hear about it," he said with irritation in his voice. "I want to speak with you before Mary Ann comes down."

Christian's palms were beginning to sweat. Mr. Stewart always made him nervous, and now was no exception. Christian wished Stewart would stop glaring at him.

"I'd like to know what your intentions are, Kent?"

"My intentions, Sir?"

"You've been courting my daughter for some months now. Do you intend proposing marriage or are you merely dallying with her?"

Christian was taken aback. "No, Sir, I'm not dallying, I can assure you. I'm very fond of Mary Ann. However, I had in mind to marry a girl of my own faith."

"Blast it, Kent! There you go again with all that quibble

about religion," Stewart thundered. "Answer the question put to you, boy."

"I'm not sure of the answer, Mr. Stewart," replied Christian evenly. There was a long pause while the two men eyed one another.

"I don't like you, Kent," said Stewart in a low voice.

"I'm aware of that, Sir."

"I only tolerate you for Mary Ann's sake. For some reason she's taken with you, though God knows her mother and I have tried our best to discourage it."

"If you'll excuse me, Sir, I find it difficult to sit here and be spoken to in this manner," Christian said, his blood rising. "If you're telling me I am no longer permitted to see your daughter, then say it outright."

"Hold on, don't get hot under the collar. All I'm saying is that if you have no intention of marrying my daughter, then tell her so and end it—which I think we both agree is the preferable course."

"And if we do decide to marry?" Christian challenged.

"Then you'll be making the mistake of your life."

Stewart's cold voice unnerved Christian. Christian stood up and walked to the door of the study. "If you'll excuse me, I'll wait for Mary Ann outside."

He turned and walked out the door, back down the hallway, and outside into the spring sunshine. He took a deep breath and leaned against the buggy. He had no idea if Mr. Stewart would allow Mary Ann to accompany him.

He determined to wait five minutes for her, and if she did not come within that time, he would get into the buggy and drive away. Stewart's groom, who still held the horse's reins, stood impassively by. Christian glanced at him, wondering how the man could abide working for Josiah Stewart.

"Christian?"

Christian straightened and put on a smile he didn't feel.

"I thought you'd be waiting inside." Mary Ann walked rapidly to Christian's side and slipped her gloved hand into his. "You must be looking forward to our picnic as much as I am. I have our lunch all packed." She held up a wicker basket for him to see.

"It smells good. Let me help you into the buggy."

"It's cold chicken and biscuits. Your favorite," she said, flashing him a coy smile.

He took the picnic basket and placed it in the buggy at Mary Ann's feet and then swung into the seat beside her. "Gid up," he said, snapping the reins.

The horse trotted off at a fast clip. Mary Ann put up her pink parasol and rested her hand lightly on Christian's arm. He looked fixedly ahead, saying nothing. She glanced sideways at him, and after several seconds, frowned and asked, "Is something the matter?"

"No, why?"

"You don't seem to be very talkative today."

"I hadn't noticed. Sorry."

She took her hand away from his arm and pursed her ruby red lips.

Christian continued to drive in silence. His horse, unused to the buggy, tossed his head and snorted, straining against the harness. Christian concentrated on keeping the animal in check.

Mary Ann heaved a great sigh. "I bought this new bonnet especially to wear today, and you haven't set eyes on it."

Christian turned and looked at her. The bonnet in question was actually a big wide-brimmed straw hat, tinted pale pink, and decorated with a cluster of pink and white flowers and a large pink satin bow. "It's very pretty. You look lovely." He meant it. She was beautiful with the sunlight playing upon her smooth face, and her golden hair tied back with a wide pink ribbon. She had on a pink full-skirted dress and a matching jacket, which came to just below her waist. White riding gloves completed her attire.

"You could sound a little more enthusiastic. Really, Christian, you're positively infuriating. What is the matter with you?" Mary Ann asked in an exasperated tone of voice.

"I guess I'm just a little preoccupied. I'll try to be better company."

Mary Ann said nothing, and the two of them rode in silence for several more minutes.

"Whoa," Christian said at last, pulling hard on the rein. The horse slowed, sidestepping against the pressure of the rein. "Let's stop here and eat."

"Here?" Mary Ann repeated. "I thought we were going to drive down by the river."

"I think this will be fine. We can spread the blanket under those trees," Christian said, indicating a small stand of oaks a few feet from the road.

Mary Ann frowned but said nothing further about the arrangement. Christian brought the horse to a stop, jumped down from the buggy, and tied the reins onto a nearby branch. Then he grasped the picnic basket and blanket in one hand and helped Mary Ann down with the other. He steered her to a spot under the tallest tree and spread out the blanket.

"Sit down," he said, patting the ground next to him.

She did, but not on the spot he'd indicated. It was several inches farther away. Wordlessly, she unpacked the basket and spread its contents out on the blanket.

Christian leaned back on his elbows and surveyed the landscape. As far as he could see, rolling hills stretched out in either direction. Ankle-high grass and colorful wildflowers rippled in the gentle breeze, and in the distance he could make out snatches of the Missouri River snaking its way around the green foliage of the river banks.

"Zion," he murmured softly, as he looked out upon the peaceful scene.

"What did you say?"

Christian rolled over onto one elbow. "I said it's beautiful country out here, isn't it?"

Mary Ann made a perfunctory glance around her. "I prefer the cities back East."

Christian looked closely at her. She was beautiful sitting there under the trees with her dress spread out around her like a billowing pink cloud. Her flaxen hair curled softly down her back, glistening in the afternoon sunlight. She met his gaze cooly, her hazel eyes clear and frank. He sat up and slipped an arm around her waist. At first she was unyielding, but as his lips met hers, she returned his kiss with an ardor he was unprepared for. He loosened her from his embrace.

"Mary Ann," he began hesitantly, taking her chin between his fingers. "Listen to me."

She looked up at him, her eyes shining expectantly.

"You know I love you."

"I love you too, Christian," she answered. She kissed him again and snuggled into his arms.

For an instant Christian reconsidered what he'd been about to say. The feel of her soft cheek against his almost drove rational thought fromhis mind. He drew a deep breath and continued. "There's more involved than the fact that we're attracted to one another."

Startled by his words, Mary Ann lifted her head. "What are you talking about?"

"When two people care for each other, they naturally want to share their thoughts, their hopes and dreams."

Mary Ann's expression was blank.

"I'm talking about companionship and understanding. A common view of life."

"I don't know what you're getting at, Christian."

Christian paused, searching for the right words. "A few minutes ago I expressed how I felt about something, but you had no idea what I was trying to convey. I wanted to tell you how I felt about the land, how much I admire its beauty, and how it makes me feel to be a part of it."

A hint of impatience crept into Mary Ann's green eyes. "Is that why you've been acting queerly—because I don't appreciate this God-forsaken wilderness like you do?"

"No, the frontier has nothing to do with it. I'm talking about us, you and me. I don't think it's going to work out between us."

Mary Ann sat bolt upright. "You can't believe that. You just told me you loved me."

"I do love you! I want us to be close, like Seth and Carrie. But we're not the same, Mary Ann. We don't have the same values. We're not striving for the same ends."

"We love each other. Isn't that enough?"

"That's the whole point. It's not enough." Christian got to his feet and began to pace. "I thought it was once, too. I thought we could iron out any differences, overcome any difficulty together. But I've come to realize you can't compromise values and still maintain self-respect."

"That's nonsense," Mary Ann said, rising to her feet also.

"You've met someone else, haven't you? All this talk about values and understanding—it's simply to cover up your cowardice in telling me the truth." Her eyes flashed and her mouth had taken on a cruel turn.

"You're wrong. There's no one else," Christian protested.

"I won't be made a fool of, Christian Kent." She scooped up the picnic lunch and dumped it back into the basket.

"Mary Ann, please, can't we—"

"You're the one who wanted this picnic," she interrupted. "You can have it!" With those words she flung the basket at Christian and stalked off.

"Wait a minute!" he cried. He hurried after her and caught her by the arm. "I don't want us to part like this."

"What did you expect?" Mary Ann hissed. "That I'd shed a few prudent tears and then slip conveniently out of your life? If so, then you've underestimated me."

"I was telling you the truth. I hoped you'd understand."

Mary Ann jerked out of his grasp. "There's one thing *you* better understand," she snapped. "I don't want to see you again—ever!"

Christian's heart hammered in his chest as he watched her climb into the buggy and sit stiffly, waiting for him to drive her home. There was nothing more for him to say—no words to express how miserable he was feeling. He got into the buggy beside her and they started back.

The sky overhead was steel gray and a drizzling rain was falling, blending its waters with those of the Blue River. Christian felt as morose as the weather. Upstream the ferry appeared as a distant dot, slowly making its way to the landing. As Christian watched, it seemed to be barely moving.

"Cheer up, Christian. It was the only thing you could do. There's no sense beating yourself over the head. Put her out of your mind and get on with your life," Seth was saying.

Christian kicked at a pebble with the toe of his boot. "I've been telling myself that same thing, but it doesn't make me feel much better."

"It's rough. There's no doubt about it. But I guarantee

you'll get over Mary Ann. Before you know it, you'll be notic-
ing every young lady on the streets of Independence."

Christian shot him a doubtful look.

The two walked along the bank of the Big Blue, occasionally looking out across the river to note the ferry's progress.

"I'm glad you decided to come with me today. Carrie was
disappointed she couldn't be here."

"How's she feeling? Any better?"

"Not much. She's sick most of the time." A soft look crept
into Seth's eyes. "She keeps telling me it will all be worth it.
She can hardly wait until the baby comes. She's like a child
looking forward to Christmas."

Christian smiled. "I can't quite picture you as a papa."

"I'm having a little difficulty with that myself," Seth
grinned. "I'm not sure I know how to take care of a child."

"Don't worry. I think that sort of thing is supposed to come
naturally."

"I hope so," Seth said, looking out again across the river.
"Here she comes."

Christian looked up to see the ferry rapidly approaching
the landing. Two men with long poles were jockeying the boat
into position. With a lurch, the ferry came to a stop against the
log pilings of the dock.

"Come on."

"What do I do?" asked Christian.

"Just smile."

Seth walked down to the landing and with one foot on the
ferry and the other on the bank, he handed the first of the passengers onto dry land. "Welcome to Independence, my name's
Seth Whitfield."

"Howdy. I'm Benjamin Perry."

"Let me take your bag, Mr. Perry. Watch your step there."
Seth saw the man safely on shore, then lent a hand to a
buxom, bright-eyed woman, who apparently was Mrs. Perry.
Six children tumbled off behind her, chattering and giggling.

"I'm Christian Kent. We've a wagon over yonder. Can we
give you a lift into town?"

"Much obliged. You wouldn't be Mormons, would ye?"

"Yes, Sir, we are."

"Lord be praised! Sarah, these here boys are Saints, come to see us safely into Zion."

"Mercy, but we're glad to see you!" cried the plump woman. She threw her arms around Christian and squeezed him until his eyes watered.

While Christian helped the Perrys put their bags in the wagon, Seth continued to greet the others disembarking the ferry. Most of the passengers were met by friends or relatives waiting for them on the landing, but a few stood uncertainly on shore by themselves. These Seth directed to the wagon. Soon, three separate families were crowded around Christian, loading their goods into the bed of the wagon.

As Christian assisted these newly arrived Saints, he glanced at the ferry to see if everyone had gotten off. Seth was speaking with the last passenger, a young woman with reddish hair. Clinging to her skirt was a small boy, and a girl not much older clutched her hand. Christian noticed that the woman looked exhausted. Seth scooped up the little boy into his arms and carried him toward the wagon, while the woman and the girl followed.

"Got room for a couple more?" Seth asked.

"I think so."

Seth swung the boy up into the wagon seat, then helped the woman and child climb in. "All set."

Seth sprang in beside Christian and the little caravan moved out in the direction of town. For the most part, the newcomers were silent during the ride, their eyes taking in every detail along the route. The wagon bounced and jostled along the dirt road, made muddy from the spring rain.

"Do you always have this many people?" Christian asked his friend in a low voice.

"Sometimes more."

"Have you places for all of them?"

Seth nodded.

Christian turned around in his seat to look back at the wagon load of immigrants. Every one of them had dirt-streaked faces and rumpled clothing, but their eyes were shining.

Seth nudged him in the ribs. "You don't know a family by

the name of Johanssen, do you?"

"Johanssen? No, I don't think so. Do they live in town?"

"I don't know. The woman with the two children asked if I knew them. Friends of hers, I suppose."

Christian stole a look at the woman in question. She was speaking to the little girl sitting at her side. Christian assumed the child to be her daughter, for she looked very much like the woman, except for her golden hair.

"I suppose you and Carrie will be taking in one of the families for a while," he said.

Seth nodded his head. "I think Carrie would enjoy having Mrs. Perry to visit with. She looks like she knows something about birthing babies." He grinned and snapped the reins, and the horses quickened their pace.

Shortly, the party arrived in Independence. When Seth stopped at the homes of three Church members, he and Christian helped each family carry their goods to the door and introduced them to the people they would be staying with until they could provide for themselves. Then he dropped Christian off at the printing house and went on home with the Perry family in tow.

It was late in the afternoon when Christian let himself inside the building. The others had already left for the day. He took off his coat and draped it across the back of a chair. A small pile of newspapers lay on his desk. He picked up the top sheet, a copy of the *St. Louis Times*. He sorted through the others, the usual papers to which Phelps subscribed that came into the office regularly. They often used excerpts from them for republication in the *Star*. He sat down at his desk and browsed through a copy of the *Missouri Courier*. It carried a piece about the cholera epidemic. Christian scanned the article quickly. He flipped through the pages, lingering on an article about a man who set fire to his house and refused to leave while it burned down around him.

Christian refolded the *Courier* and set it down on top of the rest of the papers. He put his hands behind his head and leaned back in his chair. Images of Mary Ann Stewart flickered through his mind. He saw her sitting beneath the old oak tree, her lips as soft and pink as the dress she wore. She smiled and leaned forward to kiss him. He closed his eyes against the memory. Maybe he'd been hasty in breaking off the relationship. The pain he was feeling was a high price to pay—perhaps too high.

He got up from the chair and idly looked out the window. The sky was clearing and people in the streets were scurrying home to their suppers. Across the way, he watched as Sidney Gilbert came out of his store, took a key from his pocket, and locked the door of the mercantile. Sidney stepped down from the porch and greeted a passerby. The two of them fell in step and soon disappeared around the corner of the street.

Christian turned away from the window and took his seat at the desk again. He drummed his fingers on the stack of newsprint, thoughts of Mary Ann still swimming in his head.

CHAPTER NINE

I've seen the tract, Christian, and it's the most slander-ous I've ever read," Sidney Gilbert was saying. "Pixley has been hand carrying copies from house to house for several days now. This is sure to stir up a whole new host of troubles for us."

"The Reverend is certainly zealous in carrying out what he believes to be right. I'll say that for him," Christian replied.

The two men were talking outside Gilbert's store. It was a warm June day and flies buzzed around the open barrels of produce Sidney kept stored on the porch. Sidney's voice was agitated and perspiration dotted his forehead. "I wouldn't treat the matter lightly if I were you. Trouble follows Pixley around like a dog nipping at a man's heels."

"I'm not making light of it. It concerns us. I wouldn't be surprised to see William print a rebuttal in the next number of the *Star.*"

"He should do that. We can't allow folks to believe those lies."

Christian frowned, thinking about the Reverend Pixley, of the Missionary Society. Pixley was well known among the Saints for his vitriolic attacks against the Church. He wrote inflammatory articles about the Saints, which he sent to reli-gious papers in the East, and he used his influence among the settlers to discredit the Church in Jackson County.

Christian put the rolled piece of parchment Sidney had given him under his arm. "I'll pass your feelings along to William. And thanks for the map. I'll return it after William and Oliver have had a chance to look at it."

Sidney responded with a preoccupied wave of his hand. Christian started down the porch steps.

"Tell William I'm very concerned about those tracts, and I think he ought to do something about it," Sidney called in parting.

Christian crossed the street and headed for the printing office. The road was clogged with traffic—wagons, buggies, and men on horseback clattered in every direction. The perpetual motion stirred up clouds of dust which hung in the air and covered everyone and everything with a layer of gritty dirt.

Christian picked his way through the throng, glad to leave the din of the street behind as he climbed the stairs to the printing office. The air inside was cooler and a faint breeze stirred from an open window. He found William bent over his desk, studying the galleys for the upcoming issue of the *Star*.

"Sidney wanted me to tell you he thinks you ought to print a denial of Pixley's tract," Christian said as he laid the map down on Phelps' desk.

"I've already decided to do that."

"Be careful how you handle it. We don't want to aggravate the Reverend further."

Phelps nodded. He put away the galleys and spread open the map Christian had brought.

Christian leaned over the large sheet of parchment. "Take a look here, William, where the spot for the temple is located. Sidney told me all of this land surrounding the temple lot is for sale now. He hopes to be able to purchase it soon for the Church."

Sidney Gilbert, one of the original seven men sent to Independence by Brother Joseph, had stewardship over the Lord's storehouse and the responsibility of purchasing lands for the Saints. He worked closely with Phelps and the other leaders of the Church. Though Sidney was slight in stature, Christian knew him to be a man of untiring ability.

"Does the Church have sufficient funds in hand to buy the acreage?" asked Phelps.

"Sidney thinks so, with a few more contributions from the Saints."

Christian pulled up a chair and the two of them sat together, studying the plat map. The plat had been sent to Independence by Joseph Smith as a general plan for building the city of Zion, and as a pattern for laying out future cities for the Saints. Plans for the construction of a temple were also included. Feelings about raising a temple in Zion ran deep in the hearts of the Saints. In Kirtland, ground had been broken for such an edifice just two weeks earlier. The Saints in Zion were eager to start construction on their own temple as soon as possible.

Phelps folded up the map and slipped it into his desk drawer. "Were you able to get a copy of the state law?" he asked Christian.

"Yes, I have it right here. I've written down the pertinent facts." Christian withdrew a rumpled sheet of paper from his pocket. "The law states that free negroes or mulattoes cannot settle in the state without a certificate of citizenship, and that if any person transports a free negro or mulatto into the state without papers, that person will be fined five hundred dollars."

Phelps nodded his head. "We must be careful that the brethren understand the law concerning negroes. We've already been accused of harboring abolitionist sympathies. I don't wish to publish for or against the question, but I do feel the Saints need to be made aware of the slavery laws here in Missouri."

"What do you intend to do?"

"I believe I'll simply publish the state law and perhaps briefly comment on it."

"William, do you think it's prudent to touch the subject at all? Nothing inflames the Missourians more than abolitionist talk."

"We must defend ourselves against those who arouse hatred and rebellion against us. Such men will use any weapon in their power, including the issue of slavery."

"I just question whether the *Star* is the appropriate medium to do it."

"Don't worry, Christian. I'll be tactful. I know as well as anyone how these fool Missourians can turn into a lawless mob, given the slightest provocation. That's the very reason I want to combat Pixley's tract—to prevent that sort of action."

"All right. What do you want me to do?"

"Keep working on the Book of Commandments. I'd like to

have the printing finished by the end of the month."

Christian labored throughout the week, preparing material for publication in the July number of the *Star* and readying the Book of Commandments for printing. On Saturday afternoon he visited Seth and Carrie, and the three of them went out to supper together in the evening. They'd talked briefly about Mary Ann and the possibility of Christian attempting to revive their relationship. He really didn't know how he felt about that possibility. At night when he was alone in his cabin, he longed to be with her, but the bitterness of their parting persuaded him from taking any action.

On the Sabbath, he attended services as usual. The high priests generally circulated among the churches, preaching to the congregations. This day John Corrill and John Whitmer were the speakers in Christian's branch. Christian sat near the back, his arms folded across his chest, listening to Brother Corrill. Corrill's voice rose and fell in smooth cadence as he spoke about the ordinance of baptism and the gift of the Holy Ghost. Christian paid close attention, occasionally nodding his head in agreement.

As Corrill's sermon went on, Christian took notice of those around him. The room was full and he knew most of the brethren there and their families. Near the front, on the opposite side of the room from him, sat Sister Whitmer. Next to her was seated a young woman with two small children beside her. As Christian watched, Sister Whitmer leaned over and whispered to her. The woman nodded and smiled. Christian could see her profile from where he sat. At first he did not recognize her, then he realized she was the woman he and Seth had picked up from the ferry. Seth had found a temporary home for her with the Whitmers.

He studied her idly, keeping one ear tuned to Corrill's sermon. She wore a plain black dress with a narrow white ruffle at the throat and wrists. A few unruly tendrils of auburn hair crept from beneath her close-fitting bonnet. She had a small, fine nose, a pleasant mouth, and white skin. Most redheaded women Christian knew either had splotchy freckles or a ruddy complexion, but this girl's skin was pale as milk. He tried to recall her name, but it escaped him. He vaguely wondered about her husband and why he wasn't in Independence with her.

Corrill gave a thunderous "Amen" and sat down. Then Whitmer came to the pulpit and proceeded. His sermon was in a lighter vein, and the congregation chuckled several times during his remarks. At last the time was spent, the congregation sang a closing hymn, and a benediction was rendered by one of the elders.

Christian rose to leave, but a friend coming down the aisle paused to chat with him. The two stood aside so the others could pass, and by the time they'd finished their conversation, most of the people had filed out of the church house. Christian started with his friend toward the door when he felt a tap on his shoulder. He turned to find Sister Whitmer behind him, smiling broadly. Sarah Whitmer was a small, thin woman, with laughing blue eyes and a perpetual smile. Her chestnut-colored hair was pulled up in the back and a row of three ringlets covered each ear.

"Brother Kent, how nice to see you!"

"How are you, Sister Whitmer? Your husband gave a fine sermon."

"He always does, doesn't he?" she laughed. "I'd like you to meet a friend of mine. Come here, Liddy," she said, turning to usher someone forward by the elbow. "Brother Kent, this is Lydia Dawson. She's staying with us for a spell."

Christian's eyes met the woman's. They were the deepest blue he'd ever seen.

"How do you do?" she said in a soft voice.

"Fine, thank you. I believe we've met before, haven't we?"

"Oh? I'm sorry I don't recall . . . I've met so many people in the last little while," she murmured. Christian noticed a tinge of color creep into her cheeks.

"Don't be concerned about that. We weren't even formally introduced. I was at the ferry when you came in and I helped give you a lift into town."

The woman's eyes looked puzzled for a moment. "Did you say your name was Mr. Whitfield?"

Christian smiled, "No, he's the other fellow you met. I was just giving him a hand that day. My name is Christian Kent."

"Oh."

"Brother Kent works at the printing house with Brother Phelps and Brother Cowdery," Sarah Whitmer informed her.

"I see," Mrs. Dawson answered, although by her expression Christian could tell she was unfamiliar with either Phelps or Cowdery.

"You must come to the house for a little social gathering we're holding next Saturday, Brother Kent."

"Thank you very much, Sister Whitmer, but I don't think I'll be able to—"

"I won't take no for an answer," she returned, her bright eyes sparkling. "I'll expect you at seven o'clock sharp."

"All right," Christian laughed.

"Until then, Brother Kent." Mrs. Whitmer gave Christian her hand and then bustled off toward the door.

Christian's eyes came back to the woman. "It was nice to see you again."

"Thank you." She smiled briefly, then followed Mrs. Whitmer out through the door.

Christian trailed behind them, watching as Mrs. Dawson called to her two children, who were romping in the yard of the church house. When they ran up to her, the little girl grabbed her hand and the boy began running exuberant circles around her skirt. She caught him and whispered something in his ear. He immediately settled down and took her other hand. Christian noticed the boy had on a new pair of shiny black shoes, undoubtedly purchased by Sister Whitmer.

Christian wandered back to his cabin. He prepared himself a light supper and then climbed onto his bunk and picked up one of his favorite books, a well-worn volume of Milton. He read until late into the night. When he finally slept, dreams of Mary Ann chased through his head.

Christian reined in his horse at the frame house situated at the end of the block. He tethered the animal next to several others at the post and mounted the four steps to the wide veranda. The Whitmer house was one of the finest in

Independence. John had erected the two-story structure little more than a year ago. Before that time he and his family had occupied a cabin on the banks of the Big Blue.

Sarah Whitmer answered Christian's knock. "Brother Kent, I'm so glad you've come! Please come in."

Christian removed his hat and walked into the parlor of the warm, cheerful home. Around him milled a dozen or so guests. Christian recognized several of the men and smiled in greeting. Most of them were married and their wives hovered near their sides, but a few, like Christian, were without companions.

Mrs. Whitmer took Christian's arm and steered him to the center of the room. "There's cake on the table, Brother Kent. Help yourself to it. Just make yourself right at home," she said, squeezing Christian's arm. "John's somewhere about." She made a quick glance around the room.

"Thank you, I'll find him," Christian said, carefully extricating his arm from Sarah's clasp.

"Now you enjoy yourself ," Sister Whitmer instructed, her merry blue eyes shining with heady excitement.

"I will, thank you."

She patted his arm and flashed him a bright smile, then left him to himself.

He spied John Whitmer at the other end of the room. Whitmer was a tall, lean man of about thirty, with gray-blue eyes, a long nose, and thinning light brown hair. He was historian for the Church and one of the special witnesses allowed to handle the plates Joseph Smith had translated. Christian began making his way toward him.

A young man Christian knew slightly was filling his plate at a table laden with squares of white cake and a big bowl of apple cider. Christian paused to say hello and pour himself a drink from the punch bowl. The cider was cold and tart on his tongue. As he sipped it, he studied the men and women present in the room. Most of them were farming people. Christian had toyed with the idea of farming a section of ground himself. He knew Bishop Partridge would be willing to give him stewardship over a few acres, but with his labors at the *Star*, he hadn't had time to pursue the idea. Perhaps when he found a wife . . . Mary Ann's image suddenly intruded into his thoughts. With conscious effort he blanked her out.

He put down his empty cup and started to meander through the group gathered in the Whitmers' parlor, speaking to first one acquaintance and then another. He joined a little knot of men discussing their crops and the upcoming harvest, but found he had little to contribute to the conversation. So he excused himself and moved on. Wondering exactly how long propriety demanded he stay, he threaded his way again over to the table. As he reached for a piece of cake, a woman appeared with a full tray in her hands. This time Christian recognized Mrs. Dawson immediately. She stopped at the far end of the table and began putting squares of cake from the tray onto the table. She didn't notice Christian watching her a short distance away. Occasionally, she looked out at the crowd gathered in the parlor with an anxious expression. Christian finished his cake, dusted the crumbs from his hands, and approached her.

"Good evening, Mrs. Dawson."

Her eyes darted up from the tray and for a fleeting moment she looked confused, but she quickly recovered and said, "Mr. Kent, isn't it?"

"That's right." Christian noticed that her copper hair was swept up onto her head, and she wore a dark blue dress which deepened the blue of her eyes.

She smiled faintly, then continued putting cakes onto the table. "Are you enjoying your stay with the Whitmers?" Christian asked her.

Mrs. Dawson looked up again. "Very much. They're wonderful people."

"Yes, they are," he agreed. She gave him another brief smile and returned to her work. Finding her reticence intriguing, Christian pursued the conversation. He took another piece of cake and asked, "Will you be settling in Independence?"

Her brow furrowed. "I'm not sure."

"I guess I haven't met your husband yet," Christian continued in a conversational tone.

Christian saw her hand tremble under the piece of cake she was transferring to the table. "My husband passed away a few months ago."

"I'm sorry. I didn't know." Christian felt his face redden.

The reason for his invitation to the Whitmers' party was now abundantly clear. Sarah Whitmer was attempting to include him in her matchmaking schemes. He resented being asked to come on those terms. If Sarah desired him to become better acquainted with Mrs. Dawson, she should have told him about the woman's circumstances instead of allowing him to clumsily find it out for himself.

"I guess that makes us even."

Christian looked up, startled by the woman's words. She was smiling sheepishly at him. "What?"

"I was embarrassed, too, the other day in meetin', for not recognizin' you after you were so kind to help us."

Christian grinned in return. "I suppose that does put us on equal footing."

Mrs. Dawson smiled again, this time a genuine smile.

Christian took a bite of cake. "Are you from around this area, Mrs. Dawson?"

"Illinois. I have family in Quincy."

"Quincy. I've been there. It's a nice town."

"Did you live there?"

"No, I'm originally from Philadelphia, but I was in Quincy once for a few days on business. I'm in the newspaper business," he added.

Mrs. Dawson nodded her head. "The *Star*. The Whitmers read it regularly."

"I hope they find it satisfactory," Christian laughed. She laughed too, though it was only for a moment. "Did you come by yourself all the way from Illinois, Mrs. Dawson?"

"Along with my children, 'Lizabeth and James."

She made the remark so matter-of-factly that Christian shook his head in awe. He thought she must be very courageous to make a trip of over two hundred miles without the support of a husband.

"The Whitmers have been so kind to us, takin' us in and all. I don't know how I can ever repay them." Her face clouded as she seemed to ponder the gravity of her debt to them.

"They don't expect it. They're happy to help."

"I haven't properly thanked you and Mr. Whitfield for helpin' us the day we arrived."

"We were glad to do it. You say you might not be staying in Independence, then?"

"I was hopin' to stay with friends of mine who came here a few months ago, but I haven't been able to find them. Maybe you know them—Niels and Gerta Johanssen?"

"No, I don't recognize the name."

"That's strange. I was sure this was the place they talked about comin' to."

"If you'll excuse my boldness, Mrs. Dawson, are your friends Mormons?"

She nodded. "They were baptized into the Mormon faith in Illinois and set out for here last April."

"Perhaps they've settled in one of the other counties. I have contact with quite a few people in Missouri because of my work at the *Star*. If you'd like, I could make some inquiries."

"No, I couldn't ask you to do that."

"You didn't ask. I offered." Christian took out a piece of paper and a pencil from his pocket and wrote down the name. "There. Perhaps we can locate them after all."

Lydia Dawson looked at him closely. "Are you a Mormon too, Mr. Kent?"

"Yes, I am. That's the reason I'm in Independence."

"I see."

"Fire!" someone in the room suddenly cried out. "The Johnson's barn is afire!"

For an instant everyone in the room was stunned into silence. Then the men flew into action, dashing out the door and down the street to the Johnson residence, located a few blocks away. Christian hastily made some remark to Mrs. Dawson and rushed out with the men.

John Whitmer grabbed some buckets from his shed, handing them to others to fill at a nearby stream. Christian grabbed a full bucket and passed it to another man standing close to him. In seconds the men had formed a brigade to pass the buckets of water from the stream to the burning barn. The acrid smell of smoke permeated the air, and Christian could see bright orange tongues of flame shooting from the roof of the barn. No one spoke. Every muscle was taut with the strain of getting water to the building. Christian wiped away the sweat forming on his brow. From his position near the stream, he couldn't tell how much effect the men's efforts were having on the roaring fire.

One of the men fighting the blaze came hurrying toward the stream. "We've got to have more water! Move faster. Faster!"

"Do you have it under control?" Christian shouted at him.

The man was too agitated to answer. He just kept shouting for more water. Christian worked harder at passing the heavy buckets, the water sloshing and spilling as the men frantically passed it from hand to hand.

From somewhere down the line of the human chain, a man cursed and another exclaimed, "Careful man. Don't spill it all!"

Suddenly the frenzied pace slowed, then ceased altogether. All eyes focused on the brilliant orange flames engulfing what remained of the wooden structure. Christian's arms hung limp at his side, a bucket in either hand, as he watched the fire consume the barn with a vengeance.

A movement to Christian's left distracted his attention. He turned just in time to see two shadowy figures stealthily disappear around the corner of a nearby building. Anger boiled up inside him. A few weeks earlier, someone had thrown a rock the size of a grapefruit through the window of one of the brethren's homes. The Saints would bear scurrilous lies and false charges if they must, but violence to property was another matter. Christian's eyes scoured the darkness for the fleeing culprits.

"We, the undersigned, citizens of Jackson county, believing that an important crisis is at hand, as regards our civil society, in consequence of a pretended religious sect of people that have settled, and are still settling in our county, styling themselves 'Mormons' and intending, as we do, to rid our society, peaceably if we can, forcibly if we must. . ."

The Manifesto of the Mob
Jackson County, Missouri
July 1833

CHAPTER TEN

The house where Lydia was staying was large and cozy, a two-story frame, with four windows facing the street and four in the back overlooking a section of orchard, gardens, and fields. A wide covered porch ran along the front part of the home. The room she was given, which she shared with her children, was situated in the upper west corner. It was comfortably furnished with a double bed, a dresser and washstand, and a handsome oil lamp. Her favorite niche was a seat near the window where she liked to watch the sun set in the evenings.

On this particular evening, the sky to the west was stained crimson. Lydia pushed aside the chintz curtains, letting the rosy glow fill her window. The warm July night nuzzled the pane. In the yard below, a bed of flowers nodded their colorful heads at her. A white picket fence, freshly painted, encircled the yard, and the silver leaves of two tall maples rustled in the slight breeze.

Lydia uttered a soft sigh of contentment. She felt comfortable living with the Whitmers. To earn her keep, she helped Sarah Whitmer with the household chores and took in washing and mending for several families in the neighborhood. Sarah was helping her teach Elizabeth and James their letters. Lydia, too, was picking up a few pointers, especially in her manner of speaking. Most of the Saints in Missouri were Easterners, with Eastern habits, customs, and distinctive patterns of speech. Lydia wanted her diction to conform more uniformly with theirs.

Sarah also introduced Lydia to the townspeople. She often

invited friends to her home for the evening. Invariably, there were included among the guests a number of unmarried young men. Lydia frowned slightly at the thought of those gatherings, for she always felt uneasy around Sarah's gentlemen guests. She had not yet spent her grief over Abraham's passing, and she wasn't interested in finding someone to take his place. She tried to be as inconspicuous as possible, busying herself with little duties such as refilling the punch bowl or replenishing the table with sweets.

A little more than a week ago, however, she'd had a pleasant conversation with one of the gentlemen present. His name was Kent and she'd been impressed by his polite and easy manner. He was a tall, broad-shouldered fellow of about her own age, with brown hair and eyes, and a slender face. Their exchange had been brief because that was the evening of the fire. A neighbor's barn had burned to the ground. Some said it was deliberately set by the Church's enemies. She'd overhead John Whitmer saying that this was just the latest in a series of depredations directed against the Saints. Even though she wasn't aware of all the problems that had plagued the Saints in Independence over the past few months, Lydia could easily detect the tension that existed now.

She hoped none of that would interfere with the plans for her upcoming baptism. She had made the decision to join the Church, and had expressed her desire to the Whitmers only this evening. They, of course, were overjoyed, and Mr. Whitmer had helped her select the following Saturday as her baptismal day.

Lydia knew that the Church of Jesus Christ was the only true and correct church, established by the Master himself in her own day. That testimony had been borne to her by the still, small voice after weeks of study, fasting, and prayer upon the matter. Whitmer had explained the principles of the gospel to her clearly, and they had discussed its various points together. He'd provided her with his own copy of the Book of Mormon and she'd read it carefully, savoring its words.

Now she understood the prompting that had come into her soul that evening she'd knelt, distraught, in the barren fields outside her cabin after Abraham's death. The Lord had led her by the hand all the way to Jackson County. The journey had not been easy. There were moments when doubts assailed her and the heartache of leaving home and family seemed more than she could bear. But, inevitably, the way opened before her. Even that scoundrel, Ira Slater, had ultimately been a blessing. After Lydia had reached her decision to move to Missouri, she'd ridden out to his place to ask if he was still interested in buying her farm. Slater had told her he was no longer in a position to pay what he had originally offered and suggested substantially less. That recollection made her angry even now. She'd taken the money though, just as Slater knew she would, purchased provisions for the journey, and laid the rest by.

When her brother, Philip, came for her a few weeks later, she told him of her plans. At first he thought she'd lost her mind, but Lydia succeeded in convincing him that she knew what she wanted. Although he wholeheartedly disapproved of what she was doing, he helped her pack and close up the house. She stayed with Philip and his family at their home in Quincy for a few days, and then he accompanied her as far as the Missouri, where he saw her safely aboard a riverboat. Their parting tore Lydia's heart. She knew Philip disapproved of her actions and she was uncertain when she would see him again. She'd written both Philip and her parents a letter letting them know she'd arrived safely and where she was staying.

She appreciated the Whitmers' hospitality. John made her feel like part of his family. He'd introduced her to his brothers and sisters, most of whom lived in the Whitmer settlement on the banks of the Big Blue. His youngest sister, Elizabeth, was married to Oliver Cowdery. Lydia was more friendly with Whitmer's other sister, Catherine, who was married to a man named Hiram Page. Catherine occasionally came to the house to spend an afternoon with her, or invited her to dine at the Page home.

The sound of horse's hooves outside the house interrupted Lydia's musings. She pressed her nose to the windowpane and saw Charles Allen ride up and jump off his mount. He threw the reins over the hitching post in front of the house. She recognized Mr. Allen because she did the washing for the Allens' large family. He hurried to the Whitmers' door and rapped loudly. Someone opened the door for him and he disappeared inside. Lydia wondered why he had come calling so late at night. She stood up and walked over to the bed where Elizabeth and James lay sleeping. She kissed them and pulled the blankets up around their chins, thinking how precious both of them were to her. She'd begun to change into nightclothes when a soft knock sounded at her bedroom door.

"Liddy, are you still awake?" Sarah Whitmer whispered.

"Yes, Sarah. Is something the matter?" Lydia quickly rebuttoned her dress and opened the bedroom door.

"There could be some trouble brewing. Would you mind coming downstairs for a minute? John would like to speak to you." Sarah's face was grave and Lydia noticed a tight white line circling her lips.

Lydia slipped out the door, closing it softly behind her.

"Come with me," Sarah said in a quiet voice.

John Whitmer and Mr. Allen were seated on the parlor couch. Whitmer looked up when he heard the two women approach. "Mrs. Dawson, sit down, won't you? I believe you know Brother Allen."

"Yes. Hello, Mr. Allen." Allen nodded in reply.

"Charles has brought us a bit of disturbing news. It seems a few of our neighbors have gotten up some sort of secret document calling for the Saints' removal from the county. Since you're staying with us, Mrs. Dawson, it's possible you may be in danger."

"I don't understand." Lydia questioned, "Are you sayin' they may try to force you from your homes?"

"That's what they're threatening, if we won't leave peaceably," Allen answered.

"Charles has it on good authority that the rabble plan to meet tomorrow at the courthouse to implement their plans."

"Can't the constable do something to stop them?" asked Lydia.

"The constable is one of the ringleaders," Sarah Whitmer said with disdain.

"And you can be sure Pixley is in the thick of it," Whitmer added. "That front-page piece in the *Star* didn't do much to appease the Reverend, I'm afraid."

Lydia knew which piece Whitmer was referring to. She had read it herself. The article was entitled, "Beware of False Prophets;" it was a thinly veiled repudiation of Pixley's tract of the same name which he had recently been peddling in Independence.

The real problem had come to a head, however, with the publication of another piece, also in the July issue of the *Star*, concerning slavery. The article made reference to free colored people, but the Church's enemies had construed the piece as an invitation by the Church to encourage free negroes to settle in Jackson County. The article had touched off such a public outcry that the editor of the *Star* had published an extra issue in an effort to clarify his position. This, too, was met with misunderstanding and hostility, and friction between the two groups of people intensified. Apparently, this secret document was the result of those bad feelings.

"If the Missourians band together there's no telling what they're capable of. I think it would be wise if you packed a few things for yourself and the children and left tonight. Brother Allen can take you to the home of one of the brethren who lives outside of town. You'll be safe there."

"What about the rest of you?" Lydia asked.

"I won't leave unless I'm absolutely forced to," Sarah Whitmer said, setting her jaw.

"Then I'll stay, too," Lydia answered.

Whitmer's face took on a look of exasperation. "We're not dealing with ordinary citizens here. These are vicious, lawless men. There may be real trouble. Perhaps you should at least consider sending your children, Mrs. Dawson."

"I'll take care of the children. We've been in perilous circumstances before, Mr. Whitmer. We'll cast our lot with the Saints."

Whitmers' expression softened. "All of you are to stay indoors tomorrow. No exceptions," he said.

Both women nodded.

There was some further discussion of precautions to be taken on the morrow and then Allen left to warn others. Whitmer bolted the door and the three of them went upstairs to their rooms. Lydia found it impossible to sleep. She was outraged by what she'd heard and concerned for the safety of her children and her friends. Nevertheless, her course was set. She would not abandon the Whitmers because of a few reckless men, nor would she betray her newly found faith.

Saturday, July 20th, dawned warm and clear. John Whitmer left the house shortly after noon to consult with the other brethren. He was gone nearly two hours, and when he returned he was visibly upset.

"What has happened?" Sarah asked him, breathless.

"They've held their meeting and are in the midst of delivering an address to the public outside the courthouse. Their accusations are nothing short of vile lies," Whitmer reported.

"What do you think they'll do next?" asked Lydia.

"I don't know, but I'll be surprised if we get through this day without violence."

Lydia bit her lip. Why couldn't the Saints be left alone, she wondered? What had they done to stir up such hostility and persecution against them? From everything she had seen while in Independence, the Saints proved to be peaceful, law-abiding citizens.

"There's nothing more to do now except wait," Whitmer said. "Let's have a bite to eat while we can."

Lydia and Sarah hastily prepared a light meal of bread, fruit and cheese. Lydia could scarcely eat, though. The food left a tinny taste in her mouth. They'd barely finished when an urgent knock came at the front door, sending a shiver down Lydia's spine. Whitmer jumped from his chair and hurried to the door. "Who is it?" he demanded.

"It's Christian Kent," came the muffled reply.

Whitmer quickly unslid the bolt. "Come in, Christian."

Kent slipped through the door. He glanced at the two women, giving them a quick smile. "John, about a dozen men from town are gathered at the mercantile. They want to meet with you and the other leaders of the Church to present their terms."

Lydia saw the gravity in the young man's eyes. His lithe body was tense and she noticed his hands, brown and strong, clenched at his side. His shirt sleeves were rolled up to his elbows, and perspiration glistened on his forearms.

"I'll get my hat," Whitmer answered.

"Brother Kent, do you know what their terms are?" asked Sarah.

"No, Ma'am, but I don't imagine they're favorable." He looked from Sarah to Lydia. "Perhaps you ladies should stay indoors until John gets back."

"We will," Lydia assured him. Kent's eyes held hers for a second longer.

"Let's go, Christian," Whitmer said.

"Mr. Kent, please be careful!" Lydia cried out impulsively. She flushed as soon as the words were out of her mouth.

Christian turned and gave her a studied look. "I will. Thank you."

Sarah closed the door behind them and the two women stood together in silence. Finally, Sarah spoke, "Liddy, I want you to go upstairs and shutter all the windows. Then bring the children down and we'll wait in the parlor for John to return."

Lydia fastened each shutter on the second floor, then taking Elizabeth and James by the hand, she said, "Come on, children. We're goin' to fix you somethin' to eat."

"Mama," Elizabeth said gravely as she got to her feet, "somethin's wrong, isn't it?"

"The word is 'something,' 'Lizabeth. Remember your -ings like Mrs. Whitmer has been teachin' you. A young lady must learn to speak correctly if she's goin' to live in town."

"But, Mama, you forget your -ings and never get scolded for it."

"Well, now, that's because it's harder for older folks to mend their ways than young folks. You just pay attention to Mrs. Whitmer's teachin' — er, teaching, and you'll grow up to be a right proper young woman."

"Mama?"

"Yes, 'Lizabeth?"

"Please tell me what the matter is. I know you and Mrs. Whitmer are real worried about somethin'—I mean something."

Lydia started down the staircase with the children. "There could be some trouble, 'Lizabeth. There's men in town—bad men—who want to cause trouble for good folks like the Whitmers."

"Why, Mama?"

"Well, because they don't want people who are different from themselves livin' in town with 'em."

"How are the Whitmers different?"

"They believe in a religion different from most folks."

"Why don't they just change their religion so it's the same as everyone else's? Then there won't be any trouble."

Lydia stopped on the stairway and bent down eye level to her daughter. "'Lizabeth, you listen and always remember what I'm goin' to say to you. The Whitmers', your Mama, and a lot of other righteous people believe in the gospel of Jesus Christ. I've been searchin' my whole life for the true gospel, and I finally found it, here in Missouri. We're goin' to join the Church of Christ just as soon as we can because it's the true church set up by Jesus himself, through his Prophet. You don't change your religion when you know it is true. Don't you forget that as long as you live—you either, James," she concluded, turning to look seriously at her little son.

Elizabeth looked steadfastly at her mother. "No, Mama, I won't forget."

"I won't forget either, Mama," James added in a serious tone.

Lydia kissed both children's cheeks. "Good. Now come along."

The three of them walked down the remaining few steps. Lydia directed James to a chair and motioned for Elizabeth to sit beside him. Lydia saw that the downstairs windows were all tightly secured. A lamp burning on the parlor table cast a muted glow in the darkened room.

Sarah came into the parlor carrying a tray full of food. "How would you children like some warm biscuits and gooseberry jam?"

"Thank you, Mrs. Whitmer," Elizabeth answered, popping to her feet.

Sarah spread jam over a steaming biscuit for each of them. James put the entire roll into his mouth. "More," he mumbled through the sodden mass.

Lydia smiled at him. "Eat what you have first, son."

The hours ticked slowly by. Lydia tried to remain calm, but with each passing moment it became more difficult. For Sarah, it was the same; Lydia could plainly see the strain in her face. Every few minutes Sarah glanced at the bolted door or shuttered window, and wrung her hands at the slightest sound.

All at once the color drained from Sarah's face. "What is that? Do you hear it, Lydia?"

Lydia listened closely. At first, she couldn't hear anything, but then she recognized an ominous sound. She bolted from her chair and ran to the window, flinging open the shutter. Sarah was right behind her.

"Oh, merciful heavens!" Sarah gasped over Lydia's shoulder.

They stared in horror as a large crowd of angry men advanced up the street. Their cursings and cries filled the air with a hellish noise. Some of the men waved clubs or rifles over their heads, others shook their fists in rage.

When Elizabeth and James heard the frightening din from the street, they dashed to their mother's side. "Mama, what's happening?" shouted Elizabeth, wide-eyed.

The mob turned right at the end of the block, toward the center of town. In a few moments they had disappeared from sight, but their cries and oaths continued to be heard. Sarah clutched Lydia's hand. "Close the shutter, Lydia. Close the shutter!" she cried.

Lydia fumbled at the latch with numbed fingers.

All of them stood helplessly, listening to the harangue going on outside. Now the angry voices were punctuated with the sounds of breaking glass and splintering crashes. A chill clutched Lydia's heart when she heard the terrified scream of a woman.

The tumult outside continued for an interminable period of time. Slowly the mob's fiendish cries died down, although they did not cease altogether. Now and then a spine-chilling whoop assaulted their ears. They sat huddled together, praying and listening, with only their imaginations to tell them what was taking place.

Just when Lydia thought she could not bear another minute, John Whitmer rattled the door.

Sarah opened it and fell into his arms.

"Is everything all right here?" Whitmer's eyes swept the room, taking in the frightened faces of Lydia and her children.

Sarah nodded. In a voice that trembled she asked, "What evil has befallen the Saints?"

Whitmer ran a shaky hand across his forehead. His face was streaked with sweat and dust, and there was a rip in one sleeve of his shirt. "The mob has demolished the printing house, destroyed the press and type."

Lydia gasped. "What about Mr. Phelps and the others?"

"They're in hiding. The devils threw Sister Phelps and her children out into the street, and destroyed the family's personal belongings."

"Oh, no," Sarah whispered.

"Those men have lost all reason. They covered Bishop Partridge and Brother Allen with hot tar and feathers."

"Mercy!" cried Sarah.

"The mob's sworn to kill any Mormon who doesn't leave the county," Whitmer said grimly.

Lydia swallowed hard. A dull pain began deep inside her. She had the sickening sensation that this incident was only a shadow of things to come.

CHAPTER ELEVEN

Lydia opened her bedroom window a crack. The room was stifling. She fanned her face as she peered out into the street. All was quiet except for an occasional wagon rumbling by. The last two days had passed without serious incident, although the mob continued to roam the streets of Independence, insulting and threatening Mormon citizens. Lydia found the mob's actions appalling. The injustices perpetrated against the Saints only strengthened her resolve to be numbered among them. With the situation as it was, however, it would be impractical to go ahead with her baptism as planned. The ordinance would have to be postponed until a measure of peace was restored to the community. She hoped that would happen soon.

Lydia wiped away the perspiration trickling down the children's necks as they lie napping on the bed in the afternoon heat. She and the children had stayed indoors since the trouble began, hardly daring to draw a breath of fresh air in all that time. She decided to step outside and sit in the cool of the porch for a few minutes while the children slept.

The house downstairs was still. John Whitmer had gone out while Sarah rested in her room. Lydia slipped out the front door and eased into the porch rocker. The covered porch provided a modicum of shade; she leaned back and relaxed. Two men on horseback galloped past, startling her, but they went by without glancing in her direction. She settled deeper in the chair and closed her eyes. Her mind mulled over the events of the past few days. She wondered what Abraham would have thought of it. Abraham. He was at peace, finished with the perils and travail of life. In some ways she envied him.

Her eyes flew open at the sound of approaching footsteps. Mr. Johnson, the Whitmers' neighbor, hurried toward the house. His hat was pulled low over his eyes and he walked with a purposeful stride. He reached the Whitmers' white picket fence and opened the gate. Lydia stood up to meet him.

"Afternoon, Mr. Johnson."

"Oh, Mrs. Dawson, didn't see you there. Is Sister Whitmer at home?" Johnson's voice had an urgency to it.

"She is, but she's restin' at the moment. Can I help you?"

"It's my wife. She's about to give birth. I came to ask if Sister Whitmer could come up to the house and help us."

"Sarah hasn't been feeling well ever since the trouble in town, Mr. Johnson. I know a little somethin' about birthin' babies. I'll do what I can if you'd like."

"I'd be much obliged, Ma'am. The missus needs a woman to tend to her. I'm not much good at a time like this."

Lydia could plainly see that Johnson was anxious to get back to his wife. "You go along home, Mr. Johnson. I'll ask Sarah to watch my children and get a few things together. I'll be there right away."

"Maybe I ought to wait for you. It's not safe for a woman to be out on the street alone. You don't know what those jackals might take into their heads to do next."

"I'll be fine. You go on. Mrs. Johnson will be needin' you."

Johnson tipped his hat and started back down the steps of the porch. "Thank you, Mrs. Dawson. I surely appreciate it."

Lydia went inside and quickly mounted the stairs to her room. The children were still asleep. She walked across the hall to tell Sarah about Johnson's visit. Sarah suggested she take a pot of soup for the Johnson family.

Lydia gathered several items she would need and rolled them up in a clean towel. Then she put on her bonnet and left the house with the rolled towel in one hand and the pot of soup in the other.

The road was rutted and she had to pick her way carefully in order to keep her footing. The covered pot of soup sloshed to and fro with each step. The Johnson's log home lay several houses away and across an open field; Lydia made her way through the field and came out again onto the street. She quickened her pace and had almost reached the house when a man, who had apparently been lounging in the shadows of one of the buildings, stepped in front of her, blocking her path. He stood there boldly eyeing her.

"Excuse me," Lydia said.

"Well, now, what do we have here?" The man leaned his head so close to hers she could smell the tobacco on his breath.

She stepped to one side and attempted to pass, but he moved in front of her again. She shrank back, fear gripping her. The man was large and heavy-set, with a puffy face and bulging gray eyes. His hair hung lank and long around his head, and he was slovenly dressed in a pair of baggy trousers and soiled shirt.

"I seen you comin' across the field there and I said to myself, if that ain't the prettiest little woman." He grinned, showing yellow crooked teeth.

Something inside Lydia urged her to get away as fast as possible. "Please let me by," she said.

"Not so quick, honey. You and me, we ought to get better acquainted." He bent down and peered into her face. "Say now, you wouldn't be fraternizin' with them Mormonites, would ye? I sure don't know why a purty thing like yerself would want to 'sociate with the likes of them Mormon scum." The big man roughly took hold of her arm as an angry thought flashed across his face. "You one of them Mormonites, too?"

Lydia jerked her arm away. "Let go of me!"

The burly man laughed aloud. "Feisty as well as purty, are ye? I know a sure fire way to take the spunk out of a woman like yerself. Leaves 'em purrin' like a pussycat every time." The man clutched her arm harder this time, knocking the pot from her grasp. Its contents spilled onto the road, forming a muddy puddle at her feet.

Lydia looked around frantically for someone to help her, but the street was deserted. The man jerked her to his side, leering at her out of wide, eager eyes.

She started to scream, but he clamped a hand over her

mouth before she could utter a sound. She felt herself being dragged around the corner of the building. Panic surged through her.

"Take your hands off her, Barnes. Now!" The voice came suddenly from behind her. Startled, the man addressed as Barnes released her. She sagged and would have fallen except for the strong hand which reached out to support her. She turned around to find that the hand and the voice belonged to Christian Kent.

"This ain't none of your affair, Kent," growled Lydia's burly attacker.

"I ought to have you hamstrung and dragged through the streets for this," Kent said, his voice full of fury.

"You wanna try?" Barnes took a menacing step forward.

Christian thrust Lydia behind him and crouched into an aggressive stance, fists clenched.

Barnes hesitated, taken back by Christian's savage posture.

"Come on, there's nothing I'd like better than to give you a good thrashing," Christian said, his eyes glaring.

Barnes blinked, then backed off, but not without first venting his hatred. "I'm gonna take care of you, Kent. You can count on it. Next time that little lady sees you it will be with a knife stuck in your gut." He glared at both Christian and Lydia, and then disappeared around the street corner.

Lydia stifled a cry with her hand. Christian turned to look at her, and some of the fierceness went out of his eyes. "Are you hurt?" he asked, coming to her side.

She shook her head, unable to speak.

"Let me take this for you," he said, gently loosening her grip on the rolled towel she held clutched to her side.

She let go of the parcel, struggling to control the trembling that had taken root inside her.

"You're sure you're all right?" Christian repeated.

"Yes, I think so."

"What's John thinking of, letting you out here alone with things the way they are?" Christian's voice held a trace of anger.

"He didn't know. He wasn't home when I left."

"Where were you going?"

"To Mr. Johnson's. His wife is having a baby. I promised to

help." Lydia's voice shook as she spoke.

"Mrs. Johnson will just have to get along without you. I'm taking you home."

"No, you can't. I have to help her; I told them I'd come."

Christian looked at her doubtfully. "You're sure you're up to it?"

Lydia nodded.

"All right. I'll walk you there, but you have to promise me you won't come home alone. You let Johnson see you back."

"I will."

Christian walked over to the fallen pot, picked it up and looked inside. A small quantity of muddy liquid was all that remained. "Is this yours, too?"

"Yes."

He handed the empty pot to her. "I don't imagine Mrs. Johnson feels like eating at the moment anyway," he said with a smile.

Lydia returned his smile half-heartedly. Christian offered his arm and the two walked the remaining distance to the Johnson home. He opened the gate for Lydia to pass through.

By this time Lydia had calmed down enough to gather her wits. "Thank you, Mr. Kent. This isn't the first time you've come to my assistance."

"I guess I'm just fortunate when it comes to damsels in distress."

"Whatever the reason, Mr. Kent, I'm grateful for it."

"Take care," he said, putting a hand lightly on her shoulder.

She nodded and then turned and hurried to the Johnson's door.

The following day more trouble erupted. To her dismay, Lydia learned that the mob had forced Church leaders to accept a one-sided compromise. The leading elders of the Church, along with their families, were to leave Jackson County by the first of January, and the remaining Saints must go by the following April at the latest. Gilbert & Whitney's Mercantile would be allowed to sell out their goods, but the printing office was not to be reopened nor was its newspaper, the *Evening and the Morning Star*, to be published again in the county. If these terms were complied with by the Saints, the leaders of the mob promised to use their influence to prevent further violence.

The fact which disturbed Lydia the most was that these outrages were perpetrated in large measure by county officials: the county clerk, the constable, the judge of the county court and the justice of the peace were all involved. With that being the case, seeking legal redress in Jackson County seemed futile. In spite of that, the Saints felt compelled to try. They planned to appeal to state authorities as well, including the governor, Daniel Dunklin. Bishop Partridge dispatched Oliver Cowdery to Ohio to confer with Church leaders there concerning the situation in Zion.

In the weeks that followed, the mob failed to keep their end of the agreement. Lydia repeatedly heard of incidents where Saints were insulted or subjected to humiliation and mistreatment, homes were broken into and fields and haystacks set afire. The brethren began organizing watches to protect their families and their property. John Whitmer took his turn along with the other brethren, sometimes being called upon to stand guard several nights in a row. The men stationed themselves throughout the town, wherever trouble threatened. None had occurred in the immediate vicinity of the Whitmer home, but John was taking no chances. He'd asked Christian Kent for assistance and the two of them had been alternating night watches near Whitmers' home the last few evenings.

As Lydia drew aside her patterned chintz curtains, she could see Christian's shadow near the corner of the house in the brightness of the full moon. He was slowly circling the building and as she watched he came into full view. She saw him pause and lean against the house. He held his rifle close to his side. He stood there motionless for several minutes. His face was in the shadows, but she could clearly see his tall, lean frame. His fingers drummed rhythmically on the barrel of his long rifle.

She closed the curtains and lay back on her bed. It was late, but she was far from sleepy. She thought about the young man outside her window. Each time she'd had the opportunity to talk with him, she'd been impressed by his sensitivity, his kindness, and his sense of humor. He seemed to possess a great deal of learning, but he was not pretentious about it. On the contrary, he was gracious and affable. And he was easy to talk to. In fact, she enjoyed conversing with him as much as anyone she'd met since coming to Independence. He was also very handsome. She immediately censured herself for that last thought. It was improper, and disloyal to Abraham.

She turned onto her side, her body and mind restless. She yearned for someone to talk with, a companion with whom to share her thoughts and concerns, someone she could confide in, as she had in Abraham the first years of their marriage. How she missed Gerta and their long talks together. She'd made few close friends in Independence and had no family around her. Only this evening she'd received an unsettling letter from her father, urging her to come home and disassociate herself from the "Mormon infidels."

She sighed and gave up trying to sleep. Rising from the bed, she smoothed her hair and straightened her gray-striped dress. She lifted the corner of the curtain again and looked out. Christian was still standing in the same spot. She tiptoed out of the room so as not to awaken her sleeping children, and went down the stairs. A single lamp burned in the parlor. She went to the pantry where she opened a cupboard. On the lower shelf rested a plate of biscuits left over from dinner. Lydia took three of them and then cut three thick slices of cheese. She wrapped them in a cloth and slipped out the back door.

As she rounded the corner of the house, she saw that Christian had disappeared. She turned to look for him and as she did he stepped from the shadows, his gun leveled at her.

"It's only me," she whispered, "Lydia Dawson."

He lowered his gun and strode toward her. "You'd make an excellent intruder. I barely heard you coming."

"I'm sorry. I didn't want to awaken anyone in the house."

He smiled and his tenseness seemed to ease.

"I thought you might be hungry. I brought you some cheese and biscuits." She held the folded cloth out to him.

"Thank you. I appreciate that." As he took the napkin from her hand, their fingers brushed. She drew back instinctively. Christian didn't seem to notice; he put a slice of cheese onto a biscuit and bit into it. "Mmmm," he said approvingly.

Feeling suddenly embarrassed standing next to him in the dim light, Lydia gathered her skirts and prepared to go back inside.

"Do you have to leave?" Christian asked. "I hate eating alone."

Lydia looked up into his face. He was smiling at her. She could see his even white teeth in the pale light of the moon. "Not for a few minutes, I guess," she stammered.

"Good. I'm glad." He took another bite, and made a quick sweep around the yard with his eyes. "It's been pretty quiet."

Lydia's glance followed the same course as Christian's.

"John tells me you're planning to move on with his family."

"For the time being. I'm not sure what I'll do eventually. I have the children to think of."

"They seem like fine youngsters. "It's James and uh . . ."

Lydia supplied the name, "Elizabeth Ann."

Christian nodded. "She's a pretty little girl."

"Thank you. She's a handful."

"Most girls are," Christian laughed. He put the rest of the biscuit and cheese into his mouth and folded the cloth around the remaining one. "I'll save this for later," he said, slipping it into his pocket. He glanced around the yard again. Lydia watched the shadows play on the angles and planes of his strong face. He had an expressive mouth, straight nose, and firm square jaw. There was a whisper of a cleft in the center of his chin. He wore his hair straight back off his forehead without a part, cropped short at the ears and longer at the back where it brushed his collar.

"How about you?" she asked, drawing a halting breath. "Will you be moving out of Independence soon, too?"

Christian frowned and Lydia saw a hardness come into his eyes. "Not until we've settled a few matters. The mob destroyed the press and all our books and papers. Some sort of reimbursement is due for that."

Lydia said nothing. Although she felt bad about what had happened at the printing house, she doubted Christian or any of the others would see a penny's worth of recompense.

"It's the papers I feel the worst about," Christian said almost to himself.

"Your business papers, you mean?"

"No." He paused and regarded her solemnly. "You're not a

member of the Church, are you?"

Lydia shook her head.

"We were in the midst of printing some important doc-trines for the Church which we believe came from God. They were entrusted to our care and we weren't as diligent as we should have been in completing the project. Now I'm worried that the publishing will be greatly delayed." He looked at her quickly. "You probably think that sounds foolish."

"No, I don't. If you believe those revelations are from God, then I admire your integrity in publishing them."

Christian looked at her in surprise. "Most non-Mormons wouldn't agree with you."

"I'm not altogether unfamiliar with your doctrine, Mr. Kent. If those papers were anything like your Book of Mormon, I can understand why you're upset."

"You've read the Book of Mormon?"

"Twice. Mr. Whitmer loaned me his copy."

"Yet you haven't joined the Church."

"That's only because I haven't had the opportunity. My baptism was supposed to have taken place last Saturday."

Christian stared intently at her. "I didn't realize that."

"Well, I only recently made up my mind."

"That's wonderful, Mrs. Dawson. I'm very happy for you."

"I still have every intention of joining the Church, Mr. Kent, but has it always been so difficult to be a member?"

Christian chuckled softly. "Not as difficult as it may yet become."

"Oh, dear."

"I say that partly in jest, Mrs. Dawson, but let me tell you something. The Church of Jesus Christ is the true church, divinely restored. I believe that firmly. As such it's bound to be persecuted by its enemies, just as Christ himself was perse-cuted. But it will never be destroyed. It will roll forth until it fills the whole earth."

Lydia watched Christian Kent closely as he spoke, his dark eyes luminous in the pale light. His words conveyed a power she'd felt only a few times before. They evoked the same feel-ings she'd experienced when she listened to Parley Pratt preach in the old barn in Green County.

"If you've decided to join the Church, what are you waiting for?" Christian asked.

"It's impossible now, with the mob all around us," Lydia answered, taken back by his forthrightness.

"Difficult, but not impossible."

"What do you mean?"

"It wouldn't be safe to perform your baptism in broad daylight, it's true, but what about late at night? Or better yet, just before sunrise?"

"Well, I don't know. I'd have to ask Mr. Whitmer," Lydia answered hesitantly.

"Do that. I'll bet he agrees. If you're going to be baptized, Mrs. Dawson, you want to do it while you're still in the land of promise."

He grinned at her again, with almost boyish enthusiasm. He *was* handsome, she decided, whether it was a proper thought or not.

Lydia was baptized at dawn two days later in the waters of the Big Blue. John Whitmer performed the baptism and Bishop Edward Partridge the confirmation. Christian stood guard throughout the proceedings near a grove of trees a few feet from the shore.

Only a small group of friends attended the ceremony, among them Sarah Whitmer, Mrs. Johnson and Catherine Page. When Lydia came up out of the water, they crowded around her, offering their congratulations with tears of joy in their eyes. Wrapped in a warm blanket, Lydia hugged each one of the women and shook hands with Whitmer and Bishop Partridge.

From the shadow of the trees, Christian caught her eye. He smiled broadly and nodded his head in warm approval. A tingling started at the tip of Lydia's toes and climbed up her spine. She wasn't sure if the sensation was due to excitement over her new status as a member of the Church, or because of the way Christian Kent had looked at her. It didn't matter, though. The joy and happiness she felt washed over her as completely as the river had covered her, and she reveled in the feeling.

". . . A terrible time it was."

John Riggs
Early Missouri Saint

CHAPTER TWELVE

C hristian's cabin was littered with newspapers, affidavits, and other documents, including copies of the Missouri state statutes. The brethren had determined to appeal to the governor for redress of the Saints' grievances. A petition setting forth their sufferings and a denial of the allegations made by the mob was being prepared by the Church leaders in Independence, and Christian was assisting in the research and drafting of the document. The Saints hoped the governor would order troops into the county to protect their rights and prevent the mob from further attacks upon their families and properties.

There were those among the brethren, however, who wished to take matters into their own hands. They felt they possessed the right to protect themselves, by arms if necessary, from the mob. Seth Whitfield had expressed the opinion that legal maneuverings would be too lengthy and ponderous to afford the Saints any assistance until it was too late, and that the Saints were justified in defending themselves when called upon to do so.

Christian tended to agree with him, but he felt they should exercise caution until Oliver returned from Kirtland to report what the Prophet Joseph and the brethren recommended. However, he could understand Seth and the others' feelings for they had families to consider. Seth was anxious about the safety of his wife. Carrie hadn't been well throughout her pregnancy, and naturally he wanted to protect her.

Christian picked up an affidavit one of the Saints had written and read it over. The brother's house had been unroofed by the mob and some of his household goods destroyed. He'd listed the cost of each item and underlined in bold slashes the total losses. Christian penned the numbers next to several more like it on a long sheet of paper. He was figuring the totals when a hasty knock sounded at his door.

"Christian, it's John Corrill. Open the door."

Christian thrust the numbers aside and quickly unbolted the cabin door. Corrill lunged inside, breathless.

"There's trouble down at the ferry. A mob is threatening to take some of the brethren into the river and throw them overboard. Can you come?"

"Let me get my rifle," Christian answered. He hurried to the fireside and picked up his gun, quickly checking it for powder and ball. "I'm out of shot, John. Just a minute."

"While you're getting it, I'll go ahead and meet you down by the Blue."

Christian nodded. Corrill left the cabin and disappeared into the night. Christian located his ammunition, loaded his gun, and dashed out. Though the moon was three-quarters full, the sky was overcast, making it difficult to see. Christian nearly tripped over a root in his path. He made his way toward the river, keeping in the shadows, and had the water almost in sight when he felt a heavy hand clamp down on his shoulder. As he spun around, someone kicked the rifle out of his hands.

"Where you going in such a hurry, Kent?" The man's voice was low and menacing. Christian recognized it immediately.

"Stay out of my way, Chiles."

"You talk real big for a man who's just been relieved of his gun."

From behind Chiles another figure emerged. At first Christian couldn't make out who it was in the dim light. But as the man advanced, the moon played on his face and Christian recognized Jacob Barnes. Christian's heart began pumping madly as he sensed the danger facing him.

"I believe we got some unfinished business," Barnes said, his eyes hard as stone. He came closer, picked up Christian's rifle, and leveled it at Christian's chest.

Christian glared back at him in defiance.

"It don't appear you got that purty little woman to distract you this time. That's kind of a shame, ain't it, Kent? Such a temptin' little morsel." Barnes licked his lips.

Christian took a step forward, his fists clenched at his side.

"Whoa there, boy. You wouldn't want this here piece to go off prematurely, now, would ye?" Barnes poked the barrel of the gun hard into Christian's ribs. "Now, what was we talkin' about? Oh, yeah. I was about to say how sad that little gal will be when she hears how you met with such an untimely demise. 'Course, I'll do my best to comfort her."

Chiles began to snicker. He was standing a foot or two away from Barnes, and watching Christian like a cat. Barnes rammed the rifle harder against Christian's chest, knocking him off balance. Christian lunged to one side in an attempt to escape Barnes, but Chiles blocked his path of retreat. Barnes cocked the rifle.

"Hold on, Barnes," Henry Chiles said, coming to his side. "He's just one of them. Don't forget we have a larger purpose in mind down at the Blue. If you shoot that thing, it will bring the whole town down on us."

"It's already too late." Christian spat out the words. "These woods are swarming with friends of mine. You'd be caught before you ran twenty feet."

"Shut-up, Kent!" Barnes commanded. As he spoke he struck Christian a glancing blow on the cheek with the butt of the rifle. Christian's knees nearly buckled underneath him.

"You're right, Chiles. We don't want any company jest yet." Barnes held the rifle out for Chiles to take, and then whipped something out of his pocket. The light from the moon caught the deadly gleam of a steel blade.

Christian crouched into position to defend himself. Barnes came at him, slashing the air with his knife. Christian jumped back, struggling to avoid the blade of the plunging weapon. As Barnes lunged toward his middle, the knife missed Christian by a fraction of an inch. Christian's head was pounding from the blow to his face, and his vision blurred in and out of focus. He harnessed all of his concentration at the man coming repeatedly at him with the knife. Chiles had stepped back a few paces from the struggle, but Christian didn't dare risk taking his eyes off his attacker, even knowing Chiles could easily circle behind to entrap him.

Barnes leaped toward him again, the knife flashing in the moonlight. But this time Christian grabbed his wrist, struggling and grappling with him for possession of the weapon. Barnes' heavy body fell against him, knocking them both to the ground. They rolled in the dirt—thistles and jagged brush tearing at their clothing. Barnes gained the advantage. He pinned Christian between his knees and pressed the point of the knife under Christian's chin. His bulging eyes grew wider as he forced the knife to Christian's throat.

"Christian? Is that you? Where are you?" Corrill's shout came from a few yards away.

The sound broke Barnes' concentration long enough for Christian to wrench free of the bigger man's hold. But he was not quick enough. As he scrambled to his knees, he felt a searing pain rip through his left shoulder. He fell back, and the night disappeared into oblivion.

When Christian opened his eyes, the light streaming from the window sent a thousand tiny daggers of bright pain dancing in his head. He wanted to shield his eyes with his left hand, but he couldn't raise his arm. He murmured and attempted to move. Immediately, a gentle hand restrained him. He turned his head struggling to see who was with him, but the image swam before his eyes. As he blinked, the figure steadied. A woman watched him in grave silence. The woman's features began to blur. He blinked once more, and when he looked again he could see golden hair tied up with a wide pink ribbon and the grass green color of her eyes. He called out her name and then sank helplessly into unconsciousness.

When Christian next awoke, it was dark and cool. The pain in his head was still with him, but less persistent. He tried to make sense out of his surroundings. In the dim light, he saw the outline of a table with a basin and pitcher, and curtains rustling in the night breeze. He started to roll onto his side when an excruciating pain seized his shoulder. Involuntarily, he cried out.

Instantly the door opened and a woman appeared, carrying a lighted lamp. As she lifted it toward her face, Christian recognized Lydia Dawson. She came to his bed and set the lamp on the table beside him.

"You're awake," she said softly.

"I'm not sure I'm glad of that," he answered, his head groggy. His voice sounded peculiar in his ears, as if it were detached and distant from his body. "Where am I?"

"You're in John Whitmer's home. Brother Corrill found you and brought you here."

The pain in Christian's shoulder was growing more intense; he struggled against it.

"Don't try to move," Lydia said, touching his arm. "The doctor said you must lie still until your shoulder has had time to mend."

Christian tried to recall what was wrong with his shoulder, but he couldn't concentrate on anything past the pain.

"Is it hurting terribly?" Lydia asked. Her voice reflected empathy and concern.

He breathed deeply, trying to control the pain racking his shoulder.

Lydia stepped to the table and dipped a cloth in the basin resting there and wrung out the excess water. She came back to the bedside and laid the cloth across his forehead. It felt cool and damp—soothing to his tense body.

"Are you thirsty?" she asked. He nodded weakly.

She poured him a drink of water from the pitcher and held it to his lips. He tipped his head and drank a bit of it.

"Thank you," he murmured.

She stood watching him for several minutes. He tried to smile his gratitude, but sleep relentlessly pursued him. He closed his eyes and let it carry him away.

When he awoke, Lydia was gone and Sarah Whitmer sat in a chair near his bedside, busy with a needle and thread.

"How long have I been here?" asked Christian hoarsely.

"Mercy, Brother Kent, you startled me!" Sarah cried. She put aside her sewing and leaned forward in her chair. "You've been a very sick man. The doctor says you're lucky to be alive."

Christian licked his parched lips and closed his eyes against the continuous pain in his left side.

"It's been two days. We thought you were dead, what with your shoulder streaming blood and you white as a ghost. You've been unconscious almost the whole time."

Christian slowly raised his good arm and gingerly felt his left side. His upper arm and shoulder were swathed in bandages.

"Would you like something to eat?"

Christian shook his head. "I'm not hungry."

"You need to eat, Brother Kent, to build up your strength."

"Maybe later."

Sarah stood up and gathered her sewing materials. "I'll leave you to rest then. Lydia or I will check on you in an hour or so. You're sure I can't get you anything?"

"No, thank you."

Sarah left the room and closed the door behind her. Christian groaned and gritted his teeth in pain. He twisted his head down to look at his injury and was shocked to see a splotch of scarlet staining the bandages. He sucked in his breath and lay back on his pillow. Barnes. Barnes must have got him with his knife. The whole incident was fuzzy in his memory.

At the sound of the door squeaking slowly open, Christian looked up. As he watched, a small head poked itself inside. A boy with tousled curly hair and large brown eyes peeked in at him. The child's expression was grave, but curious. He regarded Christian solemnly from his place behind the door.

Christian managed a smile. "Hello."

The boy stood completely still.

"You can come in if you want to."

The little fellow looked over his shoulder, then opened the door a crack wider and let himself through. He stood beside the door, like a soldier at attention.

"I'll bet you're James. Right?" The boy nodded. "Well, James, have you ever seen a grown man in such a fix as this?"

James shook his head. His big eyes took in every inch of Christian's bandages.

"Me, either," said Christian glumly.

James took a step closer to the bed. He raised a pudgy finger and pointed at Christian's shoulder. "Ouch," he said soberly.

"Yes, indeed. Ouch."

James' brown eyes instantly registered sympathy. Just at that moment the door opened again and James jumped aside. His mother stood in the doorway, her hands on her hips.

"James Dawson, what are you doin' in here? I told you not to bother Mr. Kent."

"I sorry, Mama."

"Out you go, young man." Lydia gave him a spat on the seat of his britches as he ran past her and out the door. "I'm sorry, Mr. Kent. I hope he didn't awaken you."

"No, I wasn't sleeping."

"How are you feeling? Any better?"

"I think so." Christian grimaced as he tried to find a more comfortable position.

"I think you look a little better. You've had several callers inquiring after you."

"I have? Who?"

"Brother Corrill has been very concerned about you. Brother Gilbert came by, and the Bishop, and Brother Whitfield has been here several times, too. Brother Whitfield mentioned he would try to contact your family."

Christian raised his eyebrows. "What for?"

"He thought they should know you'd been injured."

"Tell him not to bother. I'll be fine."

Lydia said nothing in reply. She walked over to the window and adjusted the curtain to allow more light into the room. "It's been cloudy the last couple of days, and cooler," she commented.

Christian glanced toward the window.

"Brother Whitfield mentioned that you have a brother living back East." Where she stood at the window, the sun caught her hair, heightening its deep copper color. She had it pulled up as usual, but much of the back had loosened and fallen, curling softly down her shoulders. He must have been staring at her, for she suddenly reddened and began fussing with the curtains again.

"I'm sorry, what did you ask?" he said.

"Your brother. Do you have other brothers or sisters back East?"

"No, just Jarrett and myself, that's all."

"Oh. I thought you might have a sister."

"No. Why?"

Lydia glanced at him with an uncomfortable expression, as if she regretted bringing up the subject at all. She cleared her throat and said, "That first day when you were so ill, you kept calling out someone's name."

"I did? Whose?"

"Mary Ann."

Christian swallowed and looked away. He didn't know what to say. He felt foolish that his feelings for Mary Ann should surface in such a manner.

He sensed, rather than saw, Lydia move away from the window and toward the door.

"I'll make sure James doesn't disturb you again."

Christian felt stronger the following day. Mrs. Whitmer brought him some soup and helped him eat it, and John Whitmer sat for about an hour with him. The doctor from Independence came in the early afternoon and changed the bandages. He was a thin-faced man with a gray mustache and graying hair. Even his eyes were gray. He reminded Christian of a pet mouse he'd kept as a boy. He told Christian that the knife had cut deeply into the muscle and that he had lost a great deal of blood, but with time, he should heal and regain the full use of his shoulder. The doctor also brought some powder, which he mixed with water from the bedside pitcher, and told Christian to take a spoonful whenever the pain became severe. Christian was grateful for the concoction and swallowed a mouthful as soon as the doctor left. It soon took the edge off his pain.

Later in the day, John Corrill stopped in to see him. Mrs. Whitmer showed him to Christian's room and shut the door so they could talk privately.

"What the devil happened?" Corrill asked when they were alone.

"Barnes and Chiles jumped me when I was almost to the river."

"I shouldn't have left you to come alone," Corrill replied, his brows drawn together in a deep frown.

"It wasn't your fault. I should have been on my guard in those woods. It was stupid of me."

"They pulled a knife on you?"

"Barnes did. You must have stumbled across me right after that."

"I didn't stumble on you. I heard voices and came to investigate. When I arrived on the scene, I saw two men high-tailing it into the woods, and you sprawled on the ground. Those men will be brought to justice, I promise you, Christian."

"I doubt you'll ever get a confession from them, John. It would be my word against theirs and you know what the outcome would be in the courts here. Especially now."

Corrill's frown deepened.

"What happened at the ferry? Were the brethren able to prevent an incident?" asked Christian.

"Yes, there weren't as many of the rabble as we'd been led to believe. When we caught up with them, they scattered like so many jack rabbits."

"That's good. Are we still going ahead with the petition to Governor Dunklin?"

Corrill nodded. "Sidney has written the final draft."

"Good. I've had a hard time reconciling myself to the idea of giving up my land and being driven out like a dog with its tail between its legs."

"You still feel that way after what's happened to you?"

"Of course I do. If I'd taken proper precautions, I wouldn't be lying here now. You can be assured I'll be more careful in the future. There's correspondence and figures in my cabin, John. Take them and use what you can."

"I'll stop by and pick them up. In the meantime, you get plenty of rest so that shoulder can heal. Don't worry about anything else."

"Right now there's nothing else I can do."

"Sister Whitmer cautioned me against staying too long," Corrill said with a twinkle springing into his eye. "What a lucky fellow you are to have not only one but two pretty nurses taking care of you. They have been hovering outside your door like a pair of anxious honeybees."

"They've taken good care of me, but I feel foolish lying here like a helpless child."

"Don't let them know that. They'd be mighty disappointed. Take care, boy. I'll stop by again in a day or two."

"Thanks, John, for everything." Christian took hold of the older man's arm and squeezed it.

Corrill let himself out. Christian leaned back on his pillow and closed his eyes, exhausted from the day's company. Threads from his conversation with Corrill floated through his mind. It gave him satisfaction to know the petition to the governor was going ahead without delay. But something else Corrill had said made him feel vaguely uneasy. He had to muster all his concentration to recall what it was—oh yes, Corrill's remark about the women taking care of him. Something about them hovering over him. He frowned as he recalled that Lydia Dawson had been conspicuously absent during the course of the day. He guessed the reason; they'd both been embarrassed by her questions about Mary Ann. He grimaced as he recalled their conversation the day before.

His thoughts lingered on Lydia. The woman was certainly an enigma. Although they'd had several conversations together, he really knew very little about her. He wondered what sort of fellow her husband had been, and about her life before she came to Independence. Although he didn't usually find women of Lydia's coloring attractive, yesterday when she'd stood against the window with the sun on her hair, he'd been stunned by her beauty. The whiteness of her skin and the vivid blue of her eyes created a fascinating contrast. He'd become aware of a certain quality about her, almost a vulnerability, though that, too, was a contradiction for he knew she possessed great courage and strength. Without those qualities, she never would have made the move to Independence. So long as he had to be confined at the Whitmers' while he convalesced, he resolved to get to know Lydia Dawson better.

His first opportunity came the next morning. Lydia brought in his breakfast tray and set it down on the table beside him.

"How are you this morning?" she asked lightly.

"Feeling much better."

"I'm glad to hear that. Can you manage your breakfast by

yourself?"

Christian glanced at the egg and biscuit on his tray. "I think so." He attempted to scoot himself up into a sitting position, but as he did so a sharp pain shot through his shoulder. His face registered the effect.

"Here, let me help you," Lydia said quickly. She propped up his pillow and held it in place while he eased back against it.

"Thanks."

Lydia smiled and placed his tray on his lap. "I'll stop back for your tray when you've finished."

"I'm beginning to go a little berserk staring at these four walls. Would you have time to stay?" He could see her hesitate. "Please. I'd enjoy the company."

She pulled back the chair from his bedside and sat down.

He smiled at her and picked up his fork with his good hand. "The doctor said I should be able to get up and around in a couple of days."

"That's good news."

"Yes." He took a bite of egg and broke his biscuit in half. Lydia sat silently watching him. He began to feel uncomfortable, for he could think of nothing to say to her. "Have you had your breakfast?" he asked awkwardly.

She nodded.

That was a stupid question, he berated himself. Why was it so difficult to talk to her all of a sudden?

"I guess you'll be going back to your place when you're on your feet," Lydia said.

He smiled, grateful she'd initiated some conversation. "Yes, it's just a rough cabin, but it's home."

"I know all about rough cabins. I lived in one myself."

Now here was a topic he could explore. "When you were living in Illinois?"

She nodded her head.

"What part of Illinois are you from, Mrs. Dawson?"

"Green County. We lived out in the back country."

"Farming?"

"Yes, my husband and I owned a small farm. I sold it just before I came out here."

"That was after your husband passed away."

"That's right."

Christian detected a slight quivering of her lips.

"Had your husband been ill? I don't mean to pry. If you'd rather not talk about it, I understand."

"No one has really asked me much about Abraham. Sometimes talking about a person you've lost helps to ease the pain. Abraham went to Galena to work the lead mines. He wanted to earn some extra money for fall plantin', but he was killed there in a mine accident."

"I'm sorry." He paused, watching her face. "You had family who gave you support?"

"My parents came out and stayed with us for awhile, and my brother helped with the farm. Philip—he's the one who lives in Quincy. I have another brother, John, who also has a farm in Quincy. I stayed with Philip and his family for a few days before makin' the move to Independence."

"You must have had some acquaintance with the Church to make you decide to come west," Christian commented.

A soft glow came into Lydia's eyes. "Yes, I did. Mr. Pratt was preachin' in Green County. He's the one who first told me about the Mormons. My husband wasn't interested, though." Lydia's gaze dropped.

"But your friends, the Johanssens, were."

"That's right. They joined the Church right off."

"I apologize for not making those inquiries I promised you."

Lydia smiled. "Well, you've been a bit occupied."

"I guess I have," Christian said, returning her smile.

"What will you do now that the printing office is closed?"

"I've been trying to make myself useful in securing our rights—until this happened," he answered, gesturing at his shoulder.

"Mr. Whitmer told us a little bit about the attack. Did you get a look at the man's face?"

"No," Christian lied. It would do no good to tell her about Barnes, he decided. It would only upset her. "I'm glad the brethren prevented a more general raid on the Saints along the Blue, anyway."

"What do you think is going to happen to the Saints, Mr. Kent?"

"I don't know. I hope Brother Joseph has the answer to that."

"The Prophet." She spoke the word almost with a reverence. "Have you ever met him?"

"Several times."

"What is he like?"

Christian paused for a moment, arranging his thoughts into words. "He's tall and strongly built, with light hair and blue eyes. He's a very gracious man, but at the same time straightforward and plain-spoken. There's something remarkable about Brother Joseph. I realized that the first time I met him. It's not so apparent in his outward appearance, but one senses it deep within his character. The man is a Prophet of God."

Lydia's eyes shone. "I hope I get to meet him some day," she whispered.

"You will. You're numbered among the Saints now, too, remember?"

"How could I forget?" she smiled. "On the morning of my baptism I thought surely the mob would come dashing through the trees, firing their guns at us while I was still in the water."

"You must not think much of my ability as a guard," Christian said, giving her a mischievous grin.

She laughed and the sound of it was like a flowing brook, pleasant and soothing to his ears.

"Look at that plate. You haven't eaten hardly a thing, Mr. Kent. I'm afraid I've kept you from your breakfast."

"If you have, it's been a pleasant diversion. I'm not really very hungry, though, Mrs. Dawson." He handed her the tray and leaned back on his pillow.

She stood up, carrying the tray, and prepared to leave his room. "Can I get you anything else?"

"No, I'm fine. Thank you for staying."

"I enjoyed our conversation," she replied.

"So did I."

He watched as she left the room. When she'd gone, he suddenly felt as if she'd taken the sun with her.

CHAPTER THIRTEEN

Christian awoke with a start. He looked up to find two pair of eyes staring at him, one pair blue and the other brown.

"There!" James said with a triumphant voice, pointing a short stubby finger at Christian. "There's his bad hurt."

"I can see it, James," his sister replied in a condescending tone.

Christian smiled to himself. "Good morning, James. Who have you brought with you?"

"I'm Elizabeth Ann Dawson. I live here." Elizabeth answered before her brother had a chance to say a word.

"How do you do, Miss Dawson? My name is Christian Kent."

"I know. Mama told me. She said you had a bad accident."

"That's right."

"What happened to you?" Elizabeth asked bluntly.

"Well, I got hurt with a knife."

"You shouldn't play with knives. Mama scolds us if we do."

"She's right about that," Christian answered, struggling to keep a stern face.

James took a step closer, scrutinizing Christian's bandaged wound.

"Does it hurt?" Elizabeth asked.

"Yes, it does, but it's getting better."

"James said it was all bloody." Elizabeth glanced quickly at his shoulder as if to verify the boy's account.

"It was, but the doctor came and took good care of it. How old are you, Elizabeth Ann Dawson?"

"Six, I'll soon be seven. James is only four."

"Four is pretty big," Christian answered, giving James a smile. The boy beamed in return.

"Six is bigger," Elizabeth replied stoutly.

"That's true," Christian said, nodding his head. He sat up in his bed and reached over to the bedside table for his pain killer, poured a little of the powder into a glass of water, and took a swallow.

"What's that?" asked James, wrinkling up his nose.

"It's medicine, silly," Elizabeth answered him.

"Yuck!"

Christian laughed. "It sounds like you've had a taste or two of medicine yourself."

James nodded his head fervently.

"James was real sick before we came here," Elizabeth informed Christian. "Mama cried all the time and I had to go and stay with my grandma."

"Is that a fact?"

"Yes, but he got better like Mama said you would."

"I'm glad of that."

Elizabeth gazed solemnly at Christian's bandages again, saying nothing for several seconds. Then she looked up at him and said, "My pa got hurt, too. He's dead now."

"Your mother told me. I'm very sorry. You must miss him."

She nodded and some of the brightness went out of her eyes.

"Are you happy living here with your mother?" Christian asked in an attempt to divert her troubled thoughts.

"Sometimes. Mrs. Whitmer is nice. She bought me a new blue dress and a blue ribbon for my hair."

"Me got new shoes!" James interjected, lifting up one foot for Christian to see.

"You're lucky children to have nice new clothes," Christian agreed.

"Sometimes we're not so lucky," Elizabeth informed him. "Mrs. Whitmer makes us learn letters and sums."

"You need to learn those things. Then you'll grow up to be wise."

"We have to talk correct in front of Mrs. Whitmer, too."

"You mean you have to say 'please' and 'thank you,' that sort of thing."

"Oh, Mama's always made us say those words. Mrs. Whitmer wants us to remember our -*ings*."

"Your -*ings*?"

"Yes, you know. Walk*ing*, stopp*ing*, wait*ing*. Mama tries to remember her -*ings*, too, but most of the time she forgets."

Christian chuckled. "I think you're doing very well. I've noticed every -*ing* you've said."

Elizabeth smiled broadly. "I hardly ever forget anymore. James is learning too, aren't you, James?" she said, nudging her brother in the shoulder.

"Uh huh."

"Do you like to read, Elizabeth?" Christian asked her.

She pulled a face which clearly conveyed that reading was not one of her favorite activities.

"If you'll study your letters diligently, I'll lend you some of my best books to read."

Elizabeth's blue eyes widened. "Really?"

"Really. You must study hard, though."

"I will. I promise."

James teetered on one foot and then the other restlessly. "Come on, 'Lizabeth," he said finally, tugging at his sister's arm.

Elizabeth cast a last curious look at Christian's shoulder and then took James by the hand. "We'd better go. Good-bye, Mr. Kent. We'll visit you tomorrow."

"I'll look forward to it," Christian grinned.

The two visitors made their way to the door and furtively slipped through. Christian lay back on his pillow and chuckled to himself. Lydia's children were charming and resourceful. He wondered if Lydia knew they'd been in to see him. He doubted it.

As he ran a hand across his chin, stiff bristly whiskers raked his fingers. He must look fearsome, he thought. He'd ask Seth to pick up a few personal belongings from his cabin, including his razor and fresh clothing. In a day or two he hoped to be up and moving around. He felt better just thinking about that prospect; he was weary of laying in bed, having others care for him. He sat up and bunched his pillow, but the movement brought a sudden stab of pain to his shoulder. He clenched his teeth and waited for the pain to pass.

The morning went by quickly. Whitmer brought up his breakfast and chatted with him while he ate. Later, the doctor came to change his bandages. In the late afternoon Seth stopped to see him. They had a long conversation. Seth filled him in on all the news in town, and Christian in turn explained what he could remember about his ordeal in the woods. Seth told him that Barnes had disappeared without a trace and Chiles had established an alibi to explain his whereabouts on the night in question. Christian wasn't surprised. He knew the two of them would likely escape punishment.

Seth had picked up the few things Christian wanted from his cabin and brought them with him—a razor, clothing, a few books and newspapers, and Christian's sketching pad complete with a stump of charcoal. He helped Christian change into a fresh shirt and razored the stubble off his friend's chin. With Seth to lend him a hand, Christian climbed out of bed and gingerly moved into a chair. Seth handed him a blanket to tuck around his legs.

Seth stayed a half hour more. After he left, Christian leaned back in the chair and closed his eyes. The pain in his shoulder had intensified with his movement from the bed to the chair. He wondered how long it was going to be until he could move freely again without pain. Discouragement and doubt assailed him. He covered his eyes with his good hand and released a pent-up, frustrated sigh.

Lydia spoke with Seth Whitfield at the door for a few minutes before he left the house. Although she didn't know Seth well, she liked him instinctively. He was friendly and open, and obviously devoted to Christian. After he'd gone, Lydia decided to go up to Christian's room to see if he needed anything. That was, in all honesty, more of an excuse than actual truth—she wanted to see him. The better she came to know Christian Kent, the more she enjoyed being with him. And she'd had ample opportunity for both during the last few days. While he lay upstairs in the Whitmers' spare bedroom, she'd been at his side almost constantly. It was becoming increasingly more difficult not to respond to the warmth of his smile, or the chance touch of his hand.

Since Abraham's death, no one had stirred her feelings the way Christian had. One or two of Sarah's young unmarried men friends had made solicitous overtures toward her, in particular a fellow by the name of Warren Higbee. Warren was a nice enough man, but Lydia felt nothing special for him. She'd politely let him know that she was not interested in fostering a relationship. Still, Warren managed to single her out whenever he had the opportunity.

Lydia lighted an additional lamp and started up the stairs with it. The afternoon was late and shadows had begun to move stealthily across the house. As she neared Christian's room, she saw him through the partially opened door. He was sitting in a chair, his face buried in the pages of a newspaper. She knocked softly on the door.

"Come in."

"I hope I'm not disturbing you."

"No, on the contrary. I was hoping for some company." He put aside his paper and smiled at her.

She returned his smile shyly. "You're sitting up. That's wonderful."

"Yes, but Seth practically had to carry me to the chair. I'd be lying if I said the move was easy." He grinned, but Lydia could see pain still clouding his eyes.

"How is your shoulder feeling now?"

"Sore. It's mending, though."

"That's good." Lydia set the lamp on the table beside his bed. "It's grown dark so early I thought you might like some extra light."

"Thank you. You and Sister Whitmer have certainly seen to all my needs. I appreciate it."

Lydia smiled again. She noted that Christian wore a clean white shirt and was freshly shaven. He still looked pale and drawn, however, despite his fresh apparel.

"I hope to start moving around a bit tomorrow."

"Has the doctor given you approval?"

"We won't ask him," Christian replied with a conspiratorial wink. He shifted uncomfortably in his chair. "It's been pretty quiet downstairs the last few hours. Are James and Elizabeth away?"

"Yes, Brother Whitmer took them with him while he attended to a few errands. I expect them back soon. If it's company you want, perhaps you'd enjoy a visit from Elizabeth. She's been wearying me with questions about you."

"I'd like that. She's a charming little girl. She paid me a visit the other day. James introduced us."

"Those two!" Lydia exclaimed in exasperation.

"Don't scold them. They're delightful youngsters. They lifted my spirits. Really," he added when he saw her doubtful expression.

"I'm not surprised 'Lizabeth sneaked in without permission, but I didn't expect it of James. He usually does what I ask him."

"I think his curiosity got the better of him this time." Christian chuckled out loud.

Lydia couldn't help smiling a little, too.

"James is a fine boy," Christian commented. He must look like his father. He doesn't have your coloring."

Lydia hesitated, considering what kind of reply to give him. It was evident that he was curious about Abraham for he'd asked about him on other occasions. Lydia was sure his comment was intended to draw her into talking about him.

"Yes, Abraham had dark hair and eyes, like James." Christian said nothing, encouraging her by his silence. "They're different in other ways, though," she continued haltingly. "James is happy and even-tempered. With Abraham, you never knew what might displease him. He was a quiet man, kept to himself. Did what he thought was best." She paused, swallowing hard. Without looking at him, Lydia could feel Christian's eyes boring into her, dredging up all the unhappy memories and bringing them to the surface for him to examine. "Abraham was a steady worker. He worked real hard on the farm," she stammered.

"What else?" he asked quietly.

"There's not much else, Mr. Kent. We lived a quiet life on our farm." To her consternation, Lydia felt a tear roll down her cheek and drop onto her hand. She dashed it away, embarrassed to have Christian see her unhappiness.

"I suspect it wasn't an entirely satisfactory marriage for you," he said after a moment's silence.

She darted a glance at him. He was watching her intently, his expression one of empathy and compassion.

Lydia felt the barriers slipping away. She found herself expressing her loneliness and frustrations while Christian listened with quiet understanding. She told him about her differences with Abraham and the discord in their marriage.

"Abraham had a hard time lettin' himself get close to other people. I guess that's part of the reason some folks thought he was selfish and unbending. He was a proud man, and an independent one." Lydia frowned as she thought back on their relationship. "I suppose a lot of the problems between us were my fault. I wanted him to be somethin' he wasn't."

"Perhaps that's not uncommon. Difficult as it sometimes is, accepting others as they are can save a lot of disappointment. Trying to change someone else usually results in nothing but frustration."

Lydia studied Christian's face; his brow was furrowed and his dark eyes stared past her. "Somehow I don't think we're talkin' about Abraham any more," she said.

Christian's laugh was hollow. "No, I guess not."

Neither of them said anything for several seconds, then finally Lydia spoke. "Do you want to tell me about her?"

"You're an astute woman, Mrs. Dawson."

Lydia smiled. "It doesn't take much insight to guess you must be in love with someone. Mary Ann?"

"I'm not in love with her," he answered quickly. "At least not any more. I'm not certain I ever was, to be honest with you." He looked up at Lydia and smiled briefly. "She's a girl from another county. I'm afraid we didn't have much in common."

"Is she pretty?"

Christian laughed almost bitterly. "Oh yes, she's pretty. Beautiful. Long yellow hair, hazel eyes. Slim as a reed. But that's the extent of her virtues. Any more questions?"

"No, I guess not," Lydia replied, feeling a little sheepish.

"Good. Now I've a question for you."

"What is it Mr. Kent?"

"Would you mind calling me by my given name? It's

Christian. I feel a little ridiculous sitting here in my bed-clothes, discussing our personal affairs, and having you address me as Mr. Kent."

Lydia stared at him for a moment and then she began to giggle. He started chuckling, too, and soon they were both laughing out loud.

The laughter brought a wave of pain to Christian's shoulder, but he ignored it. "Listen," he said, pretending to adopt a serious tone. "You must promise not to tell Sister Whitmer I've been entertaining ladies in my shirt tails. She'd be mortified!"

Lydia burst into another fit of laughter. Christian coughed and cleared his throat in an attempt to bring some semblance of solemnity back into their conversation. At last, when they had both composed themselves sufficiently, he asked, "May I call you Lydia?"

"I suppose that would be all right."

"Good. Then that makes it official, Lydia. We're friends."

Lydia felt herself redden, but she didn't mind. The warm feeling that rushed over her was like a welcome summer breeze.

CHAPTER FOURTEEN

A noise from the stairwell attracted Lydia's attention. She looked up from her letter and saw John Whitmer on the stair, his arm supporting Christian as the two of them slowly descended the staircase. She noted at once the expression of pain etched on Christian's face as he negotiated the steps.

"He told me he was either coming downstairs or he was going to scale the walls of his room," Whitmer said with a smile. He guided Christian over to a chair and helped him ease into it.

"Thanks, John," Christian murmured.

"Brother Kent, are you sure you should be out of bed? You look awfully pale," Sarah Whitmer said, coming to his side.

"I appreciate your concern, Sister Whitmer, but if I'm ever going to regain my strength, I need to make a start of it. He shifted his weight in the chair, and as he did so his eyes met Lydia's. He gave her a warm smile.

Elizabeth and James, who'd been studying their lessons at Lydia's feet, watched Christian with interest. He spoke a few words of greeting to each of them.

"Would you like something to eat, Brother Kent?" Sarah asked.

Christian shook his head. "No, I'm fine. Thanks."

Although he was still pale, he looked stronger and healthier than Lydia had seen him since his injury. He had on a blue cotton shirt and brown trousers, and his hair was combed loosely off his brow. His left arm lay listless, cradled in a sling against his body.

Whitmer laid down a pad of paper and a piece of charcoal he had carried downstairs for Christian and took a seat. "Maybe you'll feel up to joining us for the Sabbath tomorrow, Christian. A few of the brethren and their families are planning to meet with us here in my home."

"I'd like that."

"Can we come, too, Mr. Whitmer?" asked Elizabeth.

"Of course," laughed Whitmer. "You're a member of this household, aren't you?" Whitmer put his arm around Elizabeth and gave her a hug.

"Who will be speaking?" asked Christian.

"Bishop Partridge will be here to address us," Whitmer answered.

Since the trouble in Independence began in the latter part of July, the Saints had been holding Sabbath meetings in their homes, rotating from Sunday to Sunday. This lessened the chance of the mob coming upon them in the midst of their worship. Lydia was looking forward to hearing the Bishop's remarks.

The conversation turned to other topics. At length, Sarah arose to prepare supper and John Whitmer left to make a call. Christian moved onto the couch in the parlor and lay down. Lydia scooted the children out so he could rest, and then took up her letter again. It was from her father and its contents disturbed her. She reread his words, the sharpness of them almost bringing tears to her eyes.

"Bad news?"

Christian's question startled her. "Not really," she answered, flustered.

"From your expression, I would have thought otherwise."

Lydia looked up at him. His gaze was fixed on her face and his eyes were solemn. "It's a letter from my father. He's angry with me for coming out here to Missouri."

"Where you're living amidst the Mormon reprobates."

"Yes."

"Does he know you've joined the Church?"

Lydia shook her head. "I haven't told my parents about my baptism." She swallowed hard, afraid of what her father would have to say when he found out the complete truth of her situation. "He wants me to come home."

Christian struggled to a sitting position on the couch. He looked at her without speaking.

Lydia tried not to show how much the letter had upset her. She said in a deliberately light tone, "He calls us blasphemers and sorcerers."

Christian sighed. "It sounds as if he's heard all the falsehoods. That's the very thing we were trying to combat in the *Star*." Christian shook his head. "Idlers, liars, the dregs of society—I've heard them all, Lydia. With the newspaper to publish the truth about our people, we had a chance to correct those accusations. Without it . . ." His voice trailed off, leaving the sentence unfinished.

"I'm sure you'll have the opportunity to publish again. As soon as this trouble is over."

Christian regarded her with a sober expression. "We're fooling ourselves if we think we'll be able to stay here in Independence. We've lost Zion. By our own disobedience and foolish pride."

"Please don't say that. It frightens me to hear you talk so."

"It's the truth. We might as well recognize it."

"You only believe that because you're not feeling well. When you're stronger, you'll see that everything will work out for the Saints."

"I hope you're right."

"I know I am. This is the Lord's church and we're his people. He won't abandon us."

"The Lord chastens those he loves, is that it?" Christian said with a faint smile.

"I don't know. I only know we mustn't give up trying."

"I doubt you've given up on anything you've ever set your mind to, have you?" asked Christian. "Even though it required leaving your farm and your family, you were determined to come here and you did it."

"The Lord led me to Missouri, Mr. Kent. He must have had a purpose."

Christian's frank stare of admiration left Lydia's cheeks burning. She picked up her letter and began reading again, but the words swam in front of her eyes. All she could comprehend was Christian's eyes on her.

Christian didn't say anything else. Instead, he leaned over to the table beside him and picked up his paper and charcoal. From the corner of her eye, Lydia saw him making quick, sure strokes of the charcoal onto the paper.

She ventured a second peek at him. He was alternately eyeing her and quickly sketching on the paper. She suspected what he was drawing.

"What are you doing, Mr. Kent?" she laughed.

"Christian, please. Remember our agreement."

"May I ask what you're drawing?"

"Certainly."

"Well?"

"Well what?" he returned with a mischievous grin.

"What are you drawing?" she repeated.

"I'll show you if you'll just be patient." He deftly worked the charcoal, making long strokes with a sweeping motion.

"There," he said finally. "I'm finished." He put down the charcoal and turned the picture around so she could see it. For a moment she said nothing. All she could do was stare at the drawing.

"Don't you like it?"

"It's beautiful. You're very talented," she answered in a soft voice.

"It's yours." He held it out to her.

She stood up, walked to the couch, and hesitantly took the picture from his hand. "You want me to have it?"

"Since it's a sketch of you, I can't think of a better person to give it to."

Lydia gazed at the charcoal drawing for a long moment. "That's not me, Christian," she finally said.

"I think it's a fairly good likeness."

Lydia looked up into his face. He was staring solemnly at her. She glanced again at the picture. "This woman is beautiful. She's not me."

"Where did you get the idea that you aren't beautiful, Lydia? If your husband didn't compliment you often, he was a foolish man."

Christian's eyes held hers and the exchange that passed

between them left Lydia breathless. At that moment feelings surged and roiled within her that she had never experienced before. Not with Abraham, not with anyone. She tried to speak, but the words evaporated before she could utter them.

Christian gently took her hand, and was about to say something more when Elizabeth came bounding into the room.

"Mama, Mrs. Whitmer said supper is about ready and for you and Mr. Kent to come."

Lydia drew a breath, "All right, 'Lizabeth. We'll be there in a moment."

"Hurry, Mama. She wants you right now."

The child's words broke the spell between them. Christian cleared his throat and Lydia awkwardly removed her hand from his. She stepped back a pace. "Thank you," she said. "I'll keep it always."

Clutching the drawing in her hand, she turned and climbed the stairs to her room, slipped inside and closed the door behind her. She set the sketch on the dresser, beside the mirror, and studied it. Christian had sketched only the head and shoulders. It was true the features were hers, but they were more delicate and refined than she knew them to actually be. The curious thing about the likeness was the hair. Instead of drawing it as it was, swept into a knot at the nape of her head, he had depicted it long and flowing to the shoulders.

Her eyes moved from the drawing to the mirror beside it. She noted that her cheeks were flushed and her breast was heaving. That brief, intensely personal interlude with Christian left her heart and mind reeling. She drew a deep, ragged breath, and with one unsteady hand on the knob, opened the bedroom door and left the room.

Sunday turned out to be an especially spiritual and uplifting Sabbath day. In the morning the household gathered for morning prayer and then John Whitmer read a passage from the Bible. Throughout the scripture-reading, Lydia had felt Christian's eyes on her, and afterward, he sought her out. He wanted to speak with her later, he said, about something that was on his mind. She'd agreed, but they'd not had the opportunity to be alone all morning.

Then families began to arrive for Sunday worship service. Several of the Whitmers' friends were in attendance, including Warren Higbee. Warren immediately attached himself to her side, though Lydia tried to discourage him. When she seated herself in the parlor in preparation for the meeting to commence, he chose the seat beside her. She noticed Christian watching her from his chair in the far corner of the room, but she could not read his stoic expression. Christian looked particularly handsome dressed in his best black trousers, white shirt and black coat. His cravat was tied in a smooth knot at his throat. His dark hair had grown longish over the period of his confinement. He wore it combed back at the sides, revealing neatly groomed side whiskers. She thought him the most attractive man she'd ever met. A tingling started along her spine and traveled throughout her body, leaving her limp as jelly. She found herself eagerly awaiting their talk together.

During the opening hymn and preliminary remarks, she caught Christian staring at her, but when she glanced in his direction, he looked away. This unsettling state of affairs continued until Partridge took the floor, and then all other thoughts fled her mind as she listened to the Bishop's address. Bishop Edward Partridge was every bit the speaker Lydia expected. He was soft-spoken with a melodic voice, and he moved with a grace and confidence that befitted his holy calling. He had penetrating blue eyes, light hair, and a firm mouth. That Sabbath morning in the Whitmer home he spoke about forgiveness, and the tribulations the Saints had been called to pass through. It was a humble, yet forceful sermon and Lydia's heart soared with the majesty of his words.

When he concluded, Warren Higbee leaned over and whispered in her ear, "That was an inspiring address, wasn't it?"

"It was," Lydia agreed.

"May I say that you look particularly lovely this morning, Sister Dawson."

"Thank you, Brother Higbee."

"I would be highly honored if you would allow me to call on you one day this week."

"I do appreciate your kindness, Brother Higbee, but I'm afraid that wouldn't be possible."

"Perhaps a day the following week, then?"

"I'm afraid not. I'm sorry."

"I see," Higbee said, his face crest-fallen.

He said nothing more to her, and after the concluding speaker and prayer, he excused himself politely and joined a group of people speaking with Bishop Partridge.

Lydia looked over to the corner where Christian had been sitting. He was gone. She scanned the room but couldn't see him anywhere. A cloud of disappointment settled over her. She had wanted to talk with Christian, hear his thoughts concerning the meeting, feel the thrill of being near him.

The group lingered in the Whitmers' parlor for some time exchanging information and visiting together. Lydia hung back, preferring not to join in the conversation. Finally, the last person took his leave. Sarah began preparations for the noon meal, while Whitmer picked up his Bible and settled into a comfortable chair. When the children ran upstairs to play, Lydia found herself alone with her thoughts. She took up Whitmer's Book of Mormon and turned to the first chapter of Nephi. The prophetic words stirred her soul, just as they had when she'd read them for the first time. She thought about that day in Green County. It seemed so long ago. So much had happened to her since that time; her whole life was transformed. She offered a silent, grateful prayer, pleading for the Lord's direction to guide her path in the future.

Not long afterward, Sarah called the household to dinner. Christian entered the parlor still dressed in his Sunday finery, his left arm held against his body by the cloth sling. He greeted the others and sat down to the table. The conversation at supper revolved around the events of the day's meeting and other household matters. Christian was unusually quiet, contributing to the conversation only when specifically addressed. Lydia studied his face, but could find no clue to his reticence. She gave up trying to guess, attributing it to his injury which must be paining him more than usual.

After supper, when the dishes were scrubbed and put away, she sought him out. They exchanged a moment or two of small talk and then Lydia asked about his shoulder.

"It's feeling better," he replied. "I think I should be able to get around by myself now."

Lydia's heart skipped a beat. "Does that mean you'll be leaving here?"

"I think probably tomorrow or the next day. I can't lean on the Whitmers' hospitality forever. Or yours."

Lydia wasn't prepared for this moment. It took tremendous effort to keep her voice from revealing the tumultuous feelings churning inside her. "Is that what you wanted to talk to me about?"

He paused for a moment and she got the impression he was deliberately cloaking his real feelings. Then he answered, "No, it wasn't anything important. Forget it."

"Oh."

Neither of them said anything for several uncomfortable moments, then Christian turned and started for the stairway.

"Christian!" Lydia called out after him. He stopped and turned around. "Have I done something to offend you?"

"Of course not. Why do you say that?"

"I just thought that, well . . . I hoped I hadn't said or done anything to damage our friendship."

He retraced his steps and stopped only inches from her. He was so close she could smell the starch in his shirt. He gave her a solemn smile and took both her hands in his.

"You could never do that, Lydia. You've given me a great deal, and I thank you for it." He squeezed her hands briefly, then let them go.

Her hands felt on fire from Christian's touch. With her heart in her throat, she watched him climb the stairs.

Christian received several callers the next day. Seth Whitfield came and brought his wife, Carrie, whom Lydia had never met before but liked immediately. Because of the visitors she had little opportunity to have a private word with Christian. It was almost evening before he found time to sit down with Lydia and the Whitmers.

"I want to thank all of you for your kindness and attention on my behalf. I'm sure I would never have recovered so quickly or so well without your charitable administrations. In the morning, Seth Whitfield is coming to drive me to my cabin."

"Brother Kent, you're still not very strong. Couldn't we persuade you to stay a few more days?" Sarah implored him.

"You've done more for me already than I can ever hope to repay. Don't worry. I'll be fine. Seth's wife has promised to stop by regularly to check on me."

"Our door is always open," Whitmer said, putting a hand on Christian's good shoulder.

"I know that John, and I appreciate it."

Lydia sat quietly, not trusting herself to speak for fear of revealing her churning emotions. Christian turned to her and said, "I want to thank you, too, Mrs. Dawson, for all your help and your good company."

Lydia nodded, keeping her eyes to the floor. She could feel Sarah's scrutiny focused on her.

"Well, then, I guess that's it. I believe I'll go upstairs and pack my belongings."

Whitmer accompanied him up to his room. After they'd gone, Sarah folded her hands in her lap and leaned back in her chair, her eyes fixed on Lydia. "Liddy, dear, do I detect your silence to mean something more than your usual reserved nature?"

"I don't know what you mean," answered Lydia.

"Is it possible Brother Kent has endeared himself to you more than you're willing to let on?"

"I'm fond of him, of course. He's a fine man."

Sarah's head wagged up and down and a smile began at the corners of her mouth. "Here I've been wearing myself out trying to get you to meet some nice young men here in Independence, and you've struck up a romance of your own right under my nose."

"Mr. Kent and I are merely friends, Sarah."

"Whatever you say, Liddy. I'm certainly not one to pry into other people's affairs." The smile widened.

"I'm very tired. I think I'll get the children to bed early so I can retire myself. Good-night."

"Good-night, Liddy."

Lydia felt Sarah's merry eyes follow her all the way up the staircase.

Seth arrived early the following morning. Lydia answered

his ring at the door and they exchanged a few words, then she went upstairs and rapped softly on Christian's bedroom door.

"Come in," he answered.

When she stepped through the door, she found him bent over the bed, putting a few last things into his traveling bag. He straightened and turned around.

"Brother Whitfield is downstairs."

"Thank you. I'm just about ready." He made a quick scan of the room and then closed up his bag.

"All set?" She tried to say the words in as light a tone as she could muster.

"Yes, that's it." He took a step toward her, his bag in hand. "I appreciate all you've done for me, Lydia."

"It wasn't much. Besides, I'm the one who's been in your debt."

Christian smiled. "It's not just the care you've given me. The best part was getting to know you."

"I enjoyed getting to know you, too." Lydia's heart was pounding. Christian's nearness and the earnest look in his eye made her catch her breath. She sensed he was on the verge of saying something important to her. He seemed to be searching her eyes, her face, for some indication on her part. She held her breath, not knowing what to expect . . . or what she wanted to happen between them. All she grasped was the terrible fact that he was leaving and she might never see him again.

The moment passed and she found herself wondering if she had completely misread his expression. He smiled and hoisted his bag up under his good arm.

"After you," he said, gesturing to the door with a nod of his head. She walked out of the room ahead of him.

He closed the door and followed her down the stairs.

"Morning, Cicero." Seth called from the foot of the stairs. "Are you ready to go?"

"I'm ready."

"I brought the buggy. We'll take our time so it doesn't jostle your shoulder too badly. Let me take your bag."

Christian handed it to him.

Sarah and the children gathered around the door. Christian

spoke to each of them in turn, and shook their hands. When it came time for Lydia, she held out her hand to him.

"Good-bye," he said, taking her hand. His fingers lingered on hers a moment longer than necessary. Then he let go and turned to leave. He'd taken only a step or two when he stopped abruptly and turned back around.

"Mrs. Dawson, may I call on you in the future?" he asked in a husky voice.

Lydia's heart leaped up. "Oh, yes, Mr. Kent. I'd like that very much."

"O! how Zion mourns, her sons have fallen in the streets by the cruel hand of the enemy and her daughters weep in silence . . . . Between five and seven thousand men, women and children driven in poverty to seek for habitations where they can find them . . . . The Stakes of Zion will soon be bereft of all her children. By the river of Babylon we can sit down, yes, . . . we weep when we remember Zion."

Elizabeth Haven
Early Missouri Saint

CHAPTER FIFTEEN

hings were fairly quiet in the town of Independence over the next several weeks. Although the Saints continued to be taunted and were subjected to occasional abuse, there were no major outbreaks of violence. Several of the brethren along with their families were making preparations to leave the county, selling their homes and farms for whatever price they would bring. Christian had begun to box up a few of his belongings, but he was dragging his feet in hopes a compromise might be reached between the Saints and the Missourians. He didn't take kindly to the idea of being driven out against his will.

Lydia Dawson was another reason why he didn't wish to leave. He had called on her a little more than a week after returning from his stay at the Whitmers'. The evening had gone badly, however. He'd brought a small gift for each of Lydia's children, and they'd pressed around him throughout the evening, demanding his attention. Sarah Whitmer had insisted on acting as chaperone, as well. She never left her post for an instant. What little conversation he and Lydia had together was strained and halting. All in all, it was a frustrating visit.

Christian hoped this evening would go better. As he waited for Lydia in the Whitmers' parlor, he noticed Elizabeth peeking at him from behind the parlor door. While he watched, John Whitmer took her hand and giving Christian a quick wink, firmly shut the parlor door. Christian smiled and relaxed a bit more in his chair. The room was cool in the autumn shadows. He drew a long breath and let it out slowly.

If the right moment presented itself tonight, he intended to talk to Lydia about what was in his heart. Christian wasn't sure what her response would be, and that thought made the palms of his hands begin to sweat. He wiped them on his trouser legs nervously.

Just then Lydia entered the parlor. Christian's knees started an inexplicable shaking at the sight of her. He rose to his feet, hoping his unsteady knees would support him.

Lydia's eyes went to his left arm, which was no longer confined to a sling. "Your arm," she said laughing. "It's mobile."

Christian gingerly raised it up to a point level with his shoulder for her to see. "Good as new," he proclaimed.

"That's wonderful. Did the doctor give his permission or did you decide to abandon the sling on your own?"

"A little of both," Christian replied with a grin. He helped Lydia into a chair and then pulled his own closer to hers and sat down. "You look very pretty this evening."

Christian saw her blush. He realized that he was staring at her, but he couldn't help himself. She was beautiful. Her eyes were as clear and blue as a brilliant summer sky and her long russet hair flowed loose around her shoulders, very much like the drawing he had made of her.

"Thank you. You look much happier without your sling," she answered.

"I am. I've even been working a little bit, helping Seth at the sawmill."

"That's good. How is Brother Whitfield?"

"Fine. He and Carrie are oblivious to everything else in the world except each other. They couldn't be happier."

Lydia glanced down at her feet with a slow smile.

Christian had to force his eyes away, for her cheeks were turning a deeper shade of pink under his fixed gaze. "I received a letter from my brother this past week," he commented lightly.

"Jarrett?"

"Yes. He'd heard about the trouble in Independence and suggested I return home 'where I belong', as he put it."

"Does home mean Philadelphia?" asked Lydia.

"Yes. Jarrett is an attorney with a successful practice in

Philadelphia. My brother is very citified. He thinks anyone living west of the Mississippi is a barbarian."

Lydia chuckled softly. "What about your parents? Do they live in Philadelphia, too?"

"Mother does. My father died when I was fifteen. Father was a farmer. He worked harder than any man I've ever met. My father had no formal schooling. He felt that lack keenly and frequently talked to Jarrett and me about the importance of getting a proper education and preparing ourselves for a profession. Father scrimped and saved all his life so he'd have the means to send us to the college in Philadelphia. He was so proud of Jarrett for pursuing a legal career." Christian paused, a slight frown rumpling his brow. "I'm afraid I was a bit of a disappointment to him."

"How can you say that? You're a respected newspaper man."

"That's not what Father had in mind for me." Christian's smile was forced. "He wanted me to become a physician. To please him I enrolled in the college's medical department, but after a year it was obvious that it wasn't going to work out as he'd anticipated. I was more interested in writing for the school's monthly news-sheet than in studying textbooks."

Lydia smiled. "I suppose we do that for which we're best suited."

"Whether others think so or not, right?"

"That's right," Lydia paused, watching Christian closely. "I'm sorry about the *Star*, Christian. I know how hard you worked to make it a successful paper. What are the chances of setting up a press outside the county?"

"It's a possibility. I know Brother Phelps has been thinking about that very thing. It would be up to the Prophet, though, to make that decision."

"Do you think the Prophet will come to Independence to help settle the problems here?"

Christian considered her question, then shook his head. "No, I don't. I suspect he'll let the Church leaders here work out a solution, with his approval and support."

Lydia bowed her head and said softly. "Oh, I wish he would come. I know he could make the Missouri people see they're wrong about us."

"I don't think even Brother Joseph could do that, Lydia."

"But if he's as wise and good as you've told me, surely he can do something."

Christian bent down to look into her face. "You've the trusting faith of a child, haven't you? It's one of the things I admire most about you."

Lydia lifted her eyes to meet his. The warmth and tenderness Christian saw in them started his knees shaking all over again.

"Lydia," he began in a halting voice, "I know you're mourning Abraham and I've no right to infringe on that loss, but I wondered if perhaps later you might possibly, that is, we might . . ." He faltered, suddenly embarrassed and unsure.

"Yes?" Lydia whispered.

He plunged ahead, taking a gulping breath. "What I'm trying to say is that during these past few weeks I've come to care very strongly for you. I'm foolish enough to hope you might feel a little of the same for me. I intended to speak of it to you earlier, but then I realized you and Higbee were seeing one another and—"

Lydia interrupted him in mid-sentence. "What about Warren Higbee and me?"

"From seeing the two of you together, I gathered you were more than friends."

"Christian, is that the reason you were distant with me?" Lydia sat forward in her chair, her eyes seeking his. "There has never been anything between Warren and myself except some wishful thinking on his part which I've discouraged at every opportunity."

"You're sure?"

"Of course."

"Then he's not courting you?" She shook her head.

Christian took both of Lydia's hands into his. "Lydia, do you care for me at all? Forgive me for being brash, but I've nearly gone crazy wondering whether I should speak to you or not. If I offended you and you refused to see me again, I'd cut out my tongue in remorse, I swear it!" Tiny beads of perspiration formed on Christian's brow with this impassioned speech.

He felt Lydia's hands tremble and her voice quivered when she spoke. "I've never met anyone like you, Christian. So kind and gentle. You've been considerate of me from the first day we met. How could I not care for you?"

Christian sucked in his breath. His heart was thrashing so wildly it was difficult for him to speak. He looked into her face for a long moment. "I give you my word I'll not press you until you've had sufficient time to come to terms with Abraham's death."

She nodded and her eyes suddenly filled with tears. "Everything has happened to me so quickly this last little while. I feel as if I've been swept along in a whirlwind and I'm just beginning to get settled back on my feet. You must promise to be patient with me."

"I'll be more patient than Job!" Christian declared passionately.

"We've every right to be here, Christian. All of us paid good money for our land. I don't plan on letting some wild-eyed jackal run me off," Seth Whitfield was saying.

"I agree with you, but I think we ought to be patient and give the legal process a chance to work."

"It'll be a waste of time," Seth muttered.

Carrie looked anxiously from Seth to Christian. The couple had stopped at Christian's cabin earlier in the evening and they'd been discussing the recent turn of events. It was the last day of October and the weather was clear and bitter cold. Carrie shivered in her thin shawl. "Do you really think the lawyers will be able to help us, Christian?" she asked.

"I hope so. They've been paid a big enough fee," he answered, giving her a wry smile.

Carrie's hand fluttered unconsciously to her swollen stomach. She was nearing the end of her pregnancy—only eight weeks more, her husband had proudly told Christian. She'd had a difficult time and it showed. Carrie's pale blue eyes seemed to be sunken, and her lips were without color. She was as determined as Seth, however, to stay and give birth to the baby in Zion.

Both Carrie and Seth had been keeping abreast of events as they unfolded. They were aware of the letter from Church leaders at Kirtland advising the Saints to seek legal redress for the injuries inflicted upon them. The letter also counseled those who had not already signed an agreement to sell their lands and leave the county not to do so. Christian had opportunity to read the lengthy letter from Kirtland, signed by F. G. Williams. He was pleased with the tenor of the communication, but had been slightly piqued by the information Williams related about the purchase of a new press and a printing house being erected in Kirtland. Williams proposed to republish the *Star* under the firm name of F. G. Williams & Co.

Oliver Cowdery had already written for the names and residences of the subscribers, and Christian was helping Phelps compile that information. Christian couldn't help feeling upset when he learned that printing was to be resumed in Kirtland. It revived old feelings of jealously and guilt that Christian thought he had put to rest.

Christian had served on the committee to redress the Saints' grievances and helped draw up papers to present to the state officials. Upon receiving their petition, Governor Dunklin had encouraged the Saints to apply to the courts for restitution. Accordingly, the Church engaged the services of four attorneys to represent them. The lawyers had asked for an excessively high fee to handle the suits. Christian knew only one of them slightly, a fellow named Doniphan who seemed to be a man of principle. The others he dismissed as scoundrels.

As soon as the contract was made known, the mob again began to circulate false rumors and renew their persecutions against the Saints. There were rumors of a meeting that had taken place on the 26th of October when approximately fifty of the mob had met and voted to remove the Saints forcibly from the county. There were threats of whippings and beatings for those Saints who refused to leave, and talk of a war of extermination. Instructions had been circulated among the Saints not to be the aggressor in any confrontation which might ensue.

On the 28th, the circuit court convened. The Saints' attorneys filed their motions and affidavits. The mob was not in evidence at the courthouse, but bold threats were made against the Saints later in the day.

"If the mob attempts to carry out their threats, I'll be armed and waiting for them," Seth said heatedly.

"I hope it doesn't come to that," replied Christian. "I still believe negotiation is possible."

"You want to try to negotiate with Chiles and his kind? I would have thought you'd be fed up to here"—Seth made a quick cutting motion in the air above his head—"with their lawless shenanigans."

"I thought he and the others would abide by their word to leave us in peace until we'd had a chance to fulfill our end of the agreement."

"Are you kidding? They never had any intention of leaving us alone. Not until the last one of us is driven from the county," Seth replied bitterly.

Carrie listened silently, her face ashen in the gathering dusk.

"At least we have the consolation of knowing that some of the newspapers are recognizing our plight. The *Western Monitor* has published several articles censuring the conduct of the mob and others are following suit."

"What we need is assistance, not opinion," Seth answered with acrimony.

The men paused in their conversation as the sound of horses coming at a fast clip neared the cabin. A moment later, someone banged loudly at the door. Christian jumped to his feet and whipped open the door.

"The mob has struck!" shouted a figure standing on the porch step. In the darkness, Christian couldn't identify the speaker.

"That's right," shouted another from the street. "The mob's gathered and attacked the Whitmer settlement."

"What?" Christian cried in alarm. Seth and Carrie sprang from their seats and clustered around the man in the doorway, all of them questioning him at once.

The messenger drew a shaking hand across his mouth and relayed the details in jumbled sentences. "I've come to warn you. There's no telling where they'll strike next. Near fifty men, gone plumb crazy! They burst into Hyrum Page's house and beat him senseless. Whipped a half dozen others and threatened their wives and children. Men and women are being run off their spreads like cattle. We have to warn the other brethren!"

With that frenzied explanation, the man bolted from the porch, leaped on his horse and galloped away with the others.

Christian and Seth exchanged a grim look.

"I knew it would come to this," Seth said angrily.

Carrie clutched his arm, her eyes wide with fright.

"Let's calm down and decide on the best course of action," Christian said quickly. "Seth, take Carrie to a safe place, then get a few of the other men and spread out around town to keep watch. I'll see what I can do to help the families in the settlement."

"Let's go," Seth said, grabbing his hat and jamming it on his head. He took Carrie by the arm and slipped out of the cabin.

Christian was right behind them. Before going to the Whitmer settlement, however, he hurried up the road several blocks, past the ruined printing house, and turned onto one of the main streets. He stopped at the frame house in the center of the block, threw open the white picket gate and strode through. Lamps burned from the windows on the bottom floor of the house. As he rapped at the door, he caught sight of movement at one of the windows—a quick lifting aside of the curtain. Then Lydia thrust open the door.

"Christian!" she cried. "Thank goodness you've come. I've been so frightened."

Christian put his arms around her and held her close. The sweet scent of her hair momentarily swept everything else from his mind except the nearness of her. Finally he released her. "Are you all right?"

She nodded.

"You've heard about the raid on the settlement?"

"Yes, Brother Whitmer left as soon as we got the news. Christian, most of his family live on the Blue. We've no idea how many of them have been hurt. Do you know any details?"

"No, not yet. I'm going down to the settlement when I leave here. I'll know more when I get back. How is Sister Whitmer?"

"She's badly shaken, but she'll be fine. Can you stay a few moments?"

He nodded his head. She led him to the parlor where they took a seat close together. Christian reached for her hand.

"It's possible there may be more attacks tonight. Gather a few things together for yourself and the children in case you have to leave the house quickly. The night's cold so pack some warm blankets."

"I will," Lydia answered, her voice trembling.

He squeezed her hand as they sat huddled together, drawing comfort and reassurance from one another.

"Will you come by tomorrow?" asked Lydia.

"You can depend on it," Christian replied, gripping her hand more tightly. "Perhaps I should stay until John gets back. I don't want to leave you here alone."

"Brother Whitmer asked one of the brethren to come over. He'll be here any minute. You do what you can for those poor families along the Blue."

Christian nodded.

"Promise me you'll be careful," Lydia said, looking up at him.

"I promise. I'd better go now."

They arose and she walked with him to the door, her hand still clasped in his. They stood for a moment close together, loathe to part. Christian's heart quickened as he looked into her face. She was so lovely, so very beautiful. Her hair was pulled back away from her face, revealing the soft curve of her cheek, and the pale glow from the light of the lamps cast flickering shadows across her eyes.

He reached out and touched her cheek. Her eyes met his and in that instant he realized she had come to mean more to him than life itself. His voice echoed the thunderous feelings inside him. "I love you, Lydia." He bent forward, and with hammering heart, pressed his lips against hers.

CHAPTER SIXTEEN

Christian spent the following morning in meetings with the brethren, assessing the tragic events of the evening before. More than ten homes along the Blue had been ransacked and their occupants either molested or forced out into the cold night. It was rumored that the mob was organizing for a second attack.

It wasn't until after nightfall that Christian was able to break away to see Lydia. As he left Gilbert & Whitney's Mercantile where he'd been in conference with several of the men, Christian pulled his coat tighter around him. The air was bitter cold, cutting through him like a knife. He started up the street and hadn't gone more than half a block when he heard angry voices coming from across the square. He turned in the direction of the tumult and watched in astonishment as a knot of twenty or so enraged men surged forward. A few of them carried torches which cast long erie shadows along the ground, while others gripped rifles, clubs or long poles. Instinctively, Christian backed into the safety of a narrow alley between two buildings.

As Christian watched, one of the mob ran up onto the porch of the mercantile and thrust his pole through a front windowpane. The glass shattered with a sharp sound like the crack of rifle fire. Then the others dashed ahead and began their assault. The sound of splintering wood and cracking glass echoed in Christian's ears. A triumphant cry went up as the mob broke through the door of the store and swarmed inside. Christian watched helplessly as goods from the mercantile came flying out onto the road.

Shocked and angry, Christian hurried down the street. Rounding the corner at the end of the road, he halted suddenly, dismayed by what he saw. A few yards in front of him, another group of ten or more angry men surrounded a log dwelling. Christian saw the mob tear the front door of the house off its hinges. The realization that the mob's work was not confined to the mercantile seized Christian with a new dread. Lydia. Lydia could be in danger.

He ran down the road, keeping out of sight as best he could. But one of the mob saw him, recognized him. "There's one of them Mormonites!" Christian heard him shout. "Catch him! Catch the son of a . . ." The rest of the sentence was lost in the shouting and jarring of the crowd. Hate-filled eyes turned toward him. Men spat out foul and abusive language, their faces contorted with rage. One man made a grab for him, but Christian twisted out of his reach and shoved him roughly aside.

Then, without warning, the mob began to scramble away. In another moment Christian saw the reason for their panic. A company of Saints was bearing down upon them. In the forefront, leading the group, was Lyman Wight. Wight was a bold, fearless man, committed to preserving the rights of the Saints. In Wight's hand, Christian saw the gleam of a pistol.

Christian paused as the group of Saints ran past him in pursuit of the mob. He thought briefly about joining them, but concern over Lydia persuaded him otherwise. As the last of the Saints passed by him, someone called out his name. A figure jostled his way toward him. In the darkness it was several seconds before Christian recognized Seth Whitfield.

"Come with us, Christian. We're going to put a stop to these rampages, once and for all." Seth's eyes glowered and his voice was raspy with emotion.

"I can't. I have to see about Lydia." Seth nodded briefly and sprinted away into the blackness.

Christian ran the rest of the way to the Whitmers' house. He pulled up short when he reached the white picket fence surrounding the yard. The gate swung crazily on one hinge and portions of the fence were trampled to the ground, the wooden slats splintered and broken. He yanked the gate aside and hastened to the house. Off to his side, bulky objects lay strewn around the lawn. He distinguished a chair resting upside down in the grass, its spindly legs stretching skyward.

As he neared the front entrance, he saw more furniture, articles of clothing and other household items scattered about the lawn and porch. His heart began pumping madly when he caught sight of the shattered windows on the ground floor, and the partially opened door.

"Lydia!" he cried out. "Lydia!" He thrust open the battered door and stepped inside. From the dim light of a lamp glowing from the back part of the house, Christian discerned at a glance the condition of the room. Nothing had escaped the mob's ferocity. What little furniture that remained inside was toppled and broken, the draperies were torn from their rods, and shards of glass lay scattered everywhere. He walked to the foot of the stairs and glanced up. The upper floor was dark and quiet.

Christian turned and strode out of the house. He was beginning to feel physically ill. His head hurt and his stomach felt as if he'd swallowed hot coals. He turned down first one street and then another, searching for Lydia. His mind refused to operate clearly as he raced from block to block. Despite the frigid night air, he was perspiring profusely. At last he paused by the side of a building to catch his breath and force himself to think logically. If the Whitmers had been driven out into the night, perhaps they had taken refuge in the woods nearby, and Lydia and the children with them. He wiped his brow with the back of his hand and began running toward the wooded area at the edge of town. Christian covered the distance in record time. He plunged into the thick growth of trees, calling Lydia's name.

Christian looked throughout the night for Lydia without success. As morning broke, he learned the full extent of the havoc that had been wrought by the mob. Not only had they attacked the mercantile and several homes in Independence, the mob had also struck a settlement of Saints living on the prairie twelve or fourteen miles from town. Parley Pratt had been injured in that incident along with several others. The

Saints had managed to take two of the mobbers prisoner, which disconcerted the rest of the rabble and probably prevented more attacks. Lyman Wight and his contingent of men also captured one of the mobbers in the act of vandalizing Gilbert's store and brought him before the justice of the peace.

None of that was of consequence to Christian at the moment, however. His only ambition was to locate Lydia and find a safe place of shelter for her and her children. The whole county was in a state of upheaval and the Saints in Independence were moving about a half mile out of town in order to protect themselves and their personal belongings. The mob ranged through the streets of town unroofing vacant houses and torching barns and fields.

Christian returned to his own cabin that night and found it ransacked. His furniture had been overturned and his papers strewn about. Most of his books were ruined, their pages ripped or torn out completely. Sickened and exhausted, Christian lay down on his battered cot and slept fitfully until sunrise.

At first light Christian was up and ready to leave. He had retrieved a few of his belongings, a couple of books and some clothing, and tied them into a bundle. With the pack tucked under his arm, he strode out of the cabin, leaving the door swinging open in his wake, never once turning to glance back.

"They left early this morning for Lexington to see the circuit judge," Seth was saying. "Hopefully, they'll be able to obtain a peace warrant."

"Who went besides Pratt?" asked Christian.

The two men were standing outside an old weather-beaten cabin on the barren plain outside Independence. Seth, his wife, and another family were living temporarily inside the shelter.

"Hyrum Page and two others. I hope some good will come of it."

"So do I." Christian blew on his cold hands and stuffed them into the pockets of his coat.

"Any word of Lydia?"

"No. I'm afraid something terrible has happened to her, Seth."

"You'll find her. Our people are scattered from here to the county line. It's just a matter of time before she turns up." Seth clamped a reassuring hand on his friend's back.

"I'm going to the Whitmer settlement this afternoon. Maybe they've made their way there."

"You're probably right." Seth drew a long breath and blew it out in a stream of white vapor.

"How is Carrie holding up?" Christian asked, attempting to take his mind off his own worries.

"She's not a strong woman. Carrying this baby under the present circumstances has taken its toll on her. I'll be awfully glad to have this pregnancy over and see her regain her health."

Christian frowned, thinking how wan Carrie had looked the last time he saw her.

"I suppose the mob will make good their threat tomorrow," Seth commented, stamping his feet on the frozen ground. "Word has it they plan to drive every last one of us out of the county."

"Monday will be a bloody day," Christian said under his breath, repeating the mob's dire threat which they'd been circulating throughout the day among the residents of Independence. Those people who professed to be friendly toward the Saints were urging them to flee before it was too late. Christian knew the mob was in deadly earnest, but he refused to leave until Lydia was safely beside him.

"What I wouldn't give for a good piece of chewing tobacco right now." Seth smiled grimly.

"Better not let Carrie hear you say that."

"Wouldn't she scold me?" Seth chuckled. "I have to admit though, Cicero, every now and then I develop a fierce hankering for a chew."

"It was a nasty habit. Be glad you gave it up."

"Gave up that and a lot more, too." Seth soberly studied the toe of his boot as he dug it into the sleet-covered ground. "It's a hard religion, isn't it?"

Christian looked up at his friend. Seth's eyes were lowered, but Christian could plainly see the uncertainty marked on his face.

Christian made his way back from the Blue. The wind had come up along the river icy cold, chilling him to the bone. He'd turned his collar up around his ears, but he had no hat and the wind whipped him in the face unmercifully. As he approached the dilapidated cabin where the Whitfields were staying, Seth stepped outside and gestured for him to hurry. Christian could barely feel his frozen feet in his stiff boots as he quickened his pace. Seth held the door open for him.

"They're here. Came about an hour ago," said Seth in a low voice.

"Thank God," Christian answered. The words were a prayer. "Is Lydia all right?"

Seth nodded. "She's resting. They're all fine, but exhausted."

Christian stepped inside the cabin, where the warmth from the fireplace set his fingers and toes tingling. The cabin was a cramped story and a half, with the lower floor divided into two rooms. A steep, narrow staircase led to an additional room above. Seth answered Christian's unspoken question.

"Up there," he said, pointing in the direction of the stairs.

Christian took off his coat and flung it aside, then mounted the stairs two at a time. It was dim inside the upper room. The shutter was latched on the room's single window and there were no lamps burning. He walked over to the nearest bed where two small figures lay sleeping, their arms around one another. He smiled tenderly at the children. He smoothed James' dark hair and pulled the coverlet up around Elizabeth's shoulders, then moved on to the next bed. Lydia lay on her back, her eyes closed and her breast heaving in fitful sleep. As Christian took a chair and pulled it close to her side, she murmured and moved her head. A long copper strand of hair fell across her cheek. Christian gently brushed it aside.

The slight movement roused her. Lydia's eyes fluttered and opened. She focused on Christian with a little cry. "Christian! Oh, I was afraid I'd never see you again."

She sat up and fell into Christian's arms. He clung to her tightly, kissing her eyes, her mouth, her hair. Laughing and crying, she returned his kisses eagerly.

"Lydia, I've been looking for you for two days. I was terrified I might not ever see *you* again. Where have you been?

Are you unharmed?"

"The mob came to the house, Christian. We had to flee for our lives."

"I know. I went there. The place was a shambles. Where did you go?"

"We ran into the woods and hid there for what must have been hours. It seemed the mob was all around us. We could hear their fiendish cries from every quarter. I was so frightened, Christian."

"I know," he murmured, holding her close.

"Later, near morning, we crept to the Whitmer settlement on the Blue. Hiram and Catherine Page took us in. Brother Page brought me here a little while ago. He said you'd been inquiring in the settlement for me." She shivered, recalling the whole terrifying experience.

"It's a miracle the mob didn't hurt you." Christian looked deeply into her eyes. "I'm going to take care of you, Lydia. You and the children. There's no need for you to be afraid anymore."

Tears welled up in Lydia's eyes. He kissed her again and then helped her to her feet.

"Come on," he said softly, "Let's go downstairs where we can talk without waking the children."

Christian put his arm around her and together they descended the staircase.

CHAPTER SEVENTEEN

The following night the mob attacked the Whitmer settlement along the Blue again. Lyman Wight and his band of Saints engaged them in a fierce fight where gunfire was exchanged and several men on both sides were injured. The next morning Christian learned that the state militia had been called out at the instigation of Lieutenant-Governor Boggs. A Colonel Pitcher was given the command. Christian didn't know Pitcher, but he hoped the man would show some integrity.

Later in the day Christian went in to Independence to see what he could learn about the mob's activities. Many members of the mob were now part of the militia, and when Christian saw them assembled, he was dismayed to find the two groups almost indistinguishable. He also learned more about the character of Colonel Pitcher. Apparently, Pitcher had been in the thick of mob action from the beginning. His name was affixed to the mob's July 23rd manifesto and he'd been at the forefront of the persecution ever since. Christian was appalled that a man like Pitcher should be put in command of the militia. He wondered if the Lieutenant-Governor knew about Pitcher's activities.

As the afternoon shadows lengthened Christian started back to Seth's cabin. When he arrived he was greeted by more bad news. Seth informed him that Brother Barber, injured in the fighting the night before, had died and two of the mob had died as well. Christian feared that more trouble would erupt in retaliation for the night's bloodshed.

Christian and Lydia spent a restless night sheltered in the cramped cabin on the prairie. The other family who had been sharing the cabin with Seth and Carrie had moved on, frightened away by the mob's bold actions. Since then, Seth and Christian had been taking turns standing watch outside the cabin. Christian had been on guard duty during the midnight hours and had tumbled into bed, exhausted, after Seth came to relieve him. He was awakened at first light by voices talking in low tones outside the house. He pulled on his trousers and quietly slipped out the door. Near the corner of the cabin he found Seth in conversation with John Corrill. John gestured in greeting when he saw Christian approaching.

"Hello, John. Is there news from Independence?"

"I was just telling Seth that Pitcher has ordered the Saints to surrender their arms."

Christian wiped his hand across his brow in a gesture of futility.

"What do the brethren advise?" Seth asked, a deep scowl lining his forehead.

"The Bishop refused to comply with the order unless the mob is also disarmed. Pitcher gave his word to that effect."

"Gave his word?" Christian repeated incredulously. "The man's word is worthless."

"The Lieutenant-Governor has assured us their weapons will be confiscated along with our own. He insists it is the only way to restore order. Bishop Partridge sent me to inform you of the decision and request you to deliver up any arms you may have peaceably."

"Who do we deliver them up to? The mob?" Seth asked, his voice thick with sarcasm.

"A committee has been appointed to receive them, Seth," Corrill said evenly. "They'll arrive some time today. We'd like you to comply with the decision, brethren."

Seth and Christian exchanged helpless glances.

"Seth and I both have rifles. We'll have them ready when the committee arrives."

"Thank you. I pray this will put an end to the hostilities and we can get back to some semblance of a normal life."

Christian looked down at his feet lest his eyes betray the doubt he felt.

Corrill shook their hands and then mounted his horse and rode away to inform the others in the settlement of the decision. Seth and Christian said nothing for several seconds. Seth finally broke the silence. "Well, that's it. Unarmed, they'll fall on us like a pack of wolves among sheep."

Seth's prediction proved to be correct. The committee to receive the arms from the Saints did, indeed, arrive later that morning. Christian was especially galled to find Henry Chiles at the head of the committee. The pompous lawyer relieved Christian of his gun with a gloating sneer. It took all the control Christian could muster to keep from striking him.

Although Pitcher had pledged his honor, the mob's weapons were not confiscated. It wasn't an hour before a group of armed men fell on the prairie settlement. Cries of warning went up among the brethren as horsemen rode into the settlement firing their guns and shouting obscenities. Christian and Seth, who had been seated at the table, stood up in alarm just as the cabin door burst open and a grizzled man lunged inside, pointing a loaded pistol at them.

"Clear out of here 'fore I smather yer brains all over them walls. Move! Now!"

Lydia, Carrie and the children pressed together against the back wall of the cabin. Seth stepped in front of them and said, "We're unarmed here. Leave us in peace and we'll pack up our belongings."

"I ain't givin' you even five minutes. You Mormonites been trouble long enough. You git out now or them women will be totin' you out feet first."

"Let's do as he says," whispered Carrie, grasping her husband's arm.

The man with the gun waved it wildly over their heads. "I said move!" Seth and Christian exchanged a hesitant glance while they sized up the possibility of attacking the man and taking his gun from him, but the screams and firing coming from the other cabins in the settlement convinced them they had no choice but to comply.

"Lydia, you and the others go on outside," Christian directed in a calm voice.

Carrie and the children filed out the cabin door while the gunman watched them with a wary eye. As Lydia followed behind them, she made a quick grab for their blankets which were folded and stacked on the edge of the bunk. Christian's eye flew to the gunman to see if he would allow this slight indiscretion of his orders.

He scowled fiercely at Lydia, but made no move to relieve her of the blankets.

When the women and children were safely outside, Christian said with his voice full of scorn, "I guess Pitcher forgot to relieve you and your friends of your arms."

The gunman lunged forward and without a second's hesitation whipped the butt of his gun across Christian's jaw. Christian fell back, stunned by the blow. Seth, standing slightly behind him, grabbed Christian's arm to prevent him from falling.

"We've had our fill of your smart-talkin' kind. What's happened now to your tales of claimin' this county? The only claim you're gonna have is a place in hell." The gunman spat a jet of tobacco juice onto the floor and grinned maniacally.

"You filthy swine . . ." Seth began.

With a swoop, the gunman seized the end of a burning log from the fireplace and lifted it to the curtain covering the window next to him. The curtain ignited in a burst of flame. "Did your Joe Smith prophesy this?" he cried.

Seth jumped backward as the gunman threw the smoldering log onto the rag rug at his feet. The intruder fired his pistol into the air and shouted in a hoarse voice, "If I see you agin in these parts, I'll murder you on the spot. Now, get out!"

Seth gave the madman a final glare and headed toward the door. Christian, his chin bleeding from the blow to his jaw, angrily followed him out of the burning cabin.

Christian and the others trudged north along the Blue toward the Missouri River. A haze of smoke hung in the air from the burning cabins in the settlement; the smell of it filled Christian's nostrils. Christian carried James in his arms, while Elizabeth held tightly onto her mother's hand, white-knuckled, and too frightened to cry. When at last they spotted the

Missouri, Christian was astonished to see the throngs of people who lined its shore. Wagons, tents, campfires, and a milling crowd gave the place the appearance of a camp meeting. It seemed as if the whole population of Jackson County were camped along the river bank. The scene up and down the river was one of confusion. Christian heard the frightened cries of children and the bellowing of cattle. A jumble of people and goods lined the ferry landing waiting to be taken across the swift-flowing Missouri.

Christian and his party made their way down to the river's edge. The cold November night was rapidly closing in on them and the air was ripe with the expectation of rain. A wagon rattled across the hard ground a few feet away. From its open tail, Christian saw an elderly woman peering out from beneath her bonnet, her wrinkled face haggard and careworn.

Seth pointed to an open fire a few feet away. Christian nodded and led the group toward it.

"May we share your fire, Brother?" Christian asked the gaunt figure standing nearby.

"Aye. Sit down and warm yourselves."

Christian did not know his benefactor, but he was grateful for the man's hospitality. He and Seth spread out one of the blankets on the ground for the women and children to sit on.

The thin man who tended the fire offered them a bit of jerky from a pouch slung around his shoulder. "It's all I got, but it might help to fill the hole in your bellies."

"Thank you," Christian answered, handing the meager portions of jerky around. Until he bit into the salty stuff, Christian hadn't realized how ravenous he was. None of them had eaten since morning and it was likely they would have nothing more that night.

"You people come from Independence?" their host asked.

"Yes. We have homes in town. That is, we used to have homes. The mob drove us off and torched our fields and houses," Seth answered in a bitter voice.

"Most of these folks," the man said, taking in the panorama along the river with a sweep of his arm, "come from Independence. Some been here almost two days now, waitin' to get across the river. Burned out just like you folks."

"You're from Independence, too?" Christian asked.

"No, not me. I had a real nice little place on the prairie 'bout twelve, fourteen miles from town. Driven out, the same as you." The man lapsed into silence, his sunken eyes staring fixedly into the fire.

Christian dropped next to Lydia on the ground. She looked at him silently, her eyes gray in the night shadows. Christian took her hand. It was icy cold. "We'll be all right," he told her with a confidence he didn't feel.

She nodded, then bent down to pull the corner of the blanket over Elizabeth and James.

Christian looked over at the children; their eyes were closed and their breathing rhythmic. "Are they asleep already?" he asked softly.

"Yes. They're exhausted." She sighed and stared into the fire.

Christian leaned back and closed his eyes. The scene at the prairie settlement again closed in around him—the burning cabin, the curling smoke, the crazed man with the gun. He squeezed his eyes tightly shut in hopes of blotting out the vision.

When he opened them, he found Lydia watching him. Christian gave her a quick smile and squeezed her hand.

"Do you think they'll pursue us even here?" she asked after a moment's silence.

Christian looked out past the fires burning along the river bottoms. The barren branches of the trees assumed ghostly poses in the darkness. He shook his head. "I don't know."

A few feet away the Whitfields sat huddled against the cold. Carrie moaned softly and in the dim light from the fire Christian watched as Seth put his arm around her and pulled her close.

"In the morning I'll cut some branches to build a shelter for us until we can get a place on the ferry," Christian said.

"Christian?"

"Yes?"

"What's going to happen to us?"

Christian looked into her face. He could see the dancing flames of the fire reflected in her eyes. "We'll get through this. If we have to find a new place to live, we will. The Saints made a home in Independence; they can make another wherever the Lord directs."

Lydia's soft brows drew together. "Is he directing us still?"

Christian took her firmly by the shoulders. "Do you recall the time I asked you that same question? It was at the Whitmers', while I was recuperating. Can you remember your answer to me?"

She shook her head, avoiding his eyes.

"You said the Lord would never abandon his Saints and that we mustn't give up trying."

"Did I?" she answered faintly.

"Those were your exact words. And do you know what, Lydia? You were right. You were right," he said, repeating the words almost to himself. He lifted her chin with his fingers and gently kissed her.

When he released her, she gazed for a long moment into his eyes. "I love you so, Christian," she said quietly.

Her words sent his heart soaring. The weariness in his body and the harrowing memory of the day's events disappeared like snow on a warm April day. For that moment, Christian was the happiest man in the world.

During the night it began to rain. Christian quickly made a tent out of the blankets for Lydia and the children. He sat at the edge of the makeshift shelter, more outside than in. The rain came down in torrents and within minutes they were camped in a field of mud. Christian pulled his hat low over his forehead, but the rain ran down his neck in rivulets, soaking him to the skin. Having nothing more with which to protect himself, he spent the remainder of the night hunched against the storm.

The next morning Christian was up stretching his frozen limbs as the sun broke over the prairie. He walked through the camps, taking in the desperate circumstances of his brethren. Like himself, most had spent the night in the open air. What few had shelter from wagons or log huts had shared with others. Those who managed to escape with their wagons and goods were fortunate; most of the Saints had been driven before the mob with only the clothes on their backs. Many families had become separated from one another. Some of the men in camp were frantically searching for their wives, and children were inquiring after their parents.

As Christian started back to his campsite, he saw Lydia hurrying to meet him. Her face and clothing were streaked with dried mud from the night's rain, and her long red hair hung tangled around her shoulders. In spite of her disheveled appearance, Christian thought she was the most beautiful woman he'd ever known. A shiver of pleasure passed over him as he contemplated life with Lydia at his side. He resolved to formally ask for her hand in marriage at the first opportunity. She had said that she loved him. He fervently hoped she would not hesitate to say yes to his proposal. Christian's heart beat faster as the distance between them vanished. When she reached his side Christian suddenly noticed her look of consternation.

"Christian, Carrie is in labor."

"Are you sure?" Christian exclaimed.

"She's been having pains most of the night. Seth has moved her into one of the Saint's wagons."

"But Lydia, Carrie can't have the baby now. It's too soon." Lydia's eyes grew big and round.

"The baby's not due for six or seven weeks yet. Seth told me not more than a couple of days ago."

"Oh, Christian, giving birth is difficult enough in the best of circumstances, but here in the wilds, without proper shelter . . . and the child premature. . . ." Lydia frowned and bit her lip.

At that moment Seth came barreling out of the thick brush along the river's edge. "Lydia, you've got to help. The baby's coming!"

Lydia shot Christian a desperate look, then whirled on her heel and followed Seth to the wagon where Carrie lay.

Christian could feel his heart pounding in his throat. Quickly he threaded his way behind them, through the barren clumps of bush and rain-soaked scrub. He found Seth pacing back and forth in front of the wagon.

"Why didn't she tell me it was her time?" Seth kept repeating.

"Take it easy, Seth. Carrie probably wanted to spare you as long as she could. Babies sometimes take a long time coming into this world."

A moaning wail came from the wagon behind them. Seth froze in his steps, a wild look coming into his eyes. "What if she dies, Christian? I couldn't live without her. How can a woman have a child in circumstances like these and live through it?"

Christian racked his brain for some words of comfort and reassurance. "Indian women give birth all the time out-of-doors," he said. The analogy seemed pathetic, but it was all he could come up with. "Try not to worry, Seth. Lydia's with her and she's had some experience at this sort of thing. She delivered one of the Johnson babies in Independence."

Seth renewed his pacing, barely listening to Christian. Elizabeth and James, who sat throwing twigs into the camp-fire, watched Seth intently. Neither of the children spoke, but nothing escaped their notice.

After what seemed like an endless wait, Lydia appeared at the rear of the wagon, wiping her hands on a bit of stained cloth. Seth rushed to her.

"It's a boy, Brother Whitfield. Your wife did fine. She wants to see you."

Seth clamped his hands over Lydia's, wordlessly communicating his gratitude. Then he clamored inside the wagon.

"How is Carrie?" Christian asked, coming to Lydia's side.

"All right for the moment. The child's such a tiny little thing, Christian." She frowned, lost in thought.

Christian put an arm around her and held her close against him.

"He may not survive," she added quietly.

"What?" Christian stepped back so he could read her expression.

"The baby is struggling for his life." Lydia kept her eyes downcast, unable to meet Christian's shocked stare.

Christian swallowed hard. He'd been so concerned about Carrie, he'd given scant thought to the child. "What are the baby's chances?"

"I don't know." She shrugged helplessly.

"Then we'll hope and pray for the best."

Seth and Carrie named their child Charles Seth Whitfield. The baby lived only a day and a half. Christian helped Seth carve a grave out of the hard ground, then he and Lydia watched as Seth laid his son inside and covered him with the cold Missouri sod. It was the most heart-wrenching moment Christian had ever experienced. The sorrow he felt for the grieving parents brought stinging tears to his eyes.

The following day word came that space was available on the ferry. Carrie was still too weak to walk. Seth carried her to the little grave tucked among the trees, where they paused with heads bowed. Then all of them boarded the ferry. Christian sat close to Lydia and the children, his hand clutching Lydia's.

The ferry pulled out into the muddy, swirling waters and slowly churned ahead. Silently, Christian watched the bank recede. Slipping away with the bleak Missouri shoreline were the Saints' hopes and dreams of building Zion. Zion, the land of promise. Christian tried in vain to swallow the lump rising in his throat.

That night, camped on the other side of the river, Christian drew Lydia aside to a place where they could be alone. They sat together on the fallen branch of an old cottonwood tree. The night was clear and cold. Scores of fires burned along both sides of the Missouri. The sky, too, burned with countless points of starlight.

Christian took Lydia's hand and with pounding heart said to her, "Lydia, I don't know how all of this is going to turn out, but there is one thing I am certain of. I want to share the rest of my life with you. I need you beside me; together we can deal with whatever comes." He swallowed and his hands felt clammy against hers. "Will you marry me, Lydia?"

"Oh, yes!" She threw her arms around his neck and hugged him so tightly Christian could feel the racing of her heart. "I love you, Christian."

"I give you my word I'll be a good father to James and Elizabeth."

She drew back, giving him a solemn look. "I have no doubt of that."

Christian could hardly contain the joy that exploded inside him. He swept her into his arms and kissed her. "I love you, Lydia. I love you!"

She returned his kisses with an eagerness that sent his heart reeling.

"When will you marry me?" he asked, grinning.

"Whenever you like."

"Is tomorrow too soon?"

She laughed and gave him a hug. Her shining eyes were all the reply he needed.

"I'll see if I can locate Bishop Partridge in the morning and we'll get things started." Christian paused, his brow furrowing slightly. "Lydia, we're not far from Quincy. Would you prefer to wait until your family can be with us?"

Lydia's eyes strayed past him. "No," she answered after a moment's thought. "I don't want to wait, even if it means marrying without my family around me."

"I was hoping you'd say that."

They settled back comfortably into one another's arms, neither of them speaking, simply relishing the moment.

Lydia was the first to break the silence. "Do you know," she said in a musing tone of voice, "when I first began to love you?"

"No," he answered. "When?"

"It was the evening of Sarah Whitmer's social gathering. Do you remember? You came over to the table where I was putting out cakes and started talking to me as if we'd known one another for years. I was impressed by your manner, and I thought how handsome you were."

"Is that right? What else did you think about me?"

"I thought you must not get cake very often because you were gobbling down one piece after another."

Christian laughed. "That's because it was my only excuse for staying to talk with you."

Lydia's voice took on a melancholy note. "I thought my life was over before I met you." She sighed and leaned her head against Christian's shoulder. "It seems such a long time ago, doesn't it?"

"Yes. A lifetime ago." Christian stared pensively out across the winding Missouri, memories tumbling over one another in his head.

"We'll make a new start, Christian. Together." She looked

up into his face, her eyes luminous in the glow of the camp fires. "Let's forget the past and concentrate on the future."

"You're right. And no more log cabins. I'll build us a proper house—the finest house in Missouri."

Lydia was silent for a moment. "This may sound strange, but Missouri has been a blessing to me. It brought me the gospel. And it brought me you."

"Then some good has come out of our struggles in Missouri after all," Christian said quietly. He held her tightly in his arms. "I've waited all my life for you, Lydia," he whispered.

"The whole damage, [is] more than the State of Missouri is worth."

Amanda Barnes Smith
Early Missouri Saint

CHAPTER EIGHTEEN

L ydia bent over the big black kettle hanging from its hook on the hearth. She sniffed at the corn meal mush bubbling and roiling inside, and gave it a quick stir with her spoon. As she laid the long-handled metal spoon aside, she spied Christian's copy of the *Western Monitor* on the floor near her feet. She picked up the newspaper and put it back on the table. Smiling, she smoothed the pages of the news-sheet, thinking of her husband.

She had been Mrs. Christian Kent for nearly five weeks and in that time had been happier than she thought possible. Christian was everything she knew he would be—kind, thoughtful, gentle and loving. And he was marvelous with Elizabeth and James. James adored him and was already calling him papa. It would take a bit longer for Elizabeth.

She thought back to the afternoon when she'd taken Elizabeth aside, in the miserable bottoms of the Missouri River, and told her about Christian's proposal. Afterward, Elizabeth had one question—would Christian be her new papa? Lydia had tried to explain that Christian could never take the place of her papa, but he loved her very much, and he wanted them to be a family together. Elizabeth had just stared at her.

Even now she was a bit reticent around him, but Lydia was sure Christian would eventually win her affection. As for herself, she was completely and utterly in love with him. Sometimes she felt a tinge of guilt because of the happiness that was hers. Life had never been so sweet with Abraham. The joy and contentment she experienced in being Christian's wife colored her every thought.

She put the lid back on the kettle and began setting plates on the table for the evening meal. The square table was made of fine sturdy oak, a wedding gift from Seth and Carrie. Since her marriage, she had grown even closer to the Whitfields. The friendship had taken deep root during the trying days after the death of Carrie's baby, a time that was bittersweet in Lydia's memory.

After crossing the Missouri, Christian had found an abandoned shack several hundred yards from the shore. It was filthy and ramshackled, but Lydia was grateful for its shelter. Christian had located Bishop Partridge ministering among the destitute Saints on the Jackson side of the river. He'd brought the Bishop back across with him and Bishop Partridge had married them the following day in a clearing just a few feet from the Missouri shore. Even though their circumstances were dire, it was a glorious occasion, one Lydia would treasure forever. Christian had just recently completed the tiny, although snug and well-built, log shelter they were presently occupying. Almost everything she and Christian owned, including their food and clothing, had been donated to them by the kind citizens of Clay County.

Both Christian and Seth had since obtained work splitting rails for a farmer outside Liberty. Christian worked from sunrise to sunset. He'd just received his first wages and gone into town that morning with Seth to purchase some much needed food and supplies. Lydia expected him back shortly. Her mouth fairly watered for the tangy taste of smoked bacon and fresh-baked bread. The corn meal cooking in the hearth was the last bit of food they had on hand.

Lydia looked up when she heard the sound of wagon wheels crunching across the frost-covered yard. A moment later Christian thrust open the cabin door and stuck his head inside.

"Lydia?"

"I'm here," she answered, placing the last plate on the table.

"I've brought you home a surprise." He grinned and ducked back outside.

"What in the world . . . ?" She'd just taken a step toward

the door when Christian bobbed back inside, pulling someone along by the elbow.

Lydia gasped when she saw who it was. "Philip!" She ran
to her brother's arms. Philip hugged her while Christian
stood grinning at the pair of them.

"I been lookin' for you for over three weeks!" Philip
exclaimed.

"What are you doing here? How did you ever find us?"
Lydia asked, laughing and hugging him again.

"It was Christian who found *me,*" smiled Philip. Lydia
looked at Christian questioningly.

"I was in the Feed and Seed getting my supplies when I
overheard this fellow asking the proprietor if he knew a Lydia
Dawson. He said he was her brother. So I introduced myself."

"He came up to me, put out his hand, and said, 'How do
you do, my name is Kent. I'm Lydia's husband.' Needless to
say, I was a little surprised," Philip related.

Lydia threw back her head and laughed heartily. "That
sounds like Christian." She wrapped her arms around
Christian's neck and kissed him. He kissed her in return and
they exchanged a tender smile.

"Take off your coat, Philip, and tell me all the news," Lydia
said, as she held out her hands for his coat. "Are Ma and Pa
well, and the family?"

"They're all fine. It's *you* we've been worried about. I came
out to find you as soon as we got the news about the trouble
in Independence."

"I should have known you'd come to help me."

"It appears you've been well taken care of," he answered,
glancing at Christian.

"Did Christian tell you all about us?"

"Some. May I offer my congratulations, Liddy." Philip
kissed her cheek.

"Thank you, Philip. I'm very happy. Happier than I've ever
been in my life."

Philip looked a little discomfited. Lydia suspected the sudden change in her marital status would take some getting
used to on Philip's part.

"Here, Philip, have a seat," Christian suggested, pulling a

chair over for him. "You're welcome to stay with us as long as you can."

"You must stay, Philip. I've missed you and I have so much to tell you," Lydia added excitedly.

"You two get reacquainted while I bring in the supplies," Christian said. He smiled at Lydia, then went outside to the wagon.

"Oh, Philip, I'm so glad to see you," Lydia repeated.

"You too, Sis. I've been worried as blazes about you."

"You got my letter?"

Philip nodded. "That's why I was concerned. After I found out you'd joined with the Mormons and then with them havin' all this trouble . . ." Philip frowned.

"I know. About the Mormons, Philip," she paused, choosing her words, "I hope you'll understand my feelings and accept me as one of them."

Philip looked at her. "I can't pretend I agree with what you've done, Liddy. But if you believe the Mormon religion is right for you, I'll accept that. It may not be as easy for the rest of the family, though."

"What do you mean?"

"Pa was real angry when he got word you'd been baptized."

Lydia's eyes suddenly brimmed with tears. "I knew he would be. Please talk to him for me, Philip. Explain to him that being a member of the Mormon faith is important to me. Try to make him understand."

"These should keep us stocked up for a while," Christian announced, as he came inside carrying a large box filled with goods. He set the box down on the table and glanced over at Lydia. His smile faded when he saw her troubled eyes.

Lydia got up abruptly from her chair and began unloading the goods. "Thank you, darlin'. I'll put these things away."

Christian slipped an arm around her waist. With a quick smile, Lydia indicated that everything was all right. He nodded, then went back outside to get the remainder of the supplies.

"You haven't seen 'Lizabeth or James, yet," Lydia said to Philip in a deliberately cheerful voice.

"No, where are they?"

"They've spent most of the afternoon with the Whitfields, friends of ours. They'll be thrilled to see you. I'll ask Christian to go bring them home."

"Fine. Let me help you with those goods, Liddy."

Lydia was right about Elizabeth and James. They were overjoyed to see their uncle. They chattered and laughed with him all through supper and afterward it was a major endeavor to get them settled down for the night. When at last they fell asleep, Christian helped Philip lay out his bedroll in front of the hearth and then the three adults sat down to a quiet evening of conversation.

"Philip, has Katherine had her baby? Mother told me she was expecting, but I haven't heard the outcome," Lydia inquired, thinking of her eldest brother, John, and his large family.

"Yes, two months ago. A daughter—and bald as an eggshell." Philip chuckled with the thought.

"What did they name her?"

"Ellen. Ellen Marie, I believe it is."

"Oh, how lovely. I wish I could see her. Christian, do you think we could take a trip to Quincy in the spring?"

"Of course, as soon as you'd like." Christian took Lydia's hand and squeezed it.

"I can hardly wait. I'm so anxious to see Charlotte and the children, John, and Mother and Father."

Philip's blue eyes clouded and he glanced away. Lydia wasn't sure what the change in his expression meant. "Philip? There's nothing wrong at home you're not telling me about, is there?"

"No, everyone's fine. We'll be lookin' forward to your visit." He smiled, but the expression was forced.

"We'd be pleased to have your family come to stay with us, Philip. Any time you can," Christian told him.

"Thanks, but I don't believe we could all fit in your cabin."

Although Philip made the comment lightly, Christian's reply was in solemn earnest. "I know this place isn't suitable for Lydia and the children, but it's only temporary. I plan to build a solid home for us as soon as we get our lands back in Jackson County."

"I didn't mean to insinuate that you haven't provided properly for Lydia . . ." Philip began.

"I know that. I just want you to understand that this isn't the kind of place I'd allow my family to live under ordinary circumstances. I've five acres of ground in Independence and a strong back to build a decent home."

Philip fell silent. Lydia guessed he hadn't expected Christian to bristle at his innocent remark. She tried to explain their feelings to him.

"Jackson County's our home, Philip. The Lord has promised it to us. This trouble with the Missourians is only temporary like Christian said. We'll probably be back in Independence before the winter's over, just as soon as the brethren can settle matters there."

"I can't believe you'd want to go back there with the kind of lawlessness that's going on."

"We can't stand back and allow it to happen, Philip," Christian told him in a determined voice. "Our rights have been trampled on, our freedoms denied. Property has been either destroyed or illegally confiscated, and our reputations slandered. We intend to regain what's legally and rightfully ours. The constitution guarantees us those rights and the government is our ally."

"I gather you've taken the matter up with the authorities," Philip commented.

"The Governor intends to employ every means the Constitution and the laws of the land have placed at his disposal. I talked with Sidney Gilbert this morning in town, Lydia. He told me that our attorneys had received a letter from Mr. Wells, the attorney-general of Missouri. The Governor advised Wells that if we wish to return to our homes in Jackson County, an adequate force of state militia will be sent out to accomplish that end."

"Will the militia stay in Jackson County to enforce order?"

"Sidney didn't know the details yet. He did say that Governor Dunklin has ordered a court of inquiry into the matter. Sidney's afraid, though, that an immediate inquiry will deprive us of the opportunity of having witnesses for our defense appear at the court in Independence. Trying to bring witnesses into Independence right now would be suicidal. The mob is as active as ever and the safety of the witnesses would be in jeopardy."

"Has any word been received from the Prophet?" Lydia asked.

"None that I know of, but I don't believe Brother Joseph's had sufficient time to be fully apprised of the situation. Sidney told me that Bishop Partridge and William Phelps have both sent letters to him outlining what the circumstances are here."

"I hope things work out for you," Philip said. "It's a disgrace to the state of Missouri to allow a thing like this to happen in the first place."

Christian nodded gravely. Lydia mulled over the things Christian had told them. She, too, hoped the situation would work itself out in the Saint's favor. But the night's conversation left her with a feeling of dread.

"No! No! Leave me alone!" The terrified cry rang out in the midnight stillness of the cabin. Lydia leaped to her feet and was at Elizabeth's side in an instant. The child was curled up into a ball, her body trembling with fright.

"'Lizabeth, wake up! You're dreaming." Lydia shook the little girl's shoulder. Elizabeth's eyes fluttered open and she began to whimper. "It's only a dream, darlin'. You're safe. Shhh, now." Lydia rocked the child in her arms.

Elizabeth continued to moan softly, then said, "Mama, I was so afraid. They caught me and wouldn't let me go."

"There now, it's all over. It was only a bad dream." Lydia stroked her golden curls, clammy with perspiration, even though the night was very cold. "Lie down now and try to sleep. I'm right here and so is Christian. Go to sleep, darlin'."

Elizabeth haltingly obeyed, lying down again on her pallet next to James. James muttered and turned over onto his stomach.

"Don't leave me, Mama," Elizabeth murmured as she closed her eyes.

"I won't darlin'. I'll be right here."

When Lydia tiptoed back to her own bed a few moments later, she found Christian sitting up waiting for her.

"Is she all right?"

Lydia nodded. "She's gone back to sleep."

From his place near the hearth, Philip rose up on one elbow, his shadowy figure outlined in black by the dying embers. "Lydia, the child sounded terrified."

"It's these nightmares she's plagued with. She dreams men are chasing her, trying to hurt her," Lydia answered in a quiet voice.

"Sweet charity," Philip breathed. "Does this happen often?"

"It has for the last few weeks. Since we were driven out of Independence."

Philip stayed with Christian and Lydia for the next few days. He helped Christian put up some split rail fencing and clear a few feet of dead brush from around the cabin. When Christian was at work on his employer's farm, Philip chatted with Lydia and her children. Lydia relished his companionship and during the long hours they spent together they talked of many things. She told him about the Church and about the teachings of the gospel of Jesus Christ. He listened politely and asked a few questions, but let her know in a kindly way that he was not interested in embracing her beliefs.

One afternoon as they visited together, he said to her, "Liddy, as much as I hate to, I have to be goin'. I thought I'd leave for home in the mornin'. I been gone from my family for quite a spell."

Lydia blinked back tears that came surging to her eyes. "I knew you wouldn't be able to stay long, Philip."

He thrust his hand into his trouser pocket and took out a small stack of dollar bills, folded over and clasped together with a metal clip. He separated several bills, and held them out to Lydia. "Here, I want you to take this. It's not much, but it will help out some."

Lydia shook her head. "No, Philip. I can't take your money. Christian and I will be fine."

"Listen here, Liddy. I came all the way out here to find you and take you home with me. Charlotte and I intended to have you live with us. Now you're married, you got a place of your own, but I want to do somethin' for you. Please don't deny me that. Take this money and use it for the children if you like."

The tears spilled over and rolled down her cheeks. "I love

you, Philip. But I don't want your money, and neither would Christian."

"Hogwash. Christian won't mind. He's a sensible sort. Just tell him James and 'Lizabeth's uncle wanted to give it to them." Philip thrust the bills into her hands.

Lydia hesitantly closed her fist around the money, then leaned over to kiss Philip's cheek.

"Now, there's nothin' more that needs to be said about it," Philip replied brusquely, stuffing the remainder of the money back into his pocket. "Speakin' of that husband of yours, Liddy, I think you made one heck of a good match, even if the man is a Mormon." Philip winked his eye at her, and grinned.

The following morning Lydia prepared to send the children to the Whitfields while she and Christian accompanied Philip into Liberty. From there Philip would travel alone back to Quincy. While she helped the children dress, Philip went outside to talk with Christian. Christian was fitting a harness onto the horse and hitching him to the wagon. Philip walked up to his side.

"Ready to go?" Christian asked with a smile.

Philip nodded.

"I know Lydia has thoroughly enjoyed your company."

"I've enjoyed bein' with her, too." Christian continued harnessing the horse to the wagon. "Christian?" Christian looked over at him. "I'd like to talk to you about somethin' before Lydia comes out if you wouldn't mind."

"Sure." Christian gave Philip his full attention.

"I should have said somethin' to Lydia before, but I couldn't bear to spoil her pleasure. I haven't seen her this happy in a long time."

"What is it, Philip?"

"It concerns our Pa. You'd have to know Pa to understand his feelin's. He was brought up by the rule. A child did what his Pa told him, no exceptions. That's how he raised us. Obedience and holdin' to family traditions have always been real important to him. You see, Pa's family have been Baptists for generations."

Christian shook his head. "I know what you're going to say,

Philip. Your father is angry with Lydia for joining the Mormon church."

"It's worse than that. He's disowned her."

"What?" Christian said in consternation.

"He won't even let her name be spoken in his house. He's forbidden the rest of us to have anythin' to do with her."

"Oh, no."

"Ma's broken-hearted about it. She's not as unbending as Pa. I told her I was comin' out here to get Liddy and bring her home but Pa wouldn't have allowed it if he'd known."

"Philip, that news will break Lydia's heart."

"I know. That's why I couldn't tell her. If she's plannin' to come out to Quincy this spring, she's got to know beforehand."

"She has to be told in any event. Do you want me to do it?"

"I was thinkin' maybe she'd take it easier comin' from you."

"I'll tell her this evening."

Philip nodded, his expression glum.

"I know you'll do all you can to change your father's mind."

"I've tried. And John's tried."

"Well, don't give up. Maybe you should go back inside before Lydia suspects something is wrong. I don't want a thing like this to ruin the few remaining hours she has left with you."

Philip nodded and slowly returned to the house.

Christian and Lydia saw Philip off, then spent a few hours in Liberty seeing the town. Lydia had never been there before and Christian showed her a few of the shops and places of business, and introduced her to some of the people he had met. Lydia guessed that the town of Liberty was about the size of Independence. The people were generally friendly, and the town seemed to be growing and prosperous.

As she and Christian strolled arm in arm down the plank walkway, bundled against the cold, he commented to her, "This town has one thing Independence is lacking and that's a thriving business sector. There are banks, offices and mercantiles all up and down this street."

"There's something else Liberty has plenty of," Lydia said with a small smile.

"What's that?"

"Saloons. I've never seen so many saloons in all my life."

Christian laughed. "I guess you're right about that."

They hadn't gone more than a few feet when a woman approaching from the opposite direction stopped abruptly in front of them.

"Why, I declare, if it isn't Christian Kent!" she said in a sugar-coated voice.

Lydia didn't recognize her, but she noticed immediately the young woman's pretty face and expensive clothing. She had on a light blue velvet skirt with wide pleats and a silk ruffled blouse. A skirt-length cloak, trimmed in blue, draped her shoulders. On her blond head she wore a bonnet adorned with ribbons. The woman's eyes were a striking color of green, and her mouth ruby red.

"Hello, Mary Ann," Christian said dryly. "Lydia, this is Mary Ann Stewart. Mary Ann, my wife, Lydia."

Mary Ann Stewart's mouth dropped open and it was some seconds before she recovered herself. She put a gloved hand out for Lydia to take. "How nice to meet you, my dear." Her voice was silky, but her green eyes flashed.

Lydia took her proffered hand and they exchanged a brief touch. "It's very nice to meet you, Miss Stewart."

Mary Ann's eyes flickered over Lydia's person, and a slight expression of disdain crept into her face. Her gaze then immediately shifted to Christian. "Are you and your wife living in Liberty?" she asked him sweetly.

"No, we've a place a few miles outside of town."

"You must stop by the house and say hello to my parents while you're here. They'd love to see you."

Christian frowned. "Maybe some other time. It's nice to see you, Mary Ann." He took Lydia's hand and, tipping his hat, moved past Mary Ann. She stood for an instant looking after them, and then tossing her head, turned and stalked away.

Christian walked briskly ahead, saying nothing. Lydia glanced up at him. He was scowling fiercely. She couldn't resist teasing him just a bit. "She's very pretty, Christian."

"Harump," Christian answered in reply.

"You weren't very friendly, you know," Lydia added, trying to keep from smiling.

He looked quickly down into her face. "You're making fun of me," he smiled, giving her hand a quick squeeze.

"Only a little."

He bent down and kissed her cheek. "I suppose it's just as well you've met her. I'm embarrassed to think I was ever stupid enough to care anything about her."

"Don't be so hard on yourself. She really is very attractive."

"She's deceptive and manipulative. I can't believe I didn't perceive that at the time. Did you hear her say how her parents would 'love to see me'?" His mouth took on a distasteful look. "Her parents despise me."

"Now, Christian, you don't know that."

"They told me so! Let's forget it, shall we? The subject's not worth the breath it takes to talk about it."

He took a firm hold of Lydia's hand as they continued down the plank walk.

The night after Philip left for Quincy, Christian had related to Lydia as gently as he could the devastating news Philip had told him. At first Lydia couldn't believe her ears, and then as the fact settled in that she had been disowned by her father, she wept with shock and dismay. Christian had held her in his arms while she sobbed like a child. All through the winter months she struggled with this new burden. Both Philip and John had written her letters, but the one person she yearned to hear from remained stonily silent. The hurt she carried weighed upon her heart.

With the birth of spring Lydia's spirits lifted, buoyed by the reawakening of life surrounding her. She tenderly cultivated the wildflowers that sprang up beside the cabin door, and planted squash, peas, and beans in the garden spot Christian had cleared for her. She and Christian clung to their hope of returning to Jackson County, even though the pleas to Missouri officials had failed to produce results. The Prophet had written from Kirtland advising the Saints not to sell their lands in Zion, and expressing his sympathy for their plight. Some of the brethren had sent money to aid the Saints in the West. News arrived from Kirtland that many of the brethren were preparing to come to their assistance. In the meanwhile, the Saints in Clay County were pursuing every method of civil and judicial redress available to them, and Church leaders had written to the President of the United States asking for his help. But still the Saints were no closer to having their properties and rights restored.

"I'm astounded by President Jackson's refusal to help us," Christian was saying as he and Lydia visited with the Whitfields. "I always believed he was a champion of the common people, but I can see I was badly mistaken."

"You sound like one of those Whigs calling for the President's head," Seth replied.

"Maybe I am. Jackson should have offered us some assistance."

"He probably doesn't wish to become embroiled in another states' rights controversy and that's how he views this issue."

"Religious persecution is a violation of federal, not state, laws," Christian replied indignantly. "The federal government has the authority and the duty to intervene in such matters."

Lydia listened closely to the conversation, nodding in agreement. She and Christian had eaten supper with the Whitfields in their cozy cabin. Seth's cabin was very much like the Kent's. Both had a new addition built onto the back to make them roomier. The men had prepared a patch of ground for a common garden and the warm July sun was doing its best to encourage their plants to grow.

"Apparently, the President doesn't look at it that way," Seth continued. "Perhaps he's right in referring the problem back to Governor Dunklin. In any case, Dunklin's the one who's shown himself to be a coward."

"You can say that again," Christian answered in a disgusted tone of voice. "The governor's letters are filled with patriotic rhetoric, but when it comes down to it he lacks the moral courage to act against the mob."

"It's a sad commentary on the officials of the state," Carrie remarked, her pale blue eyes shrouded in the gathering shadows.

"The mob has possession of our weapons, they've burned our homes and now they're stirring up the citizens of *this* county against us. And the governor continues to allow it," Seth said heatedly.

Lydia noted Seth's tense expression. His face was etched with harsh lines and his dark wavy hair fell in his eyes, unheeded.

Christian reached for her hand, "We'll just have to depend on our own people."

"Depend on ourselves?" Seth repeated skeptically. "I don't think the brethren from Kirtland are in a situation to give us much help."

Lydia knew what Seth meant. The Saints from Kirtland comprising Zion's Camp had recently arrived in Missouri. While camped near Rush Creek, an epidemic of cholera had broken out among them. A few of the brethren from Kirtland had died from the disease. And Sidney Gilbert, laboring at Rush Creek on behalf of the brethren, fell ill of the cholera and soon afterward died. Christian was heartsick about Sidney's passing. Lydia felt him grip her hand tighter.

Seth frowned. "Those brethren were supposed to be on the Lord's errand. Why did he allow them to contract cholera?"

No one offered a reply to Seth's query. Christian sat silently beside Lydia, his eyes lowered.

"Now it looks like we'll never get our land back," Seth said bitterly.

Lydia sagged in her chair. Perhaps Seth was right. Perhaps they'd never return to Jackson County.

CHAPTER NINETEEN

Lydia put the finishing touches on the table, then stood back to survey her work. The tablecloth was patched and faded from repeated washings, but the polished dishes and the vase full of freshly cut geraniums lent the table the kind of festive air Lydia wanted to achieve. She straightened one errant fork and smiled. It was perfect. Everything was in readiness. All she had to do now was wait for Christian to return from Liberty. She sat down but popped to her feet again in seconds, too excited to sit still. The good tidings she had for Christian had been long awaited. Almost three years. Now she could barely wait a moment more to tell him about the glorious secret she had been harboring. She first suspected she was with child some weeks ago, but she hadn't wanted to say anything to Christian until she was certain. And more importantly, until she was reasonably sure that this pregnancy would terminate in the birth of a full-term, healthy child.

She had conceived twice before, and both times miscarried. With her last pregnancy she had carried the child nearly to term before it had been born, dead. It had been a son, with a patch of dark fuzz on its tiny head. She had been devastated by the loss and afterwards slipped into a long period of melancholia.

Christian had done everything possible to cheer her. And Carrie had been a godsend. She'd taken James and Elizabeth for days at a time so Lydia could rest, and on many other occasions came to the house simply to buoy her up. Carrie had recently given birth to a beautiful daughter named Rachel.

Sharing Carrie's joy over the birth of her child helped assuage Lydia's own grief. With both Christian and Carrie's caring ministrations, Lydia began to regain her emotional balance.

Now all the sadness was past and forgotten in the joy of this new life she was carrying within her. By some happy chance the doctor from Liberty had stopped that morning on his round of patients. He had wanted to speak with Christian, and not finding him at home, was about to leave when Lydia hesitantly told him about her suspected condition. He examined her, declared her fit and healthy and twelve weeks pregnant. Somehow she knew everything would be fine this time. The jubilant feelings inside her bore testimony to that.

She glanced at the table one last time as she heard Christian's wagon pull into the yard. She knew she was smiling like a witless child, but she couldn't help it. She stood near the table, one hand on the back of a chair to steady her soaring emotions, and waited for Christian to come inside.

He opened the door and stepped through. When he saw her, he walked over and kissed her. She clung to him, wanting, needing him close.

"I take it you're glad I'm home," Christian said with a smile in his voice as he gently unraveled her arms from around his neck.

"I miss you when you're away working," Lydia answered, the huge grin still lighting her face.

He looked at her with a curious expression. "Lydia, are you all right? You're grinning like the cat who just ate the proverbial canary."

Lydia laughed and clutched his arm. "I love you so, Christian. And I have something wonderful to tell you."

"What is it?"

"Come and sit down with me, sweetheart." She led him to the table and pulled two chairs close together for them.

"What is it, Lydia?" he repeated as she took both his hands into hers.

"Doctor Walker stopped by the house this morning, wanting to see you," Lydia began. She stopped abruptly, seeing the sudden change that came over his face.

"What did he say to you?" Christian's jaw tightened and his eyes became grave.

"About what?" she asked, confused.

"Did he mention anything to you about—never mind, it's not important."

Lydia was alarmed by her husband's angry, concentrated stare and his obvious attempt to shield her from whatever was bothering him. "Tell me," she pressed. "Something's wrong and if it concerns you I want to know about it."

He paused, and looked into her face. "I didn't want to worry you, but there's some talk in town about the citizens wanting our people to move out of Clay County."

"What?" Lydia asked incredulously.

"Evidently they've written a petition of some sort asking us to leave. I heard about it this morning."

All the feelings she'd experienced when they'd been driven out of Jackson County came tumbling back. Scenes of the mobbings and beatings and burnings crowded upon her mind. It was as if she were reliving that nightmare all over again. Her hands trembled in Christian's grasp. "You can't be serious. The people of Clay County have treated us with nothing but kindness."

"I guess their generosity has run out. I understand they're raising the same old complaints against us."

"But what does that have to do with Doctor Walker?" Lydia asked.

"I saw Doctor Walker in Liberty a few weeks ago. He mentioned to me then that things were beginning to heat up. He promised to let me know if the feelings against us worsened. That's why I wondered if he had said anything."

"No, not a thing. Can you trust his word, Christian?"

Christian shrugged. "I don't know. Right now I don't trust any Missourian."

Lydia glanced over at the table. All of a sudden it didn't look so gay and inviting. Even the flowers were beginning to wilt in the heat of the hot summer sun. Lydia sagged in her chair.

"There now, I've spoiled your surprise," Christian said abjectly.

She gave him a thin smile and tried to recapture some of the enthusiasm she'd felt. "Nothing the mob can do will spoil my happiness, Christian. We're going to have a baby. Doctor

Walker confirmed it this morning and said there's no reason why everything shouldn't go well this time."

Christian's eyes widened and his mouth slowly broke into a grin. "Lydia! That's wonderful!" He grasped her by the shoulders and pulled her to him. She readily returned his embrace.

"I'm so pleased, Lydia," he said, his eyes shining. "When?"

"December. Six more months."

"December," he echoed. "It will be the best Christmas present we've ever had."

"Yes," she laughed, kissing him.

"You mustn't work too hard. I want you to get plenty of rest. Let Elizabeth help you more. She's nearly nine now and she can be a big help to you."

"I will. I promise."

"A baby for Christmas!" Christian shouted exultantly.

If Lydia hadn't been so excited about telling Christian her good news, she would have seen the concern in his face as soon as he stepped in the door. He was clearly upset over the fact that they might be forced out of their homes again. While he'd been in Liberty that morning, he'd encountered some disturbing developments. A crowd of considerable size had been gathered in the town square listening to the rantings of a young man perched atop a packing crate. It had taken a moment before Christian realized that the man was delivering a vitriolic attack against the Saints. Christian had been stunned by the ferocity of the man's remarks. He accused the Saints of scheming with the Indians to take over by force the lands in Missouri, and he claimed to have conclusive proof to that effect. His tirade went on for several minutes. Christian could feel the crowd responding. Several of the men standing next to him scowled and shook their fists above their heads. Others were shouting out their agreement. The speaker made an impassioned plea for the good citizens of Clay County to rid themselves of the Mormon menace and then stepped down.

As soon as the man finished, another took his place. Christian had heard all he cared to; he had a stomach full of the Missourians' lies and accusations. He began to back his way out of the growing crowd and had almost extricated himself from the group when the new speaker began his attack. A familiar tone in the voice stopped Christian in his tracks. He strained to look over the heads of the men in front of him. At first all he could see of the speaker was a glimpse of his coat—an expensive, well-tailored coat. When the man's face came into his view, Christian wasn't the least surprised to see that it was Josiah Stewart.

Stewart's speech was even more inflammatory than the first one. Skillfully couched in convincing terms, Stewart brought his listeners from mild indignation to a fever pitch. He related the circumstances that had brought the Mormons into Clay County, and outlined in vivid detail their threat to the community. The crux of his attack rested on the Saints' purported opposition to slavery, a topic which was guaranteed to excite the passions of the listeners. Christian knew very well that Stewart didn't care a whit about the Saints' abolitionist sympathies. He only used that as a tool to stir up the crowd. Stewart's sole concern was his own political aspirations. He was heavily involved in county politics and didn't wish to see his influence diminished by an ever-growing number of Mormon voters who would not likely be partisan to his views. That realization made Christian angry. Stewart's high-handedness and duplicity had always disturbed Christian, but never as deeply as now. He waited impatiently for Stewart to finish his diatribe. When at last he concluded and stepped down among the crowd, Christian shouldered his way toward him. Stewart's back was to him. Christian tapped his shoulder and the older man turned around.

"That was quite a speech, Mr. Stewart," Christian said, his voice cold as ice.

Stewart's gray eyes narrowed in recognition. "I hope you paid heed to it, Kent."

"Oh, I did. You were quite persuasive. I'm sure you convinced many of the good townsfolk here. Of course, you and I both know that every word you spoke was an outright lie."

A group of men standing around Stewart suddenly fell silent. Stewart blanched and his shaggy red brows lowered like thunderheads. "I'd be careful what I say if I were you," he said in a threatening voice.

"Careful? I don't believe you were particularly careful in delivering that speech of yours. Innocent men and women, thousands of them, have been either burned out or run off their own property because of careful speeches such as yours."

"Run off and deserving of it," Stewart snapped. "You people have been nothing but trouble ever since you arrived in this state. You couldn't survive in Jackson County and you won't survive here."

"Oh, we'll survive, Mr. Stewart. Survive and flourish. It may not be in Missouri, but you can depend on the Saints making an impression for a long time to come."

"You're courting disaster, Kent, and I for one won't be sorry to see you get what you deserve." With that, Stewart turned on his heel and roughly shoved his way through the crowd.

Christian watched him go, anger smoldering inside him. Stewart had reached the fringe of the crowd when a slim young woman stepped out and took his arm. As she did so, her eyes bore into Christian's. She had evidently been watching the exchange going on between Christian and her father the whole time. Mary Ann Stewart lifted her head and gave Christian a withering stare. Her green eyes echoed contempt and the smug smile she wore sent a signal of warning shooting through his veins.

Christian shivered as he thought about his encounter with the Stewarts. It was people like them who would always cause trouble for the Saints. Haughty, proud, and totally unfeeling of the Lord's spirit, they and their kind would continue to torment and oppress the Saints until they had filled up the measure of their iniquity. Christian feared for them. The Lord had promised to pour out his wrath without measure on his enemies and to let fall the sword of his indignation. The Lord's enemies had prevailed for a time, it was true. The Saints had been driven out of their promised land, beaten, robbed and murdered. But the day would come when the Saints would possess the land, as was promised. Christian would bide his time and wait upon the Lord.

Over the next few days, Christian and the other Saints dwelling in Clay County waited uneasily for word concerning their fate. They didn't have to wait long. In a public meeting held at Liberty on June 29th, it was resolved by the citizens of Clay County to ask the Mormons to leave peaceably. The leaders of the Church in Clay County agreed to their request, and by October many of the Saints had left the county and gathered around the vicinity of Shoal Creek. The Kents and the Whitfields packed their meager belongings and moved with them.

Alexander Doniphan, the Church's attorney in Jackson County, was instrumental in the preparation and passage of a bill to create new counties for the Saints to settle in. A sparsely populated region in the northern part of the state was chosen where the Saints could dwell in peace. The new governor, Lilburn W. Boggs, signed the bill on December 29, 1836, creating two counties, one to be called Caldwell and the other Daviess County. A settlement was located at a place called Far West, in Caldwell County. It was there Christian and Lydia made their home.

Two weeks after they settled into the cabin Christian had hastily built for them, Lydia gave birth to a daughter. They named her Roxana Jane Kent, after Christian's mother, and both Christian and Lydia were overjoyed. She was a beautiful healthy baby, with soft dark curls and deep blue eyes. Her family called her Roxie and she quickly became the center of their affections.

Far West was located on a high swell of ground on the rolling prairie, about a mile south of Shoal Creek. The site had been chosen by John Whitmer and William Phelps, and it proved to be a favorable spot for the gathering of the Saints. By the spring of 1837, there were nearly 4,000 Saints living there. They had established a school, stores, half a dozen blacksmith shops, hotels, and a printing house.

As they'd done in Clay County, the Kents and the Whitfields built their cabins in close proximity to one another. Their children freely roamed from one house to the other, and were warmly welcomed in both. Rachel Whitfield had grown into a sturdy, vivacious two-year-old. She had flaxen hair like her mother's and her eyes were large and blue. Seth spoiled her shamelessly. Seth had obtained employment in one of the town's blacksmith shops, and in his spare time he pursued his carpentry skills, fashioning cupboards, chests and chairs for his own home and those of his friends. In the short time they'd been at Far West, Seth had succeeded in making a fair amount of money. That spring, however, the country experienced a financial crisis brought on by the effects of reckless speculation and excessive banking practices. A mania to invest in property had swept the country during the preceding two or three years until President Jackson, alarmed by the speculative appetite, issued the Specie Circular in the summer of 1836, which provided that purchasers must henceforth pay for public land in gold or silver. At once the rush to buy land ground to a halt. When demand slackened, prices fell. Depositors sought to withdraw their money in the form of specie, and soon the banks had exhausted their supplies. Panic was sweeping across the country as many banks failed and others were forced to suspend specie payments. Much of Seth's money was deposited in the bank at Liberty, and he was distressed about its safety.

Seth was also well aware of the financial debacle at Kirtland, centered in the Kirtland Safety Society Bank. Land had been purchased around Kirtland at excessively high prices, and on credit, with the expectation of new Saints moving in to possess it. When the prices in real estate dropped, the lands purchased by the Saints could not be sold except at a loss. In November of 1836, some of the brethren in Kirtland, including the Church presidency, applied for a charter for a bank to be known as the Kirtland Safety Society Bank, but the legislature refused to grant the charter. In the meantime, Oliver Cowdery had been sent to Philadelphia to have plates engraved on which to print the proposed bank's currency. When the charter was refused, the Saints instead organized a stock company called the Kirtland Safety Society Anti-Banking Company. In issuing their notes, however, the Saints used the plates prepared for their bank issue, reading Kirtland Safety Society Bank, instead of the proper name of the anti-banking company. Having no state charter and hence no legal standing as currency, the notes of the Safety Society were rejected by its creditors. The Kirtland Safety Society

Anti-Banking Company failed, involving members of the Church in financial distress.

Many of the Saints at Kirtland blamed their financial troubles on the Prophet. Some said that the Bank had been instituted by God, through revelation to Joseph Smith. The Prophet reportedly denied this, but the information coming out of Kirtland was so contradictory that the Saints in Far West were unsure of the truth of the matter. During the previous month, the Prophet and Sidney Rigdon had been arrested upon a charge of violating the banking laws of Ohio.

All of this greatly troubled Seth. He had talked to Christian about it on a couple of occasions. Joseph's involvement in the whole affair had raised questions in his mind—doubts concerning Joseph's role as a prophet. Christian sensed a gradual change in Seth's attitudes and a preoccupation with worldly matters that hadn't been apparent before. He hoped things would soon right themselves in Seth's mind.

Aside from his normal concerns, Christian was happy and content. He'd taken a teaching position in the town's large, newly-constructed schoolhouse which served also as a courthouse and a church. Both Elizabeth and James attended the school. James was eager to learn, though he struggled with his studies. Elizabeth, on the other hand, was a quick, bright student who excelled with little effort. Christian found a good deal of satisfaction in teaching, but his first love continued to be his writing. He edited a small town paper and wrote many of its articles. He also corresponded with friends in Kirtland and occasionally contributed to the Church's newspaper, the *Latter-Day Saint Messenger and Advocate,* which had supplanted the *Star* in October of 1834.

The *Star*, with Oliver Cowdery as editor, had published ten issues at Kirtland. Christian had heard that there were some difficulties connected with the management of the newspaper. He didn't know the nature of the problems, but he'd learned that William Phelps and John Whitmer had gone to Ohio in May of 1835, and that Whitmer had been appointed to take the place of Oliver Cowdery in conducting the new paper, the *Messenger and Advocate.* A year and a half later, the firm of Oliver Cowdery & Co. was dissolved and the entire establishment was transferred to Joseph Smith and Sidney Rigdon.

Christian wasn't sure of all that was taking place at Kirtland, but he felt comfortable with his own circumstances in Far West. He had a warm cabin, a loving wife, and three fine children. He and Lydia were building their home on gospel principles and endeavoring to rear their children according to God's revealed word. Although he enjoyed a close relationship with James, Elizabeth continued to remain aloof. Christian tried to gain her confidence, but there always seemed to be a sense of distance that separated them. Four-month-old Roxana more than made up for Elizabeth's coolness. She was a delight and elicited feelings Christian never suspected he possessed. Altogether, Christian was more at peace with himself than he could ever remember.

CHAPTER TWENTY

Sweetheart, are you listening to me?"

"What? I'm sorry, Lydia. I guess my mind was else-
where. What did you say?"

Lydia finished unbuttoning her dress and slipped
out of it. She quickly put on warm nightclothes, for the meager warmth coming from the cabin's hearth did little to dispel
the icy December air.

"Did you notice Elizabeth Cowdery's dress? It must have
cost her a small fortune. It was all covered with lace and ribbons. It really was beautiful."

Christian frowned. He hadn't noticed Sister Cowdery's
gown, but he had taken note of Oliver's fine new clothes. He'd
thought at the time that Oliver looked out of character in the
expensively tailored coat and tails. It was the first time he'd
seen Oliver in over four years, since he'd left Jackson County
back in 1833, bound for Kirtland. He'd been in Kirtland for the
most part, all that time, and he'd only recently come to Far
West. There was something different about Oliver, something
Christian couldn't quite put his finger on. More than just the
new clothes. Christian's scowl deepened.

"Christian, is something the matter? You haven't said two
words since we left the party and now you're scowling like an
Indian." Lydia put an arm around his waist. "What's bothering you, sweetheart?"

Christian pecked her cheek and smiled briefly. "I don't
know exactly. I feel unsettled about Oliver."

"What about Oliver?"

"It's just a feeling I had at the party tonight. I can't seem to shake it."

Christian and Lydia had spent the evening at a Christmas social held in Seth Whitfield's home. The Whitfield's had invited several couples, among them some of Christian's old friends whom he hadn't seen for months—John Corrill, William Phelps, Oliver Cowdery, John Whitmer, and their wives. The evening had started out pleasantly enough. The group had chatted and then enjoyed a superb dinner. The Whitfields' home was merrily decorated with ribbon, holly, and wreaths, and a huge Christmas tree stood in the center of the parlor, festooned with strings of popcorn and colored candies.

It was after dinner that he noticed the tension. Christian had spent some time visiting with Corrill before the two of them moved to a knot of men engaged in conversation. Phelps, John Whitmer, and Oliver were at the center of the conversation, and when Christian and Corrill joined them, Christian noted a guarded tone creep into their speech. They had evidently been discussing matters dealing with the Church in Kirtland, and Christian caught a fragment of a sentence concerning Joseph Smith just as he and Corrill joined them. He'd been struck that what was said about the Prophet was not complimentary. That put him on his guard. Nothing more was mentioned about Joseph in his hearing, but he received the unmistakable impression that these men were dissatisfied about something having to do with Joseph and the Church at Kirtland.

Christian had heard the reports from Kirtland. Some of the brethren were in rebellion against the Church. Important men. Men who held high and trusted positions. Three of the Quorum of the Twelve Apostles were said to be openly hostile against the Prophet, and even Oliver Cowdery had been censured by Joseph for misconduct. Some members had become disaffected over the failure of the Kirtland Bank; others claimed that the Church authorities had departed from the true order of things by calling the Church by a new name, "The Church of the Latter-Day Saints." This new title had been adopted in May of 1834 by a conference of elders in Kirtland, in an effort to give the Church a more distinctive name, and hopefully to escape the derogatory terms of Mormonite and Mormon. Because of these and other reasons, many in Kirtland were clamoring that Joseph was a fallen prophet. Apostasy, false accusations and bitterness abounded in the city. And some of it was spilling into Far West.

When Joseph had come to Clay County with Zion's Camp, he'd organized the Saints into a stake, with a high council and Stake Presidency. David Whitmer had been called as the Stake President, with Phelps and John Whitmer as his counselors. Shortly after this work was accomplished, Zion's Camp was disbanded and the Prophet and most of those who came with him returned to Kirtland.

As much as he admired John Whitmer and William Phelps, Christian felt they had over-stepped their bounds in connection with certain of their Church duties in Missouri. When Phelps and Whitmer purchased the land at Far West in 1836, difficulty arose over the manner in which they handled the transaction. Some members of the high council accused them of acting independently of the council and conducting matters in their own interest and for their own gain. While David Whitmer was away in Kirtland, Phelps and Whitmer laid out the town sites, appointed a committee to supervise the building of a temple, and then appropriated the profits arising from the sale of town lots for themselves, pledging a considerable sum out of those funds, however, toward the building of the proposed temple. This led to an investigation of their conduct by the high council in the spring of 1837. Both Whitmer and Phelps made explanation for their conduct and confessed their error. The town site entered by Whitmer and Phelps, together with the profits arising from the sale of the lands, was turned over to Bishop Partridge for the benefit of Zion and the situation was thus amicably resolved.

Christian was glad the whole distasteful affair was over, but he noticed that both Phelps and Whitmer continued to display a somewhat proud and rebellious attitude. He suddenly realized that was the same kind of spirit he had recognized in Oliver Cowdery tonight.

"What sort of feeling?" Lydia persisted, as she pulled back the covers of the bed and climbed in.

Christian hurriedly changed his clothes and crawled into bed beside her. "Maybe it's just my imagination," Christian said slowly, as he pulled the blankets up to his chin, "but I didn't feel good about some discussion going on between a few of the brethren."

Lydia sighed as she snuggled comfortably close to Christian's side.

"The words struck me as disloyal and vindictive."

"What in the world was said, Christian?" Lydia asked, turning onto her side to face him.

"It wasn't so much what was said as the manner in which it was said."

"Something Oliver was saying, you mean?"

"Oliver and a few of the others. William. John. They were talking about some difference of opinion Oliver evidently had with the Prophet. I didn't hear what the problem was, but the feeling I got was that it caused a considerable amount of concern."

"Perhaps it wasn't as serious as you supposed. There isn't anyone closer to the Prophet than Oliver, or anyone who loves and sustains him more. I'm sure if there was some misunderstanding between the two of them, they'll straighten it out."

"You're probably right," Christian answered, but he wasn't convinced. He turned onto his side, put his arm around Lydia and pulled her to him. Her hair smelled sweet, like clover in the summer's sun. He kissed her.

"Mm," she murmured, cuddling against him.

"Did you have a nice time at the party?" he asked, stroking her long auburn hair.

"Yes, I enjoyed visiting with our old friends again. We must go over and see John and Sarah's new baby. They named her Sarah Elizabeth, did you know?"

Christian shook his head.

"Sarah told me she's quite a handful," said Lydia, chuckling.

"I can relate to that. The three of ours aren't exactly a picnic."

"No, they're not. But they're a joy, aren't they?" Lydia leaned on one elbow. "Do you know what James did the other day? I left him in charge of Roxie while I did my chores.

While he was watching her, she fell down on the hearthstones and cut her knee a bit. The next thing I knew, James had her whole leg bandaged. It was quite a sight." Lydia laughed at the memory.

"James enjoys doctoring. Several times I've seen him trying to coax the girls into acting as his patients. It's not all play, either. James is genuinely concerned about people. At school he's always the first to help if there's a problem with one of the other children. His is a compassionate and sympathetic nature."

"He can also be a little ruffian," Lydia laughed. "But he's a good, obedient boy. We're very lucky, aren't we, Christian?"

"We are, indeed." He kissed her hair. "The most fortunate one is myself. I'm the one who was lucky enough to marry you."

Christian trudged through ankle-deep snow, his hands in his pockets. The air was still and frosty cold. A snowstorm the night before had cleansed the sky and left the ground sparkling. Few people were out. Most were at home enjoying their firesides or busy at their employment. Since school was in recess for the Christmas holidays, Christian had some spare time on his hands. He rounded the corner and walked toward the blacksmith's shop. He hadn't seen Seth since the evening of the Christmas party, and he was glad for an opportunity to visit with him.

When he arrived at the smithy, he pulled open the big double doors and walked inside. Seth was a few feet away, tugging at the bellows. Christian strode over to him.

"Morning."

"Hello, Cicero. How are you?" Seth gave the huge bellows a shove and then pulled out a handkerchief from his pocket and mopped his brow. Although the day was cold, the heat generated from the open furnace of the smithy made the room warm and close. "What's on your mind?"

"Nothing special." Christian glanced up at the big bellows overhead that Seth had been patiently working. "That's hard labor. Why don't you open your own carpentry shop? Do what you do best."

"This pays better, Cicero. Besides, it's not so bad. How's Lydia and the young 'uns?"

"They're all fine. What about Carrie and Rachel?"

"Ah, Rachel, sweet Rachel. She's led her mother and me on a merry chase this past week. She refuses to go to bed at night and she's discovered that her favorite word in the English language is 'no!'" Seth laughed and took another swath across his forehead.

"She sounds like a typical two-year-old. How's the house coming along?"

"Slow. The bad weather has taken its toll." Seth was in the midst of adding a second story to his already roomy cabin. Christian had been helping him whenever he had some free time.

"I'm out of a job for a few days now with the holidays. I can give you a hand."

"Thanks. If President Van Buren would do something about the economic situation, I could better afford to build my house."

"He's not about to. He's concerned with government, not people. He refuses to assume any responsibility for the general welfare. 'Let the people shift for themselves,' as Webster aptly put it. A fitting epitaph for Jacksonian democracy," Christian said cynically.

"You've never forgiven Jackson for withholding his aid during our troubles in Jackson County, have you?"

"Have *you*?"

"Well, I'm not quite as adamant on the subject as you are."

"You should be." Christian spoke the words sharper than he intended.

"Why should I, Christian? Not everyone is as zealous as yourself. Once you've committed yourself to something, there's no turning aside. It's either black or white. Right or wrong." Seth frowned and dropped his gaze.

"What's that supposed to mean?" Christian asked, surprised by the censure.

"Just because you feel strongly about something doesn't necessarily make it right. There is room for difference of opinion."

Christian was silent for several seconds. There was something gnawing at Seth which had nothing to do with personal or political viewpoints. It went deeper than that. "Why don't we back up here? We were talking about your house. Do you want me to come give you a hand or not?" Christian said in a conciliatory tone.

"I don't know. That is, I'm not sure that I'm going to keep the house."

"You're thinking of moving?"

"Not exactly. A fellow I did some work for in Liberty is looking for property to buy. I told him I might be interested in selling mine."

"Oh."

"I'm thinking about also selling him my land in Jackson County."

"You're what?" Christian exploded.

"I don't want to hear any of your lectures, Christian. It's my land and I'll decide what to do with it."

"You know as well as I do the brethren have told us not to sell our lands in Jackson County. You can't be serious."

"It's true they did say that. But circumstances have changed since then. We're settled here in Caldwell County now and it looks highly unlikely that we'll ever return to Jackson."

"The circumstances make no difference. We've been admonished to hold on to our Jackson County property as long as it's feasible. What you're proposing to do, Seth, is in direct violation of the commandments."

"I don't look at it that way. I've an opportunity here to sell my land for a handsome price. The money I make on it can be used to further the cause of Zion, which is better than doing nothing at all, which seems to be the case at the present."

"That's a false and dangerous argument. You'd be making a big mistake."

"Listen, Christian, I'm not the only one who feels this way. There are plenty of the brethren who think they should sell their lands. The other night at the Christmas party, John pointed out that we should be using our means to take care of our present needs, and trust to the future to find ways to redeem Zion. I agree with him."

Christian shook his head. He couldn't believe what he was hearing. "You're heading down the wrong road, Seth. What you want to do is wrong, and you know it."

"It's my decision. If you don't agree with it, I'd appreciate it if you wouldn't impose your views on me."

The chill in Seth's voice made Christian's stomach tighten.

"Apparently we don't see eye to eye anymore," Seth said. "If we're going to travel different roads, it might behoove you to consider that the one *you've* chosen just might be false." Seth stared at Christian for a long moment and then he walked over to the bellows, grasped the handle and pulled it down with a fury.

There was nothing left for Christian to say. He turned and walked out of the blacksmith shop.

Christian filed out of the meetinghouse with the rest of the brethren. There were no smiles or exchanges of greeting among them. Every face was somber. Sorrowful. A few men were quietly weeping. Christian walked home alone. He needed a few moments to himself to mull over the action that had taken place at this specially called general assembly. Three of the finest men he knew had been stripped of their positions in the Church. The high council had presented charges against David Whitmer, William W. Phelps and John Whitmer, members of the presidency of the stake of Zion, and asked the assembled brethren for their sustaining vote in removing these men from the presidency. The motion had been unanimously carried.

Christian felt torn in two. If committed and courageous men like Phelps and the Whitmers had fallen, where did the blame lie? There were many in Missouri who were disaffected, brethren falling away on every hand. Bitterness, accusations and apostasy were rife. Was it possible the apostates were justified in their beliefs? Had Church leaders departed from true and correct principles as some charged? It seemed to Christian that the Church was being torn asunder, and he didn't know where in all the wreckage to grasp a hold.

It was several weeks before Christian's spirits lifted. The Prophet arrived at Far West, driven out of Kirtland by embittered, vengeful men who had once been Joseph's trusted companions and brethren in the gospel. Joseph's presence at

Far West, along with other staunch men such as Brigham
Young, Sidney Rigdon, and Hyrum Smith, infused a new
vitality into the Church in Missouri. Joseph called new
brethren to fill the vacancies left by those who had been disfellowshipped or excommunicated.

As Christian approached his house after a tiring day of
teaching, he noticed Seth's buggy drawn up in front. He'd
seen little of Seth since their disagreement. He'd felt miserable
about the altercation. Seth was his best and closest friend. A
senseless misunderstanding was certainly not worth sacrific-
ing their friendship. Two days after he and Seth had
quarreled, Christian had gone to his home and apologized to
him. They had shaken hands and expressed their desire to be
reconciled. But bad feelings still existed between them, much
to Christian's dismay. His heart lifted when he saw Seth's carriage in front of his house.

But it wasn't Seth who had come to visit. When Christian
opened the door and stepped inside, he found Carrie weeping on Lydia's shoulder. Lydia looked up at the sound of his
step, and motioned for him to come inside.

"Here, Carrie, take this and dry your eyes," Lydia directed,
handing Carrie her handkerchief. "Everything is going to be
all right. Christian's here. Maybe you'd like to talk with him."

Carrie obediently wiped her eyes, sniffed a few times, then
sat wringing the handkerchief in her hands.

"What is it, Carrie? Is something wrong with Rachel?"
asked Christian in alarm.

Carrie shook her head. "No, Rachel's fine. It's Seth. I'm so
worried about him." Carrie's pale blue eyes filled again with
tears.

"Is he ill?"

Lydia answered for her. "No, Seth's not ill. Carrie is concerned about something potentially more serious. Brother
Hinkle came to their home this morning and asked Seth to
appear before the High Council next week. He said that certain charges have been brought against him which could
jeopardize his standing in the Church, and the brethren
wanted to discuss it with him."

Christian sank down in a chair. "Oh, no."

"Seth says he won't appear before the Council, that they have no jurisdiction over his temporal affairs," Carrie told him, her voice quivering. "We had a disagreement over it. He stalked out of the house and hasn't been back all day."

Christian didn't know what to say to comfort her. He was as stunned by the news as she.

"Carrie said he's been keeping company with some of the apostates in town, that he and the Whitmers have become especially close," Lydia related.

"It's not just that he's become involved with a new circle of friends," Carrie added, "he's made such a change. The things that were important to us no longer seem so to him." Carrie twisted and pulled at the handkerchief in her lap.

Christian shook his head silently.

"Seth's unhappy with Joseph and some of the other brethren because he feels they should reimburse him for the time and money he's spent laboring to build up the kingdom here in Missouri. He's dwelling on what he perceives to be all the injustices he's suffered for the sake of the Church."

"Carrie, I didn't know it was as bad as that," said Christian. His head was beginning to ache with the grievous news Carrie bore.

"I'm so afraid for him, Christian. He's a proud man, and stubborn. You know that as well as anyone. He was upset over the trouble between the two of you, but he wouldn't swallow his pride long enough to come and talk with you about it. If you hadn't come when you did, he would still be fuming. Will you talk to him, Christian? He's always respected your opinion. He loves you like a brother."

"Maybe that was true once, but I'm afraid it isn't anymore," Christian answered quietly.

"If you'll only try. He'll listen to you. I'm sure of it. Please, Christian. I don't know who else to turn to." The tears spilled over and ran down Carrie's cheeks.

Christian wiped them gently away. "All right, Carrie, I'll talk to him."

Christian stood uneasily on the Whitfield's porch, waiting for Seth to answer his knock. He didn't know what he was going to say to his friend, or how best to approach him. He was almost sorry now that he had promised Carrie he would talk to Seth. He remembered only too well how their last conversation concerning the Church had turned out.

Seth opened the door and stood in the entrance, with Rachel in his arms. "Hello, Christian. I wasn't expecting to see you this evening. Come in."

"Thanks, Seth. How are you, Rachel?" Christian reached over and playfully tweaked the child's nose. She giggled and clung to her father's neck.

"Can't you say hello to Brother Kent, Rachel? You little rascal." Seth tickled the little girl until she shrieked with laughter, then he swung her down to the floor. "Go and play now, sweetheart."

"She's getting to be a beauty, Seth. Looks just like her mother."

"It's a good thing she doesn't take after me, huh? Come in, Christian, and sit down."

As Christian moved past Seth toward the couch, he was startled by the unmistakable odor of tobacco on Seth's breath. He tried not to let the shock and disappointment show on his face.

"Carrie's gone out, so I'm watching Rachel. We've been playing dolls and having quite a time of it," Seth said with a grin.

Christian tried to summon a convincing smile.

"How's everything going for you?" Seth asked.

"Fine. I've been doing a little writing."

Seth nodded, but didn't make any reply.

"And yourself?"

"There's more work than we can do at the smithy."

"That's good." Christian hoped Seth would open up and confide in him about the summons before the High Council. It would make Christian's task easier.

"How are the little ones?" Seth asked casually.

"Keeping us busy, as usual." Christian took a breath and plunged ahead. "Are you still planning to sell your property here in Far West, Seth?"

"There's been some problem develop over that. The fellow who wanted to buy it has changed his mind. He gave me a little bit of cash down and now he wants it back. I don't intend to give it to him. We had a firm agreement and his backing out now has put me to some expense. I had the papers already drawn up for the sale."

"I'm sorry to hear that."

"Yes, well, so am I. Oliver thinks I should bring a suit against him, and he's willing to do the legal work for me."

"Oliver is?" Christian was surprised to hear that Oliver had taken up his law practice and was urging Seth to initiate legal action.

"Yes. I think I may take him up on it."

"What about your land in Jackson County?" Christian asked cautiously. "Do you still plan to sell it?"

Seth's eyes narrowed and a defensive expression flickered across his face. "After what's happened to Whitmer and Phelps, I don't think that would be very prudent. Do you?"

Christian knew exactly what he was referring to. William Phelps and John Whitmer had just recently been disfellowshipped from the Church for the same general reasons they had been rejected as a stake presidency. Their troubles stemmed from the unsavory affair over the town plots taken out at Far West and their persistence in claiming money which rightfully belonged to the Church. Both were charged with unchristianlike conduct and denying the faith by selling their lands in Jackson County.

"Seth, Carrie came by the house yesterday to talk to Lydia. I happened to walk in on them. Carrie was pretty upset."

Seth stared at him for a second and then his gaze dropped to the floor. "She told you about the summons."

"Yes. She's worried about you. She asked me to talk to you."

"There isn't anything you can say that will change my mind, Christian. I won't appear before the High Council's court. They've made up their minds about me already, anyway. Look what they did to Phelps and Whitmer. They didn't even give them a chance to speak in their own defense."

"That's not true, Seth. John and William refused to appear before the Council to plead their case. It was their own decision to absent themselves, not the Council's. If you'll just explain to them how you feel, it will clear up this misunderstanding. They're good, honest men. Righteous men. They're not out to get you."

"If I told them how I feel, Christian, they'd boot me out of the Church before you could wink your eye," Seth answered sourly.

"What are you saying? That you no longer believe in the Church? That you've lost your faith?"

Seth rose to his feet and began pacing the room. "I don't know any more, Christian. I just don't know."

"Is this business about the Kirtland Bank still troubling you?"

Seth ceased his pacing, pulled his chair close to Christian's and sat down. He leaned forward and said in a low tone, "Frankly, yes it is—that and several other things. Oliver's told me about some pretty serious charges leveled against the Prophet. Smith is apparently preaching one thing and doing the opposite. Even the apostles in Kirtland have turned against him. They knew what he was up to, and tried to stop him."

Christian let his breath out slowly. "I've heard the rumors, Seth. But I'd hardly call men like Luke Johnson and John Boynton reliable sources. They've shown their colors in outright rebellion against the Church."

"And Oliver?"

"I don't know about Oliver. Oliver's changed, that much I'm aware of."

Seth put a shaking hand to his forehead. "We've sacrificed our money, our time, our very lives doing what Smith has asked us to do. I buried my son on the banks of the Missouri because of the Church. Have we been wearing ourselves out chasing after a false prophet?" Seth asked in anguish.

"Do you remember all the slanderous rumors making the rounds while we were in Jackson County? We even joked about some of them because they were so ridiculous. You didn't believe them then, Seth. This is nothing new. The attack is more insidious, that's all. You believed Joseph Smith was a true prophet then. He still is today."

"I believe Joseph was a prophet. I believe he translated the Book of Mormon from ancient plates just as he said. I believe he organized the Church under the direction of God. But I also believe since that time he's transgressed and is no longer the Lord's spokesman."

"Who is, then? The Whitmers? Phelps? Oliver Cowdery?"

Seth shook his head. "I don't know."

"Then find out. There's only one way to do that—get down on your knees, man, and ask! Don't be persuaded by what others say. Find out the truth for yourself, Seth."

Seth looked into Christian's face for a long moment, but he didn't speak.

The two of them rose to their feet and Seth walked with Christian to the door. "Thanks for coming, Christian. I appreciate your concern." Seth paused, searching for the right words. "I can't make you any promises."

Christian nodded. "I know."

Christian took him by the shoulders and embraced him. The two men clung to one another in silence.

Christian left the house and walked toward home, consumed in thought. Lydia was waiting for him when he got there.

"How did it go?" she asked anxiously.

"All right, I think. We talked. I hope it helped." He pulled Lydia to him and hugged her with a sudden urgency. "Dear Lord, I hope it helped."

Less than a week later, Christian learned that Oliver Cowdery and David Whitmer had withdrawn their membership from the Church in consequence of numerous charges brought against them by the High Council. Among other things, Cowdery had been charged with persecuting the Saints by urging on vexatious law suits against them, forsaking the cause of God, and seeking to destroy the character of Joseph Smith. Whitmer's charges were much the same as those initiated against him earlier— using tea, coffee and tobacco in violation of the Word of Wisdom, as well as other acts of rebellion. Both men were excommunicated by the Council. Although Christian agreed with the Council's decision, he nevertheless felt deep sorrow. These men had been his friends and brethren in the gospel. Christian mourned the loss of their fellowship.

CHAPTER TWENTY-ONE

Seth refused to attend the hearing before the High Council where charges were brought against him for conduct unbecoming to a Saint and failure to keep the Word of Wisdom. He was shortly thereafter notified that he had been disfellowshipped from the Church until he could make restitution. The actions of the High Council only served to increase Seth's hostility toward the Church. Gradually he cut himself off from his former friends and fraternized with the apostates in town. Carrie was distraught by this turn of events. She neither shared Seth's attitude toward the Church, nor condoned his rebellious actions, but she stood by him and did all within her power to convince him of his error. She spent a good deal of time at the Kent's home, where she received support and encouragement from Lydia and Christian. As for Seth, Christian seldom saw him any more. What little information he gleaned came from Carrie. Seth apparently had abandoned all his old beliefs, although he had not allied himself completely with the apostates.

Christian's concern over Seth was abruptly overshadowed by other, more serious problems in the late summer of 1838. At an election held at Gallatin, Daviess County, fighting broke out between Mormons and some Missourians who tried toprevent the Saints from voting. The altercation ignited smoldering feelings in other counties of Mormon settlement, resulting in escalating violence. Governor Boggs activated the state militia to quell the hostilities between the Mormons and the mob.

To Christian's consternation, mobbings, burnings and killings ensued. A battle between mob forces and a Mormon company of militia at Crooked River resulted in the deaths of three members of the Church. News of this encounter spread rapidly, with the accounts being greatly exaggerated. Boggs ordered out more militia. A savage attack by the militia on the Mormon settlement of Haun's Mill on October 30th left seventeen Saints murdered, many of them women and children. A few days later, troops under the command of Colonel S.D. Lucas arrived outside Far West, sent by the governor to put an end to the "Mormon insurrection." Lucas had orders to assault the city.

The leader of the Mormon militia at Far West, George M. Hinkle, succeeded in obtaining a private interview with Lucas. Afterward, Hinkle treacherously delivered the Prophet, Joseph Smith, into Lucas' hands. He also agreed to surrender all arms and conceded to the Saints' withdrawal from the state.

Christian, a volunteer with the Mormon militia, was infuriated by the actions he witnessed. If he had been able to get hold of Hinkle, he would have wrung the man's neck. Hinkle had totally capitulated to the Saints' enemies, paving the way for their destruction. Brother Joseph had been taken prisoner and threatened with death. Armed bands of Lucas' militia roamed the town committing all manner of plunder and pillage under the pretext of searching for arms. And the governor had issued an order calling for the extermination of all Mormons who did not leave the state.

Although the Saints had been given until spring to vacate Missouri, the mob militia made it intolerable for them to stay that long. Christian and Lydia determined to leave after the first of the year. They spent their remaining weeks disposing of their property. Most of the Saints were forced to sell their possessions for a pittance. It wasn't unusual for a valuable farm to go for the price of a wagon and two mules for transportation. Nor was the mob content with thievery and greed. They meted out abuse whenever they found the opportunity.

Christian urged Seth to leave Missouri with them, but he

refused. He told Christian that he wasn't about to lose his house and land again without proper recompense. As the weeks went by, Carrie became increasingly distressed. She feared for the safety of her child, and for Seth who seemed to be taking a dangerous middle-of-the-road position. Lydia spent as much time with her as she could spare. On one occasion when Lydia was present, Carrie broke into frantic weeping, begging Seth to allow them to leave with the Kents. Seth was visibly shaken by her outburst, but he still clung to his determination to remain behind.

As the day neared for the Kents to leave Missouri, Christian made what remaining preparations he could. Brigham Young, who assumed leadership of the Church while the Prophet was kept prisoner at Liberty jail, organized a relief movement for the poor and distressed. Christian was able to obtain food and clothing and other necessary provisions for the journey.

Late one afternoon, as he and Lydia were on their way home with an armload of provisions, they were accosted on the street by the mob. One of the men roughly shoved Christian and accused him of stealing the goods he carried in his arms. Two others circled around Lydia, taunting her and making lewd and vulgar comments. Dusk was settling in, making it difficult to see the faces of their attackers, but as one of the mob loomed up to Lydia's side she noticed a flicker of recognition light his eyes. He immediately skulked away toward the edge of the group, but not before Lydia plucked him from her memory.

"Jens? Jens Johanssen, is that you?" she gasped.

The young man wheeled around and glared at her defiantly. Suddenly, Lydia wasn't sure of his identification. The youth appeared to be about eighteen or nineteen years of age, possessed the same shock of yellow-white hair Jens had and the same round, florid face. But the eyes! They were so cruel and filled with malice. How could those eyes possibly belong to Jens?

The rest of the rabble were staring at the young man curiously after hearing Lydia's outburst. He scowled and whispered something to one of his companions. The companion's reply brought a smirk to the youth's face. There was no mistaking that sneer. It was as familiar to Lydia as Gerta's big hearty smile.

Lydia pulled away from the safety of Christian's grasp and walked boldly over to the young man standing at the side of the road. "It is you, isn't it, Jens? I can hardly believe it. How disappointed your parents must be in you."

The young man stiffened and his face flushed under her biting words. "I don't know what you're talkin' about," he mumbled. "You got me mixed up with someone else."

"I don't think so," Lydia replied angrily. "I wouldn't forget the son of two of the finest people I've ever known. Your behavior here is a disgrace to their name." She gave him a chilling stare, then turned and stalked away. The other ruffians were taken aback by the exchange and made no further attempt to molest them. Christian took Lydia's arm and steered her quickly out of the mob's way.

"What got into you, Lydia?" asked Christian through clenched teeth as he hurried her along.

"That was the Johanssen boy, I'm sure of it. I've told you about Niels and Gerta. How they sold their farm in Green County so they could come out here to Missouri to be with the Saints. Imagine Jens trying to destroy the very thing dearest to his parents' heart. I can't believe it," she sputtered.

"Well, you better believe it. That boy's face was as cold and hard as any Missourian's. We're getting out now, Lydia. I won't have you exposed to any more danger."

Christian shifted the goods in his arms and quickened his pace.

Lydia handed Carrie her handkerchief. The only sound in the Whitfield's cabin was Carrie's muffled sobs. Lydia noted how pale and thin Carrie had grown; her slight frame barely filled the chair she sat upon.

"You're sure Seth won't change his mind?" Lydia asked quietly.

Carrie shook her head. A few strands of blond hair fell across her brow. She brushed them back with a trembling hand.

"Christian wants to leave at dawn in hopes of avoiding a run-in with any ruffians."

"I know. He was here yesterday to tell Seth," Carrie answered. She wiped her nose with the cloth clutched in her hand. "Seth was cold as ice toward him. He wouldn't even discuss the possibility of leaving Missouri."

Lydia was already aware of that. Christian had come home in low spirits after his call at the Whitfields.

"Seth's hardly spoken to me all week," Carrie revealed in a quivering voice. "He's forbidden me to bring up the matter again."

Lydia reached for Carrie's hand. "Seth's a good man. He thinks he's doing the right thing, that's all."

"I know," Carrie murmured into her handkerchief.

"You'll have to be strong, Carrie. Seth needs you—now, probably more than ever before. Perhaps Seth will find the strength he needs from you."

Carrie looked up out of red-rimmed eyes. "If I thought that was true I could wait forever for Seth to regain his testimony."

"It is true." Lydia gave Carrie's hand a squeeze. "The Lord will be with you, Carrie, to sustain and support you. You mustn't ever forget that."

Lydia saw a glimmer of hope appear in Carrie's round blue eyes.

"May his spirit go with you, too," Carrie whispered. "Though I don't know how I'll get along without you." The words caught in her throat.

Lydia felt her own eyes filling with tears. This parting wrenched her heart. Leaving Seth and Carrie and their home in Missouri was as hard to bear as anything she'd passed through over the last six years.

For six long years the Saints had been hated, driven and persecuted. They had suffered cold and hunger, humiliation and fear. And for what purpose? Simply because they had embraced the gospel of Jesus Christ. Lydia looked into Carrie's stricken face. People should be rejoicing over Christ's restored gospel, she thought sadly, not raising their hand against it. The memory of Jens Johanssen's cold, cruel eyes rose like a spectre in Lydia's mind. His mother, who had accepted the gospel so readily, had been instrumental in preparing Lydia to recieve God's restored word, too. Though Lydia had not seen Gerta and Niels since coming to Missouri, she'd heard they had left for Illinois with the other Saints.

Almost unbidden, passages of scripture Lydia had memorized years ago paraded through her mind. Scriptures about wickedness versus righteousness, and God's promises to the faithful. She realized that the Saints must trust in the strength of the Lord. Whether they were leaving their homes in Missouri, or remaining behind, this was a season for strength—a season to exercise faith, to depend on the Lord to bring them safely through all their trials.

Lydia summoned a smile. "I'll never forget you, Carrie, and the sweet friendship you've given me. I'll cherish that for all the days of my life."

Carrie lifted her head, her eyes clear for the first time since Lydia's visit. "God grant that we may meet again, Lydia."

The sun was a red disk at the edge of the sky. In the gathering shadows of late afternoon, Christian struggled to make a place in the crowded wagon for Lydia's big iron skillet. The haywagon was nearly loaded now, piled with blankets, dry goods, seeds, nails, and the family's few personal belongings. Lashed to the side of the wagon was a precious barrel of flour Christian had managed to salvage when the mob militia ransacked his home. He cast a caustic glance at the log house he had built for Lydia. He'd promised her a respectable home that night on the Missouri bottoms when he'd asked her to be his wife, and still he had not been able to fulfill that promise.

Christian's thoughts were bitter as he cleared a spot for the skillet. Once again the Saints were being driven from their homes. Once again they were being stripped of their lands and possessions. Only this time they were being forced to abandon their beloved land of promise—Zion. As the Prophet Joseph languished in a dank Missouri dungeon, the Saints were trudging out of the state with only the barest of necessities. Joseph's only crime, and the Saints' as well, was choosing to live in accordance with God's revealed word. Christian shook his head as he pondered the incongruity of it all.

Distressed with his thoughts, Christian tossed a box of crockery into the wagon harder than he should have. The crockery rattled and a sharp crack echoed from somewhere deep inside the box. He grimaced and moved the box more gently into a protected spot against the side of the wagon. He was so absorbed in his task, that he failed to hear footsteps approaching from behind.

"Hello, Cicero."

For an instant Christian's hand froze on the wagon, then he whirled around. "Seth?"

Seth Whitfield stepped forward after a moment's hesitation. His face wore a frown and his wavy brown hair fell unattended across his brow. He put a hand on the tail of the wagon. "It looks like you're about ready to clear out," he said in a flat voice.

"Yes. First thing in the morning."

Seth glanced wordlessly at the loaded wagon.

"We plan to stay with Lydia's brother in Quincy for a spell. After that we'll be gathering with the Saints in Illinois."

An uncomfortable silence fell between the two men. Christian couldn't read Seth's stoic expression, but he knew his friend well enough to guess that Seth's visit did not mean he'd changed his mind about staying behind in Missouri. "Will you come inside the house to talk?" Christian asked.

"No. I can't. I just wanted to wish you and Lydia good luck." Seth put out his hand uncertainly.

Christian grasped Seth's outstretched hand without reservation. In spite of the tension between them, Christian felt impelled to make one last effort to persuade him. Christian's chest heaved with sudden emotion. "Come with us, Seth! We'll wait for you in Quincy."

"No, Christian. It's much too late for that."

Christian swallowed hard. He put a hand on Seth's shoulder. "I'm glad you came. It means a lot to me."

Some of the hardness left Seth's eyes. "You have a safe journey," he said.

Christian nodded.

"When you get to Illinois, build Lydia that fancy house you've always been so intent on," Seth commented with a semblance of his old grin.

"I'll do that," Christian returned, smiling.

"Take care, Christian."

"You, too."

Seth gave him a lingering glance and then turned around and rapidly strode away.

Christian sagged against the wheel of the wagon. The unexpected visit from Seth left him drained. It shook Christian to the core to accept the realization that his friend's mind and heart were darkened as to the things of the Spirit. The persecutions the Saints had suffered had surely done its winnowing, sifting them like chaff before the wind. Christian recalled a revelation the Lord had given to Joseph Smith explaining that the Saints must be chastened and tried in all things, for those who could not endure chastening cannot be sanctified.

Like Seth, many of the Saints had not been able to endure the Lord's chastening hand. Christian was humbly grateful that he and Lydia had grasped firmly onto the rod, and on the spot he offered a silent, urgent prayer that they might continue to endure whatever trials the Lord still had in store for them.

Suddenly, leaving Missouri did not seem as tragic as it had a few minutes earlier. The faithful Saints had established God's word and were striving to live by his precepts. They had done as they were commanded. If they must wait a season to redeem Zion it made little difference, for the Saints would carry Zion in their hearts. He would not despair. The Lord would be with them, as he had always been. Christian's heart swelled within him as the Spirit touched his soul, speaking peace.

Lydia stepped outside the cabin to watch, for the last time, the sun rise over the rolling prairies of Missouri. The sky was tinted pink in the early morning light. Rosy fingers reached across the expanse above her head, lifting the darkness from snow-covered fields, the humble log homes, and the steepled meeting house. In the distance, the frozen waters of Shoal Creek shimmered in the pink dawn. Already the town of Far West was astir. Lydia could hear the lowing of oxen, and the scraping of heavy boxes being slid into wagons. The Kent's own open wagon waited in the yard, loaded and ready to begin the trip to Illinois. Lydia glanced up at the sky again.

She wondered if the sunrise was as beautiful in Illinois this morning as it was here.

She turned at the sound of a door opening. Christian came out of the cabin, pulling his coat over his coarse woolen shirt and patched trousers. He smiled when he saw her. Lydia thought how strikingly handsome he looked, even with his dark hair barely tamed from the night's sleep. The snow crunched under his leather boots as he came to her side.

"Is there room in the wagon for these?" Christian asked. He held out two books.

"We'll make room, sweetheart." Lydia read the titles. One was a slim volume of poetry, and the other a collection of Thomas Paine's essays. "What about your other books?"

Christian shrugged. "What's left of them is still at the schoolhouse. My gift to the mob," he added sardonically.

"Let's stop at the schoolhouse and get them, Christian. There's no sense in letting good books go to ruin."

"Let's forget about the books," he said quietly. "They're not important. Is everything else loaded?"

Lydia nodded. She watched him rummage through the wagon bed to find a spot for the books. She knew full well the importance of these books to Christian, these as well as the ones he was leaving behind. Lydia considered the sacrifices each member of the family was making. Leaving their home and possessions behind was difficult not only for her and Christian, but for the children as well. She formed a mental picture of Elizabeth's freckled face and clear blue eyes. Elizabeth was twelve, almost a young woman. But in many ways she was still such a child. The trials and suffering Elizabeth had experienced in her young life gave Lydia cause for concern. Perhaps they would leave scars which Elizabeth would have to deal with as she grew older. Then, too, Elizabeth's natural tendencies were very much like Abraham's. She could be as stubborn and unfeeling as he had been. And yet she was quick to help Lydia with the chores and diligent in caring for her younger brother and sister. Elizabeth was a bundle of contradictions. Lydia hoped the influence of the gospel would soften the more negative attributes in Elizabeth's nature.

If Elizabeth's personality was a complex one, James' was easy to define. Though only nine years old, James was old enough for Lydia to determine that he possessed a mild temperament. He was a quiet, obedient child, given to tender feelings. Tucked away in the corner of Lydia's heart was the memory of the priesthood blessing James had received at the hands of Parley Pratt. She was certain that blessing had saved James' life, and it proved to be a comfort and beacon in Lydia's own life. The reality of priesthood power, combined with hope and faith, had been the foundation for Lydia's testimony. She suspected that she would need to hold fast to those things in the uncertain days ahead.

"I found just the spot for them," Christian announced, stuffing the books into a cranny in the corner of the wagon.

"That's good." Lydia circled her arms around Christian's waist. His tall, sturdy frame felt comfortably reassuring.

"I think that takes care of everything," Christian said, surveying the filled wagon.

"Did you remember to pack your drawing paper?"

"Certainly. You don't think I'd miss an opportunity to sketch that pretty face of yours."

Lydia laid her head against his shoulder. "Do you have any idea how much I love you?"

"No," he replied, grinning. The dimple in his chin showed clearly when he smiled. "Tell me how much."

Lydia pushed his dark hair off his brow. "Sometimes when I wake up in the night and feel you beside me, I still can hardly believe you're mine. You're the miracle in my life, Christian."

Christian bent to kiss her. When he straightened, his face was solemn. "I love you, too, Lydia. In addition to all the reasons you already know, I love you for your courage and your faith." He paused, giving her a grave look. "We can meet this challenge, Lydia. Just as we have all the others."

Lydia contemplated his statement. She and Christian had faced many adversities. They had given up a great deal in embracing the gospel of Jesus Christ: home, family, friends. But she knew that the gospel, as restored through the Prophet Joseph Smith, embodied true and correct principles. In spite of the persecution and personal heartaches they had suffered, she was grateful to be a member of the Church.

She looked up into Christian's face. He smiled at her, and covered her hand with his. She noted the strong set of his jaw, and the glint of determination in his eyes. His courage bolstered her own resolve. She knew more difficulties awaited them. Even when they reached their destination, there would be hardships to overcome. But the strength she had gained from surmounting their trials was like a deep well of cool water. A well she could draw from to sustain and strengthen her in the future—a reservoir of strength she could pass on to generations after her.

"You're right, Christian, " she replied in a voice firm and confident. "We will be fine. Wherever the Lord directs his Saints to gather, that place will be our home. Not only will the Saints build homes—we'll build a whole city," she added, excitement mounting in her voice.

"A city?" Christian chuckled at her enthusiasm.

"Yes, a city. With tree-lined streets, and brick homes, and a magnificent temple set on a hill."

Lydia gazed up at the sky. The pink sheen of morning had changed to gold with the sun's appearance on the horizon. She put both hands in Christian's. "Oh, it will be a beautiful city, Christian. You'll see."